Peterkin and the First Dog

to Sarah

with best wishes —

Peterkin and the First Dog

Simon King-Spooner

Simon King-Spooner

Illustrated by Jane King-Spooner

Published by Simon King-Spooner

www.simonking-spooner.com

All illustrations by Jane King-Spooner
Text formatted by Katie Slesser
Cover formatted by Katie Slesser and Jack King-
Spooner, with lettering by Jennifer Gorrod

ISBN: 978 1 7394472 0 5

To Rosie who inspired the first version, and whose exhortations prodded me into trying to write it up; and to Jane, Jack, Jenny and Katie for all they've done to help turn the text into a book

Part 1: The Valley

Chapter 1: Orphans

eterkin walked out one morning in spring, swung back the door of his hut on its leather hinges and walked into the day.

It was late – soon the rim of the sun would keek up at the skyline, seeing off the last cool grey of dawn. He'd meant to be out at first light to chase the crows from his barley field, but he'd stayed up with a suffering ewe till the lamb at last slid from her and was up on its legs and feeding.

He hurried, carrying his sling. They took off as soon as they saw him, fanning out under the skyline to not make a target, kraaking as if in mockery. He slung a stone from his pouch but it fell way short.

No major damage. He'd raked the seed under and they hadn't found much. He had another handful or two, he'd use a poke-stick a seed at a time.

Nice to be busy he said aloud, mocking his mother's voice. He sniffed a little laugh to himself, shaking his head.

But then he took a sudden breath and blinked his eyes a half dozen times, then tilted back his head and smoothed at one side of his face with the heel of his

hand, looking almost down his nose at the fall of the narrow valley.

He often stood here first thing, at the toe-end of the half-acre field, planning the day as much as there was to plan, looking down and across at the world he knew: scrub and rough pasture, pines and birches climbing the valley sides, the scraggy birches speckled with brilliant green.

The rough fall of land to the first fields of the village. The far mountain skyline across the Great Valley, black angles beneath the now-risen sun.

He was fifteen years old or thereabouts and he owned the highest farm, three tiny fields and first right to the grazing, water and wood enough for a town, whatever he could hunt or trap. Oats and barley, turnip and kale; sixteen ewes giving milk and lambs. His mother had died in the autumn (a whole year in the dying) but she'd coached him when she couldn't lift a hand, and anyway he'd known from a child every inch of the farm and every job to be done, and every mountain ledge where a ewe might seek an excuse to fall to her death.

He stood in the cool morning air as was his custom, squinting against the sun, not especially looking at anything. He felt the pull of his ewes, wanting out of their fold, three still to drop their lambs. He was just about to turn and go.

Then he saw the wolf.

He froze, everything in him went tight. It was downhill from him, barely fifty yards, watching. He could almost see its eyes. Making the best of the patchy cover, the ears sleeked back. His hand closed on his sling, the other felt for his stone pouch, but then they let go.

Slowly but not sneakily – as if he hadn't seen, as if he was just enjoying the morning still – he started to cross the slope along the top edge of his field, keeping the wolf in the tail of his eye, wanting a better viewpoint. But it saw that he had seen and it was off, soundlessly, heading for the trees. He saw that it was skinny and that it was limping. Fast enough though, on its three-and-a-bit legs.

He watched very hard as it went, the quick grey slipping image, staring after it when it vanished. That strange trick of a fleeing creature, as if it pulled back its presence behind it the way a spider does its strings, so you wonder if you ever really saw it.

He jogged back to check his sheep, thanking Luck that they were still in fold.

There was a new lamb born, still wet, wobbling on its new legs, butting for the udder.

He spoke to the sheep – the way he always did, impatient but amused, calling them by their names. He told them about the wolf but they showed no interest, braying as they queued for him to lift the wicker gate. He made them wait while he went for his bow, thinking of the safest place to take them, how to keep the lambs from dancing off.

There'd been no wolf in the high side-valley in Peterkin's lifetime. The valley was a bottle trap for wolves, lone or in a pack. One way in and no way out – a narrow gorge climbed steeply from the greater valley below, then fanned out and rose more gently. Its sides were impassable, so were the mountains it backed against. When wolves last found their way up – the older men were forever telling the story – a dragnet of bawling hunters with boy drummers between drove them into a corrie and wiped out the pack. (A wolf tried to break through the drive and two hunters shot each other as it sped between them. One suffered a permanent limp, its cause retold with joy when drink was taken.)

But none for thirty years, till now. This is what had happened.

The Great Valley downriver pack needed more room. It had made the best of a good season but now winter had come and the wolves were hungry. They pushed into the upriver pack's terrain, making war. Every night the intruders would set up a howl, a dozen voices soaring and looping, raising in fear the hair on the backs of the smaller upriver pack, who howled back as best they could, sounding well to themselves till their voices dropped and they heard the other pack's howl reach for them through the night.

In a sprawling nearby village men went out with torches, noisily checking cow house and sheepfold, shouting one to another, trying to reclaim the night. A great bull bellowed in his stall, to tell the wolves how big he was, and their howls came back to tell him how many they were.

The big pack drove the upriver wolves from their kills, ambushed them, followed their scent trails as if they were prey. As winter wore on all the elder wolves, male and female, were killed by ones and twos.

Three brothers from the year's spring brood were all that was left. They kept a good distance from the strangers, and made a meagre living on mountain hares and carrion. But one day when the wind blew down the valley they took a roebuck in scrubby woodland, their first decent meal for a week, and the incomers caught the scent and the old male and four others were up and sniffed and wove round each other keenly and then they set off.

They stalked close, the three brothers preoccupied, then rushed them. One of the brothers was over-whelmed, dead in seconds; one the old male had pinned by a foreleg, waiting his moment to switch to a throat bite. The third brother fled, but in twisting to dodge his chaser he saw the big male with his brother pinned and something must have turned within him for he wheeled back full pelt and onto the big male, and the pinned brother was free and bolted with two in pursuit while his liberator vanished beneath the attackers' fury.

The rescued brother ran well at first but his punctured leg was weakening fast. He ran downhill, angling towards the river, narrow and wild this far up the valley. He knew they were catching him. He curved right for steeper descent, careering through thickening scrub. He crashed through to the steep rocky bank with a chaser nearly on him, and skidded and sprawled down the bank and into the huge momentum of the water. The chaser pulled up at the edge and watched him carry away, swimming aslant across the great pull of the river, bobbing in its heave. In the moments it took for the second wolf to arrive he'd disappeared. The two stood taut and parallel and stared at where he'd vanished as if they were trying to solve some puzzle. Then they turned together and clambered unhurriedly back up the bank.

He swam as best he could, skidding off boulders. Twice he was pushed right under. Then, at the thinnest end of his strength, the water abrading his lungs and his movements loose and chaotic, the river swung left and his feet hit shingle and he scrabbled ashore on the right hand bank and stood head drooped and then stepped up the bank very slowly, then paused till he found the strength to shake himself.

A slushy, muddy track ran alongside the river, thick with the odours of men and their beasts. Beyond it rose a steep rocky cliff. He turned to his left and followed the track downstream, limping on the injured leg, corridor'd between river and cliff. Still in fear, though less so – no smell of stranger wolves, and the day-old human scent held less alarm.

But when a side-stream joined the river, with a side-track climbing beside it, he took the sidetrack for being less used and having less human odour. The slush turned to snow as he climbed. Ice footprints, sheep dottles melted in. When the sheer slope on the right-hand side of the path began to ease he climbed away from the stream and the track, taking a line as high as he could, for there billowed down increasingly the massive packed smell of a village, of people and smoke, of cattle and sheep, of their wastes.

He circuited above the village, pressing away from its stench. When it was well behind him he looked for a den and found a jutting rock and squeezed under and squirmed to lie on hock and elbow facing out, and he licked his wounded leg with care and watched the piecemeal view through boulders and pines of the high side-valley that fell away below.

Peterkin always threw out the last crust of a loaf, breaking it into thumb-tip sized crumbs, to show Hunger he didn't fear him. As well as which if the birds were eating his crumbs they weren't eating his seed. One evening he did so and next morning at dawn, after a night of soft spring rain, he unwound the thong that held his door and eased the door a crack ajar to watch the birds and he saw straightaway that the bread had gone in the night. He stepped into his clogs and went to check and he saw in the mud of the path a footprint of the wolf, just one, blurry-edged in the mud but there couldn't be any doubt.

When he first saw it he'd gone to tell the Headman.

He went unwillingly. He didn't want to think of the wolf cornered and punctured with arrows and pikes. But he knew that he ought to, that he *had* to. All the old stories of wolves and sheep, wolves and sheep: he'd never seen one before but he knew what it was in a second. So springy and quick it had been for all its bad leg, so scared of him.

But he'd gone at the end of the day to tell Mulda the Headman, fat and smirky in the Big Hut with a couple of his cronies, a cup of barley beer in his hand, and Mulda had asked a few sceptical questions and told him no, there'd been no wolf up here in thirty years and there wasn't now, no tracks no scat no howling in the night no ripped-open sheep. A couple of lambs missing but no signs, maybe a lynx or an eagle or just got lost. Pray well to Luck to keep sheep alive, as they say.

Mulda's tone was as sleek as his belly, persuasive, I-know-best. He spoke to his cronies more than to Peterkin. A wonder how big some dog-foxes get, how grey they can look in an early light or a late. How would you know it's a wolf if you've never *seen* a wolf?

So he'd picked his way back up the track the three-quarter mile to his hut, the only light a thin cold moon in and out of the clouds. He felt relieved that they hadn't believed it, that the wolf wouldn't be hunted. Not yet anyway. He felt it might be watching him – a moment's dread at the thought and he touched the handle of the knife in his belt, but then he recalled its fear and the grace of its three-legged flight and felt quite easy in the wolf's imagined gaze, as his mind's eye guessed out the path in the thin-mooned dark and his feet warily followed.

Since then half a month had passed. Two more lambs had vanished: no tracks, and both new enough for an eagle to lift off a slope. Peterkin thought the wolf had gone back where it came from. Not so much as a foot-print. Not till now.

He thought he should go and tell Mulda about the print, but he didn't. Somehow it felt like a secret.

Later that day he checked his flour store and made an extra loaf and left it to cool. When it got too dark for the crows to fly he cut off a third and smeared the crusty end in his dish of dripping and took the boiled-out soup bone from the pot and went out.

The last light of the day silhouetted the great peaks that rose above him to the west. To the east hung the now-huge moon, above the lesser mountains across the Great Valley, picking out each blade of grass at his feet.

Ten paces from the door he dropped the soup bone on the path. The same distance again he pulled off chunks of bread and scattered them, till all he had left was the greasy end of the crust. He closed his eyes and turned around twice or thrice, and when he had no notion which way he faced he flung it backwards over his shoulder, then looked to see where it had gone. It was right by the hut, somewhere in among the tussocks, almost under the single shuttered window.

Then he jammed open the door and unshuttered the window and sat in the hut with his back against the back wall and settled himself to watch.

A lot of his life was spent watching. Sheep around him on the hill; sheep in the fold that might or might not be thinking of giving birth; just-sown fields, with the birds waiting their chance; the evening sky from his doorway, with everything settled down for the night. He was good at it – he'd fall into a watchfulness that suited what he was doing, but was at the same time a kind of dream, a kind of trance. The sheep (he knew all their personalities), the raked-under barley seed (you'd swear the crows could see it through the earth), the stars whose names he knew and the stars with no names. These things as he watched were in the world and in a dreamworld both at once, but only in the dream world did they come into themselves, were the crows really crows and the stars really stars, and then he was content in his solitude.

He sat with his back to the far wall of the hut and watched for the wolf, in the square of moonlight bounded by the doorway, the path stretching off. The moon climbed higher and higher, the evening star fell away.

His eyelids began to droop. He wrestled his eyes wide open and blinked fiercely a few times and got back his focus. But then the night softened around him, its soft weight on his eyelids, and then he was asleep.

A sound woke him. Outside, just under the window – movement, stealthy movement through the high grass. Quick furtive gulping, a wet whisper of tongue and saliva. Peterkin was instantly awake, his skin prickling, mouth wide open trying to silence his breath. More soft steps out there and the brush of the animal against the high grass as it wheeled away. Then he saw it.

It had circled out and was moving back in towards the bread and the door. It knew the door was dangerous – could it see him? The moon was behind it, a shape coming towards him, ears must be lying back. moving in very warily. Hardly a trace of the limp. It seemed a lot bigger than before, in the moonlight. All around very silent, very still. Even the sheep were silent in the fold.

It reached the bread and took each piece with a quick nose-and-gulp. Now he saw more of it, tail curved under, ears down, crouched, watching the door. Surely it could see him. Skinny – its belly roached up, the long face jabbing deftly at the bread.

And then it crouched lower, moving in straight towards him. The hair on its back had risen, catching the moonlight; its face was in darkness. Suddenly Peterkin thought it might be coming for *him*, not the soup bone – an icy hand stroked his neck, he stopped himself just in time from clutching his knife. Now he was as awake as he'd ever been in his life.

The wolf reached the bone and darted its long mouth and whisked about and trotted away down the path. At sixty yards it turned side on, staring back at the hut a moment as if in puzzlement. Then in two steps it was gone.

Peterkin jumped up and through the door to see it if he could, but it had vanished. The moonlight lay over all as silent as snow.

Chapter 2: Luck and the Trickster

He baked two loaves again, one for the wolf. Every evening he put out bread.

Then the last of the new lambs was born very late and dead. He gutted it with care, and at the fading of the day he placed the innards about as far from the door as he'd scatter the bread. A fine white coil, luminous almost in the last grey light.

Peterkin sat in the doorway, sure that the wolf would see him. Sidelong and sprawled, trying to look at his ease, as if he cared nothing for wolves and was anyway half asleep.

It was nearly dark when the wolf appeared at the far bend of the path and it saw him straightaway. It froze and crouched, watching him. He slowly turned his head away in a show of indifference, keeping it in the tail of his eye. The moon was up and clear of the running clouds; he could make the beast out but no more.

He kept still and by and by the wolf crept nearer, crouching low. The day had been warm, a soft wind blew, the innards had a sweet pungency. It was as if the wolf was being dragged, half against its will. Peterkin sat slumped and watching sidelong, curbing the urge to turn his head.

The coil of intestine lay barely fifteen yards from where he sat in the doorway. The closer the animal crept the more it looked to be dragged against the pull of its fear, ears flat to its head and the tail curled under, the hair risen along its back.

A few yards to go and it seems to stall completely – then in an instant it catapults forward, snatches up the entrails and whirls and away, a pallid string trailing to one side. Peterkin almost jumped up with the shock.

He stayed completely still in case it turned and so it did, almost at the bend, hard to make out in the light of the moon. The white loops drooped from its mouth were the clearest thing.

What it could see of him sprawled in the doorway he didn't know but he sensed its eye on him, a beast's intensity and puzzlement. Then it whisked away and the night continued to close on in as if it had all never happened.

Peterkin had lived all his life with beasts – sheep, a few goats, a milk cow for a while. He followed his mother's way with them, patient, careful, cajoling. The lambing, the milking, out on the hill. When they found a lost lamb with its eyes both gone she wished no ill on the raven, smiling drily and shaking her head as she ended its little ruined life. She even did that gently, a careful quick dip of her knife between the neck bones – the lamb's life-force magicked away, legs instantly unstrung.

And she told him all her tricks, the times they'd worked and the times they hadn't, always with that wry amusement. Most of all how to use small pleasures to draw a beast to your purpose. Be its second mother, she'd say. Get it so you see an eagle, you call the lamb, it comes to you. But have your sling ready in case. And then, don't miss and hit the lamb.

They went every year from when he could walk that far to the summer fair in the Great Valley. His father was long gone by then.

It became a piece of his life – red-faced drunken strangers, pipers and dancing, wrestling, a great muddy open-air market. There was always an animal trickster with a hat of feathers and a coat of many skins. He had a fox that walked at his heel and a snake that coiled round his neck and a rat that lived in his pocket. One year it was a weasel.

He carried with him everywhere on his back, the top of it jutting way above his head, a narrow cage of maybe a dozen doves. He'd ease it down and open a door and they'd hurry out, but instead of flying away they'd dance, each one whirling on its spot. Then he would sit on a stool and the doves flapped up and perched all over him and he'd feed them titbits; then he'd clap his hands and they'd fly away and you'd think they'd gone; but he'd take out a fife and blow a two-note tune and they'd come flapping back and land and dance again and he'd feed them once more and they'd all in a line troop back into their cage. More tricks with the fox and the rat; he'd play his fife and they'd dance together, after a fashion – the fox kept making to snatch up the rat and then stopping, the rat each time rearing up – while the trickster rolled his eyes in wry critique.

To finish he'd lie on his back and feed the snake into one leg of his breeches and the rat into the other, and give a droll commentary as they made their way up to the waistband. At last he'd hand his hat to the prettiest girl in the crowd with a warning not to bring it back until it was full of silver and stones, and she'd blushingly take it round the four-deep circle of gawpers and gather enough to keep him in bread and beer for maybe a month.

Peterkin's mother would talk with him. She'd have a fat silver bead in her purse, or maybe an amethyst wrapped in mouse skin, not for the hat but to take to him after, and use the gift to start a conversation. At first he thought she was coming on to him, a lusty man as were most of the itinerants, but she quickly put him right, claiming a distant husband. No, she said, man of the hat that fills with the savings of fools, let me speak plainly. They say that the folk you meet at a fair are all liars, but me I lack the gift. I only tell the truth – though you're thinking that's a lie. The truth is, I want to know how you do it. I know you won't tell me, you think I'd be down next year with a cage full of birds and a feathery hat, but let me find you a plate of beef and three or four quarts of beer and I'll learn from your lies. This is my fine son Peterkin by the way. she said, patting the five-year-old's head. He means to thrash you if you misbehave.

The animal trickster looked down on Peterkin, who stared up unblinking in wonder and fear.

You've picked yourself a remarkable mother fine Peterkin, said the man. Tell her I'll do as she says, eat and drink her wealth and pay her with beer-tales.

Peterkin, flummoxed by the incomprehensible words, looked up at his mother. But she just tousled his hair and squeezed his arm, and he looked back up at the man's trickster face, the laughing eyes and rubber smile.

And what do they call you? the trickster asked, with a quarter turn of his head, still looking down at Peterkin.

They call me all sorts of things, said Peterkin's mother. But you can call me Ella.

Peterkin's task was to ease the wolf to his presence by tiny degrees and his days were spent in thinking how. He killed an old ewe who'd gone barren and slow afoot – he'd thought to let her live through the summer, then smoke the meat for winter. He skinned and butchered her on a rock by the stream, well away from the fold. He wrapped the shoulders in smoked hide and stowed them in the slab pantry in his hut. He stripped naked, all but his clogs, to spare his clothes from the blood and fat, and wrestled the headless and legless carcase onto the shoulder-high grid in his smoke hut, and started the fire and choked it with leaves and then washed himself, gasping in the ice-cold stream.

When he'd dressed again, wet under his clothes, he punctured the skull with his knife tip and chivvied out the brain, and dabbed the small portions onto a dockleaf and packaged the little heap with a thread of wool to add to the larder, Then, holding his breath, he added the head to the smoke-shed grill. Likewise the liver and kidneys and heart, plated on cross-hatched birch twigs. The hindlegs he put aside to carry to the village, one for his uncle and aunt and ten cousins, one for the Headsman's sharing as was the rule.

The rest was for the wolf. Legs below the hock, the rest of the innards, the tail. Maybe he'd add some sweeter portions, according to the moment. When all was done he went to the shrine to Luck at the foot of a streamside knoll and pricked the back of his hand, and smeared a drop of blood on the white quartz pebble set in the heart of the shrine and mouthed some words and turned and came back.

Ella had taken ill when she was pregnant. The birth was hard, and for months she felt she was moving in a dream, moving at half speed and not knowing how she did it. She felt so emptied out she could hardly believe her body was solid – emptied out into her baby, emptied by the cough, emptied into her milk. She wept as she suckled the child, small weary sobs coming like hiccups; but as she wept she planned for him, working the problem round and round, the one care that stood up from a floor of utter indifference.

The bloody cough had come to the village and all those it fell on began a drift towards death, a slow drift with rises and falls but with only one end. They said it came from the south – sold by the pedlars along with their knives and spices, or borne on the southern wind by flying ants, or beamed down by the Sun herself, angry with them for something or other, people argued what. Ella went through in her mind those who'd had it: there wasn't one who'd lasted ten years.

Her good man knew it, and she felt him shrink back from her. He did his lukewarm duty but he wasn't really there. She sensed he felt she'd let him down, though he'd never say such a thing. Sometimes she'd watch him sidelong as he stared across at them, she suckling the boy between bouts of the cough, as bleak of eye as a gambler staring at the empty fold when he's wagered away his sheep. Cursing Luck without words, in case that dangerous one should hear. But he answered to his duties and said nothing. At worst he had nowhere to run; and if she lasted a couple of years till the boy was past the troublesome age, and able to dod about on the farm and touch his father's heart with his babble and would-be helpfulness – she could go when the time came, and not be stuck haunting the walls.

But these were queasy times, the first years of Peter-kin's life. Then worse came. When the boy was two years old there was war, somewhere no-one had heard of; the

Alliance was at risk the herald proclaimed, the forces of evil, our lands and our children. One man in ten. Recruitment before the full moon, prepare. The village saw an outbreak of hefty limps and mortal back pain, of old wounds never healed, of unsocial quirks of bowel and of water. Lusty unmarried youths turned back into boys, parents counting their years and frowning, surprised to find the sum so low.

When the mustering gang arrived with war-bows and swords no tenth had been agreed. The Marshal, with a notched scar where an eye had been but a devil in the other, ordered all the men to the meeting ground, no exceptions. Reclassified boys were turned back to manhood at the toe of a boot; the huts were searched and those found hidden were whipped to the muster, where they squirmed from toe to toe in their welts.

Seventy men, shoved and kicked into lines. The Marshal's unblinking eye scanned the motley crowd. Then he walked the lines and the men in the lines froze before him. Thessel, Peterkin's father, Ella's man, big for the village and square-made, less quailing of eye than most, was the third to be picked – the Marshal gave a small jerk of his head and a flip of his hand, Thessel stood a moment unsure till a burly number two thumped him in the back, and he hardly had time to kiss farewell his now appealing wife and child before he was speed-marched along with the other six to the track to the Great Valley and the war.

He didn't come back. Only two of the seven did, and they didn't know, such had been the chaos of battle, whether he'd been killed or been captured, marched off to the unknown land in slavery. For Ella it made no practical difference, although she'd rather think of him dead than chained and soul-broken in some galley or some mine.

And so Luck, whose laughter shapes the world, toyed with the little household like a forest cat with a wounded bird. Ella never cursed Luck but made the shrine to him, offering there a cup of blood from a slaughtered sheep, the first seeds of a harvest. She prayed, appealing to his sense of humour, conceding his mastery. And Luck showed a soft side to his happy wickedness, letting her live for twelve more years, most of the time with little sign of illness; giving her a death clear-headed and not too grotesque, when the boy had the strength to take it, and a steady mind to manage the tough little farm.

The animal trickster was a side-plan – learn his tricks, they'd surely be useful somehow. Maybe persuade him to take on the boy as apprentice once she'd gone, she hadn't thought it through. But he stopped coming to the fair. Some said the snake had bitten him. She had Peterkin try out what she'd gleaned of his methods – he got a couple of finches to feed from his hand, but you'd hardly make a living with that, and the notion faded away. But she'd sing him a rhyme she'd learned from the trickster, changing the words here and there:

Underground the tireless mole
Has a dark worm-loving soul.
Eagle's soul is in his eyes
And the lonesome hare he spies.

Every dawn and every day
Through the ewes' souls on the brae
The cold green world in which they live
Falls like water through a sieve.

Through the bat's soul in the night
Black dreams flicker with his flight.
Raven soars, his soul is drawn
Down upon the lamb new-born.

Fox sniffs birth and has likewise
A soul of wily enterprise
While the great slow ox so strong
Is placid as the day is long –
His soul, uncomplaining, vast
All vexation will outlast.

From the eagle to the mole
Every creature has a soul
From the dog-fox to the bat
Mother Sun decided that.

Cow and calf, ewe and lamb,
She-goat, he-goat, ox and ram,
Mother Sun she gave us these
To make use of as we please

And the wild beasts on the hill
All to do with as we will –
But remember when you do
They have souls the same as you.

Do not rule by fear and pain –
You will lose more than you gain.
Softness, cunning, patience, and
You will hold them in your hand.

There'd been verses about what tricks to use, but Ella remembered only a line or two. She had no desire for a weasel to live in her pocket. What she grasped worked well enough – her sheep stayed close, came when she hollered, she could make them call in their lambs if the eagle was in the sky.

But she kept an exact recall of the last few lines of the song, and sang them under her breath in awkward live-stock moments:

Mother Sun she gave us these
To make use of as we please –
To make use of flesh and bone
But their souls are theirs alone.

She above calls on us to
Give the kindness they'd be due
If you were them and they were you.

Night followed night and Peterkin fed the wolf, not much but always something. He'd sit in the doorway, less recumbent now.

One night he put out only a tiny piece of meat, now pungent with the warming weather. The wolf came and took it and looked about for more. Peterkin gave the low whistle of a dusk owl and as he did tossed out another. The wolf jerked back in shock, crouched low, ears down. Peterkin kept very still. It crept up on the morsel and snatched it and backed off and gulped it down. Peterkin let some long moments pass, then did the same again – the low whistle, the toss, aiming to land the meat a couple of yards from the wolf, so that it would have to move towards him to take it. And so he went on, tossing out six of the seven morsels he had spaced out on a burdock leaf beside him. A real dusk owl came and perched in a tree and called back, bemused and indignant, its little tuft-eared silhouette against the twilit sky.

When he'd done he raised his hands to show the wolf that one was empty and the other held the final morsel of meat. Then, making the movement slow and smooth, he rose directly from his cross-legged seat – the wolf crouched and backed – and owl-whistled three times, then tossed out the morsel with a slow underarm lob and as if absent-mindedly stepped back into the hut, owl-calling a few times more as he went.

He closed the door decisively and barred it, then quietly went to the window. He'd left the shutter open a crack. The wolf had taken the final piece of meat and was staring at the hut, perhaps in hope. Then it turned and trotted away.

The little dusk owl had flown down and was calling from a fence post, insisting that its rival come out and fight.

Chapter 3: Auntie Irmin

ut the wind turned in a day or two from easterlies that blew the scent of the wolf uphill to southerlies that carried to the fold, and the sheep got his scent when he came and were frantic in their pens and Peterkin feared for the lambs. So he walked out in the falling light as if to meet the wolf, giving the owl whistle each few steps. In a satchel he carried a piece of the old ewe's intestine. He'd cut the hefty innards into lengths and washed them out in the stream and hung them from the alder tree by the hut to dry in the sun – even so they were odorous, in the sweet spring air.

He thought as he went how the wolf might be watching and might use his absence to wheel and cut in behind him, and he saw in his mind it leaping the fence round the fold, proof against nothing more than a fox, and his mind's eye saw the frenzy and the carnage – the tales he'd heard of the doings of wolves, how they'll kill all they can, how more than any other beast Destruction possesses them, how Luck shares the joy in the farmer's ruin. He chanted a prayer to Luck as he went, over and over, giving the call after each repetition.

Open birch woodland climbed the valley side a quarter mile from his hut, and here he stopped at a low-branched tree and took out the strip of intestine and wound it round a branch at shoulder height, tying it in a half-hitch to fix it there. Then he went aside thirty yards and waited, giving the low whistle, whispering the prayer to Luck.

The wolf has indeed been watching, crouched on its hocks at its viewpoint on the hill, tucked between boulders.

It sees the boy walk away from his steading and hears the owl-call and catches whiffs of intestine on the breeze and saliva runs from its mouth, With its other ear it can hear the sheep in the fold, oblivious low-key bleatings and shufflings.

It has watched him with the sheep many times with desire for them in its mouth, once or twice very close to snatching a wandering lamb when he was turned away, but always the boy's gaze whipped round as if he'd felt the intent, and he'd make a call and the ewes in turn would call in their lambs and he'd feed each ewe some titbit from his satchel as her lamb thuds up at the udder.

The wolf has in all its senses a fine intelligence of danger. Danger pushes it, and hunger pulls it – mostly the wolf is found precisely where the balanced forces place it. Danger and hunger fight for the soul of a wolf – danger in stranger wolves, in greater beasts, but above all in man. Man the other, man the eternal enemy, whose smell and presence are the bone of fear.

And so the wolf crouches in the twilight, not settled but pulled two ways: the steading, the boy away, the sheep there somewhere (it hasn't seen), no other human guard either seen or smelt – the boy and his call and easy food (if never enough), the ripe waft of the entrail of the ewe. And danger both ways: the unexplored steading, the sense of a trap, of too easy a chance – the boy out in the open, up to something new.

The bleat of a lamb thin and tiny against the breeze lifts the wolf to its feet and turns it towards the hut and the fold. But as it stands that same breeze brings the thick salivary odour of the intestine, and it rears turning and trots aslant towards the odour, to circuit and stalk in far-sided from the boy.

Peterkin's had time to consider the slow creep of the moon and stars across the deepening sky, time for the early night to sink in. It's very different, out here, from sitting in his doorway. He is open on every side; anything could be out there. The wolf is out there. He's thought momentarily before that he might be the prey, alone in the open in the night. He's heard the stories – now they flood back, not in any detail but a single icy gist. He thinks: wolves eat people. Not often, but often enough. Starving packs in winter mostly, forgetting their dread; but does this parentless youngster know better? And haven't I been teaching him, night on night, not to fear me?

Peterkin sits, still and cold, and somewhere in the surrounding night is the wolf. It can stalk in absolute silence; it can see in the dark. His arm is aquiver as he finds his knife and draws it. The handle feels wrong, as if he hasn't properly grasped it, or maybe a toy has been put in its place. So he sits. But then he hears a real dusk owl call way off on the breeze and he lets go the knife and mimics the call himself and hands his soul to Luck and to the sky, and in that moment the shape of the wolf is suddenly there at the dangling bait and it rears and is tearing it.

On the next day the boy's Aunt Irmin, short for Irmin-bruga, mother of his ten cousins, sister of Headman Mulda, was speaking with Aylard the Man of Law. There was, by order, a Man of Law in each village of more than a hundred souls, schooled to memorise the core legis-lation, with relevant amendments and novel edicts as they arrived – a matter of perhaps five thousand words. The land was not yet literate; the law lived among the people in half-chanted recitation, like prayer to the Sun or the Powers. An official of the regional court, with rights of penalty and dismissal, appeared at random to check on exactitude of recall, but his coming was whispered ahead and he was pleased to accept small respectful gifts, and a fumble or two would be smiled at, and *sotto voce* reminders given, and cups of sweet mead would follow.

Irmin has some concerns about property law. Matters of interpretation. Tricky passages, seemingly ambigu-ous. She has Aylard go over them, as is anyone's right. An owner absent, of unknown condition but possibly alive – how is 'abandonment' defined? Inheritance by a youth, without adult support. Who counts as 'nearest male kin' – brother or ungrown son? What if a minor, left alone on a farm, struggles to manage – can concerned relations intervene? Perhaps unasked, but we're speaking of a youngster?

Aunt Irmin's voice was quiet, inexpressive, her face moon-like and bland. No names were mentioned. When Ella finally died she'd watched discreetly with a hopeful eye, but was disappointed by Peterkin's competence. But she watched still – how much left fallow, what more could be tilled, the lowish yields, when many had to squeeze all they could from not enough land. She and her good man Jepkin and their ten, Jepkin as close to Ella by blood as the boy – their natural right is obvious, surely there must be something in law to back it.

Jepkin was no help. Their marriage, a sickly creature already, had died on the same night as Ella – he'd gone quite mad, beating his head and his chest with his fists, swearing in the grating, gasping voice of some possessing demon that she'd played a game to keep him from his sister, that he'd given up his soul for a peaceful life, that in Ella's very last days she'd concocted dilemmas to keep him away. Between his rantings he'd howl like a beast, and pound at his head, or clamp it between his forearms, as if he were a wrestler and himself his own opponent.

When his madness passed she let him know that so had her devotion, what little was left. 'No more of that' she said in the dark, when he pressed her arm and she heard his coarse breath. 'Aren't ten enough?' He said nothing and rolled and turned his back, and so from then on – silence, back turned to back.

The Man of Law knew what she was about. So did the whole village. He was politely unhelpful, as she'd expected. She knew the passage as well as he did – inheriting minor

unable to manage: disinterested stewardship arranged by local leaders. That meant Brother Mulda, always a soft-hearted fool for Ella and the boy – Irminbruga was sure he'd tried it on with her, on feast days, in his cups. But that was the best she had – mismanagement; work on Mulda: 'Let your nephews help out ...'

Peterkin was keeping the sheep in their pens till the sun was high, he'd put off sewing the smallest field with barley till almost too late, the field now weedy and needing the hoe. He'd be out on the hill at dawn, in the wooded sides of the valley, way up on the patchy slopes of tussock and juniper-mat past the treeline. He'd sense the wolf following him, sometimes he'd see it. Every now and then he gave the owl call and dropped it a morsel.

One morning he came on fresh roe tracks, a mother and fawn on a faint brush-parted trail. Next day he came with his bow, in the earliest grey of dawn. He'd worked out they were coming to drink where a branch stream purled over rock and slipped in a yard of braided fall into a lively pool. He'd already picked a hiding spot uphill and upwind of the pool and the trail, with the chance of a decent twenty-yard shot. He'd owl-whistled on his way now and then, not knowing whether the wolf could hear, and once he was settled and hid he did again.

The mother roe and fawn weren't long in showing but long enough for the cold to get into his bones, jaw starting to quiver, the mucus to run from his nose. A far-spreading network of birdsong had risen, in the thin chilly air. He had an arrow notched and two more at hand. He clenched and unclenched his fists in turn to keep them from growing clumsy and he gave himself to watchfulness.

He heard a rustle of movement so small that it might have been nothing and then there they were, the half-awkward grace of deer, the mother and fawn in their quiet world. He half-rose very slowly and eased back the string of his bow, and the arrow too fast to see from the forty-pound bow thumped into her as if she'd been hit with a branch, and she screamed and fell and was scrabbling chaotically as Peterkin crashed down the slope, drawing his knife. She had purchase with her front hooves when he got to her, the back hooves kicking aslant, head down and mouth agape coughing blood. He grabbed an ear to hold her still and the bucking animal strength jarred his arm and broke his grip, destroyed as she was, and the hard-structured body jerked and bucked with great force but he found a join in the bone-crest of her neck and rammed in the knife at the second attempt, and her soul and her physical torsion were gone and she was dead.

Such was the kerfuffle he'd had only a blurred and eye-corner sense of something else going on. It happened that the fawn had bolted through the pool and as she did the wolf burst out from nowhere and seized it at the neck with such side-on momentum it was taken clean off its thin precarious legs, and they both bowled over and the wolf re-set its grip and the fawn kicked vaguely for a little time and then it was still.

And the boy and the wolf each with his kill stared at each other across the stream. The wolf had his hackles up. He was in a crouch but showing his teeth, ears drawn back as if he was snarling into a wind.

Peterkin had one idea, vague but there was no question. They had to share their kills. He had no sense of how to make it happen. He let his hands and feet feel out a plan, with a razor-edged watchfulness.

He slowly dragged the doe to the edge of the stream to give the wolf clear sight of it, making no sudden movements. He arched back her head and slit the vein in her throat so the blood ran down, spreading, over her chest. The wolf watched, rigid, seeming about to catapult into action. Peterkin remembered the owl call, then he thought to toss the wolf some titbit. The tight bone-braced hide of the doe seemed entirely resistant, so – perhaps a demon worked him, he still had no conscious plan – he prised open her mouth as slow as he could and as if in a dream or a ritual sliced across the base of her little sharp-pointed tongue, and with a low whistle, smoothly, underarm, tossed it to land a yard from the wolf. The wolf jerked back as if into itself, and then darted and snatched the tongue and the tongue was gone.

Peterkin felt what he had to do next and the nausea of fear came on him. He had to take some of the fawn for himself. He thought about hefting the doe across the stream, to make a kind of swap, but he knew it'd be a failing and a weakness. So he slowly stood upright and slowly, a step at a time, waded the icy pool. The knife was in his hand. The wolf shrank back by inches, snarling.

Thus he covered the few yards to the fawn, the wolf backing to keep an exact distance. Peterkin sensed a shift, a touch of resignation in its snarl, but kept to his dream-like pace. When he got to the fawn he slowly crouched and keeping an eye on the wolf, which stood four yards off displaying its teeth in an intermittent sneer, he severed a hind leg, his hand shaky but skilled (the joint like a lamb's), and took it and stepped a pace or two back, and then gave three low whistles and breathed a prayer to Luck and turned away from the wolf and stepped back slowly across the pool.

He gralloched the doe and took off the head and lower legs. He left the innards, offal and all. His broadhead arrow had split a rib and gone clean through one lung; he whittled off the arrowhead with care and eased out the shaft and wiped all as best he could. He gathered his bow and his quiver and made ready to go back, to his hut and his farm and his too-long- penned sheep, the lamb-lost ewes unmilked. He watched the wolf, now settled to its task, as it tugged and ripped at the fawn. He felt like a curl of the stream or a piece of the cloud-blown sky, chilled and euphoric and somehow mineral, great breaths coming and going through him. Still not quite knowing what he was doing he took the doe's heart and whistled low and tossed it across the pool, and the wolf was on it and awkwardly trying to tear it, pinning the heart with its front paws and gnawing and tugging.

Peterkin tucked the fawn's leg into the empty carcase of the doe and shouldered the carcase, then squatted to take up his quiver and bow, and took a last look at the wolf and gave a last whistle. It gave him a long, unreadable stare, then it went back to tearing at the heart.

Peterkin turned and hefting the carcase began to pick his way downhill.

Irminbruga heard a whisper that Peterkin's sheep were being left in pen, and she sent up her second and third sons to see how it went. For years the three had gone out early to hunt small game on the hill, though never quite so soon in the season. Peterkin was up and out with the sheep the first time the cousins came by, and so again the second; but the third time he was nowhere around. The ewes were bleating in the fold, the sun well up.

Later in the day he turned up with a roe deer haunch and shoulder. Gratefully received of course. A little too keen on hunting over farming then, but hardly mismanagement – there were many such. But something else – when the boys asked him when and where he was jokey and guarded; Irmin felt something furtive in his jokey avoidance. Something to work on, to press on, to pick at till an aperture appeared or else the breach closed over.

 The cold late spring moved on to a cold early summer. The wolf would den up for

most of the day, favouring the long late dusk and the long early dawn.

Way above Peterkin's hut the wolf had his kingdom, wide and lonely, far from the smell and sound of the village. Above the hut the high valley widened to country of little appeal to a farmer. The grazing where Peterkin had option was the last reach worth calling on with a flock of sheep. Above it were woods, stumpier and more tousled as you climbed: in the end no higher than a man, their tops crooked over where they broke through the winter snow and into the searing wind. Up there the valley a widening traverse, cut by streams that jinked through boulderfields, lost themselves in peatbog. Above the treeline tussock grass and ling, willow-mat and juniper-mat; higher still lank khaki moss in tasselled spreads; and then pure rock, degrading in castings of gravel and scree.

This spare world a tilted contouring shelf beneath the high tops, cut off by cliffs from below, the little valley its only access. Maybe four miles in span, anything up to half a mile in width, everywhere steep and awkward. Once goat-girls had come in summer – you could still see the roofless shielings, dissolving into the hill. No longer: only hunters, seasoned men and intrepid boys – the sharper demands of the farm now met, with the fields sown and the lambing done – coming after ptarmigan and mountain hare, and goats now long gone wild.

This is what had happened.

Chapter 4: Sixty Years Earlier

hen the oldest of the villagers were barely past childhood sixteen desperadoes appeared from over the mountains, wild plait-haired men speaking an unknown tongue. They captured the goat-girls in the shielings; for three days and nights they feasted on goat meat and took turns with the girls.

On the third night one of the girls slipped away and gave the alarm and at dawn every man in the village was out. Their arms were hunting bows, slings, a few spears. Pitchforks, axes – not one in ten had a sword. They surged up to the high land in a single loose mass, the Headman yelling to keep the hotheads in check.

A party of six barbarians was scouting the hill for the escapee. They were caught in a defile and quickly surrounded; but fighting men with seventy-pound war bows, two village men were killed and four injured before the last intruder, blood-masked from a head-wound, charged from his hopeless cover bellowing a war-cry and was almost on them before he fell, sprouting arrows.

That first encounter was a sobering one. Their casualties were taken aside to help down or carry down later, the wounded to keep the carrion birds from the dead. The enemy bows were tried and picked up by the few who could draw them. Fulko the Headman took tighter control for the stand-off that followed. By gesture and mime he presented a deal: let go the girls and you leave unharmed; hurt them we burn you alive. Men – fathers, brothers, sweethearts – shouted to the girls words of sentiment and hope.

But the incomers knew they'd not be let free, to maybe come back with a hundred, to avenge their comrades and take these weaklings' lands. They gave back a counter-mime: we're taking the girls, attack and we cut their throats.

And so they processed: five desperadoes each paired with a girl, shoving her along or holding her by the hair, a knife in his hand that he waved now and then for the village men to see; the other five behind with arrows snibbed ready, walking backwards and drawing in threat if the villagers came too close. Who followed in a pack, tensely but lamely, shrinking back when a bow was drawn, like a hunting beast bemused by a porcupine.

The procession made a slanting climb to the furthest region of passable land, angled under the peaks. There was realisation, muttered side to side, that the incomers and their captives were heading for the Notch.

Everyone there in his boyhood or youth would have been to the Notch. A deep vee with peaks rising either side, the only place in the villagers' world with a view to the west, down and across to its unknown lands. The far side falls sheer but they must know a way down. Back to the world from which they had conjured themselves, now perhaps with a booty of goat-girls.

Two youths spoke to Headman Fulko. There's a way, not even a goat-track, that climbs to a yard-square precarious sloping ledge that looks down on the Notch. Room for two bowmen kneeling, a third standing behind. Fulko by gesture called in the six best bowmen, three and three reserves, and told the boys to lead them. Don't let them see you. Pick your man but don't let fly till you hear me shout 'fire down!' Whatever happens don't risk hitting a girl.

A run of scree led up to the Notch, shale sliding down as the girls and barbarians climbed. The two-part procession slowed and then halted, the village men below closing to thirty-odd yards, the rearmost intruders flat-handing them back and half-drawing their bows.

The crowd of village men watched two girls and their captors appear in the Notch above, backed by the vast summer sky. The other girls on the scree just below, walled in by the five-bowman rearguard.

There was a pause. It seemed very long. Fulko glanced over one shoulder then the other. The men had already fanned out as best they could for line of sight.

Ready an arrow but don't let them see you move he said, as if to the man beside him. Most already had. Don't fire till I say. Get the five nearest, keep clear of the girls.

Every eye was on the party of four skylined in the Notch. A dispute was going on: barks of command, violent gestures, the girls' voices coming faintly, chanting as if in prayer.

One of the two men eased himself over the edge and disappeared by section, warily starting the downward climb. Their leader came up to replace him, tall in the gap, formidable in demeanour. It seemed Biddy was to follow the climber, Biddeka, the tallest girl, lithe and wide-shouldered. She held back, shaking her head, chanting louder. The leader seized her hair one-handed and shook her, jabbing his knife towards the drop. She raised her hands in appeal, nodding in urgent submission against his grip on her hair. He let her go.

From below the villagers watched her silhouetted quandary as she squatted by the edge, her hand-and-shoulder gesture of bewilderment. The big man crouched above her, shouting, directing.

Then in an eyeblink she gripped his jacket two-handed and with a bursting scream she threw herself to one side with a twist of her torso and he was on his toes flapping for balance and then he was gone, his braying wail disappearing behind him.

Drop Girls Drop! she screamed, Drop!

Fire! Fire Down! shouted Fulko, surfacing from blank astonishment.

Stay Down Girls Stay Down ...

A war arrow thunked into his chest and poked right through, an inch above his lung. He staggered with the impact but kept his feet, shouting Not Near the Girls, Not Near the Girls.

The other desperadoes fell quickly – no cover, outnumbered five to one. Thanks to Luck and the sidefire from above no girl was hurt and no village man killed, though four as well as Fulko were variously pierced.

Fulko, arrow-punctured but numb to all pain, raised his two fists high and shouted to the Sun his gratitude. Above the girls were whooping and shrieking and clutching each other and hugging every man that came up, and soon the little region was dangerously packed and Biddeka led back down the scree, shoving and caressing in happy play the hands that reached for her.

The bodies of the intruders were slung over the cliff as if in a hurry, no-one even stopping to take their rings and accoutrements – embossed arm-guards, the silver combs in their hair.

Below, at first forgotten, the man who set off climbing, and clamped to the rock when first his wailing leader and then his silent comrades came thudding and cartwheeling past him, was almost down before he was noticed. The villagers made target practice of him; five times punctured he still got down, sprouting arrows from his shoulders, one from his head, one angled downwards through his thigh. Such is the will to live. So badly hurt, his comrades dead, back in the land that he'd fled from, a few last optimistic arrows clattering on the rocks behind him, he lurches like a drunk down through a boulderfield and into scrubby forest and is gone.

They tease out Fulko's arrow while his body's still in shock, whittling off the tail and easing it out the way it was going already. Blood streams, his jerkin is sodden. He insists on walking but after a mile his steps are getting clumsy and they shoulder-ride him down in turns. Praises are called, they reach to support him but really just to touch him, in casual veneration.

Biddy is shouldered too, beaming with enormous pride. Fulko gestures her and her bearer into the lead. She writhes still with surplus energy; losing touch with the other girls she ululates and they reply, exchanging a shrill and caterwauling joy.

The rest of the villagers who have been watching all day surge up to meet the party. Dusk is falling. Mothers, older sisters, sobbing with relief; the sixth girl, Gode, the escapee, touching and stroking the others as if needing proof; a mass of women, children, toddlers, babes in carry-shawls; the old, creaking up last.

The tale is told, for the first of a thousand times, while Fulko and the other injured men have their wounds stuffed with honey and poulticed over.

From out of the echo of events the tale throws itself together, a montage of doings, of hyper-lit seeings, of turmoils and causations, each facet from a different viewpoint, all flung out in approximate sequence with side-storms of yesses and nos and corrections, mockeries, refinements, buts and ands. A narrational landslide of the events.

After come hundreds of small conversations, of two or three or five, working over the detail, correcting misrememberings, miscorrecting true ones, linking and linking, going over and over. Always the same incandescent moments: the lone barbarian's suicidal charge, the distance he made in his harvest of arrows. The long pause at the Notch, Fulko's composure, the company's trust in him; then holding his command with an arrow clean through him. But above all, the nub of the story forever, Biddy's scheme and its perfect conclusion, though few had seen it clearly – the other girls, two or three on the side ledge, not counting the dead barbarians.

With telling over and over the story smooths out and sets, firmer and firmer in shape. And so down to Peterkin's time, when only one of the goat-girls is still alive, and a couple of the rescuers: the longest day in the life of the valley, the closest it came to history.

The girls' side of the tale came out more slowly. They'd been round the fire in the early night when the men came out of nowhere. Gode, quick as an eel, nearly slipped through but one grabbed her smock.

Their speech was incomprehensible, as was the girls' to them. When they tried to talk to each other the men got angry, cuffed them or shook them by the hair. They seemed so different from men of the village – strong, scarred, tough as beasts, their movements sudden and ballistic, their lust and their tempers ferocious. You knew there was nothing they wouldn't do.

On the first day of their captivity half the men had gone to scout the terrain. When they came back there was loud conversation in their tongue, a long ill-tempered debate. Staccato barks, fist-clenching, sudden backhand sweeps. Someone gestured towards the girls with a questioning lift of the shoulders and their leader, turning slightly away, shrugged and ran his thumb across his throat.

It was Colwen, always a flirt, who found a way for the girls to converse. She squirmed in pretend fondness against the man who'd most recently lain with her, cooing as if in grateful praise.

This one stinks worst of all, she purred. But look on the bright side (she nuzzles) – his prick's so titchy you hardly know it's there.

Gode picked it up, pressing the arm of the man at her side.

Are they human, d'you think? Or low-grade demons? We should have gone with the he-goat, he's got better manners. O, but what are we going to do girls? What are we going to do?

The game gave strength. Talking back and forth across the barbarians, who smirked and basked in their seeming praise, gave a lift to their souls. And perhaps it was good for more than deceitful insult: guile, surely, could open doors, find escape routes, conjure up fathers and brothers.

They found new lyrics to milking songs; re-worded ancient prayers to dawn and to noon and to sunset; muttered as if to themselves at awkward tasks, at tending the fire, even at the latrine trench. Morsels of joy in the risk of a squirt of unstoppable laughter, at foxing these thugs who thought them so helpless.

They were all different and all the same. Their order of respect was as clear as with a herd of beasts: who took the floor, the best of the goatmeat, the prettier girls. A couple had wounds no more than a few weeks old, of which they took no notice. Wounds that seeped and stuck to their clothing, which stank worse than their bodies. And many older injuries: battered faces, ill-healed cuts and punctures, the criss-cross scars of floggings.

Gode, slight and lithe, escaped in the third night, threading herself past the guard who dozed in the doorway. The other two in her shieling were to simper and squirm distractingly to any who woke but the ruse wasn't needed.

The men didn't notice Gode's absence right away. Colwen, always quick, seeing a chance to sidestep blame, cried out in dismay: Where's Gode? Where's Gode? – shouting accusingly at the men, tugging at their sleeves.

The six pursuers who would die in the defile left with their weapons at a bent-legged trot, heavy and graceless and surprisingly fast. The guard was beaten to the ground by his comrades and three, led by their headman, kicked him for a while with deliberate precision. The girls watched, sick at the stomach. But their turn didn't come. Colwen you darling, mouthed Hilla the normally shy, I'll wash your drawers for a hundred years.

When the time came, and they headed at knife-point for the Notch, Biddeka improvised variations on an ancient hymn:

> Mother Sun O Mother Sun
> You who hold our lives hold mine
> Mother Sun shine
> down shine down
> I'll try and make a diversion girls
> Drop down when I shout

Give the guys clear targets
Fathers, brothers, don't you miss
Mother of us all O Sun
Smile on me once more once more
Or else we're dead, or slaves to these animals
Sun Sun Mother Sun
Drop when I shout, drop when I shout

 She'd guessed where they were going, the Notch they
knew well, a place of curiosity and dreams, to stare out
at unknown lands of the west, vast mist-draped forest
and distant patch clearings and minuscule smoke-braids
from hearths in unseen huts. The notion when it came
on her brought dread, but it wouldn't let her go, she
who beat most of the boys in her wrestling days before
she became a woman:

Mother a hip wheel Mother a hip wheel
Give me the moment, give me the grip
My life is yours my life is yours
The moment I pray you I pray you the moment ...

The next day but one, after discussion, six men headed
up to the place of the first skirmish. The two best dykers
in the village, two volunteers with butchering gear and
headstrap baskets, a shawm player, a drummer. The villagers, easing back into their mundane lives, watched
them go – from sheepfold, from porch, from a herd on
the hill. The shawm gave out a single long phrase of de-

fiance, over and over, falling silent on only the steepest stretches; the drum kept up a sullen rhythm throughout.

When they got to the place the volunteer butchers severed the incomers' heads. The heads already eyeless, flies buzzing in the summer heat. They stripped the bodies of jerkins and footwear and the coloured random insignia they wore, and piled heads and clothing into the baskets. All of value – swords, knives, rings, circlets, fine-buckled belts, undamaged arrows from both sides – was laid out with care to pick up on their return.

A hundred yards off in the complex terrain a scree-slope dropped away, bevelling to a sheerer drop. Here they dragged the headless bodies, hefting them awkwardly onto the scree. Four slid down with no hitch and disappeared; a couple jammed, some precarious toeing helped them complete their journey.

The men had brought up food but no-one touched it. Wearily in the sticky heat they went on, the musicians skirling and thudding, the dykers and butchers taking turns with the baskets – past the very still and silent shielings, on towards the Notch, even the drum falling silent on the last climb.

They built a buttress cairn at each side of the Notch with the heads incorporated, faced to meet an intruder as he came to the top of his climb. The jackets, boots, insignia were likewise interwoven.

Thenceforward the shielings were abandoned, the practice of summer goat-herding fell away. The surviving goats escaped in the stramash and turned feral. Young men and boys went up every summer to hunt them, and the spring-born marmots and hares and ptarmigan, but if they stayed overnight they'd sleep beneath a shelter stone or the stars. The shielings, built and rebuilt over centuries, with their turf roofs and peat stacks and hearthsides imbued with the girl generations of squabbles and singing games and endless ribald speculation, now stained beyond cleansing by Darkness, were left to the elements, and the timbers rotted and the roofs fell in and tempests toppled unbraced walls, and by Peterkin's time they were blurred rectangles of rubble, chest high at most, woven into the moorland, sinister only when night fell and Darkness came out to reclaim his holdings.

But the Notch retained its allure. Here every boy would come, some just once, some over and over. Not many girls, even those free to – the whole upland terrain was thought unlucky. Biddy herself never went back, to the place of her fame.

The boys and young men would inspect the cairns with fascinated reverence, and some would stare to the west with a kind of longing, as if a spirit were whispering their name. The boldest would make the first few moves of descent, their comrades watching through their fingers – but even that was forbidden: the village council made a law that the world of the valley stopped at the two cairns forever, and the world beyond likewise.

Chapter 5: Discovery

p in the higher country the wolf had easy pickings of the new crop of goat kids and marmots and leverets. Way above the human stench of the village, men's jerky doings and shoutings. Each evening though, as the light fell, he came down by habit and found the boy, by scent and by the small sounds of his movements and by the call that fooled indignant dusk owls but not him. There would be titbits, unnecessary now but a shapely occasion in the day. And the boy was his only company.

So with slow familiarity the wolf came closer and closer to him, almost to touching.

Irminbruga had the idea of meeting with Peterkin face to face, just the two of them. Taking him by surprise, like a bearer of sudden news. Taking him off balance. The force of her big, quick-minded personality; the demands of senior relative respect.

Of the age and condition she was, mother of ten and not much given to walking, she set herself off on the uphill track one evening. She worked her way up slowly, breathing heavily, favoured by a near-half moon and a brisk and cooling downhill wind. She gave thought to her purpose as she walked.

Worry, would be her opening – we're worried about you, up here alone. Trying to manage, the struggle to manage. So much easier it'd be, she'd say when she felt the moment, to have cousins Jep and Beri up here to help. To make it easier, not be lonely. Your mother always loved the boys. Two lines of negotiation if he blank-walled her: 'Just young Beri then, you've always been close to Beri ...'; 'Just for the summer while it's so busy, just till the harvest's in ...'

Go canny. How well had that creature his mother trained him? Ella with her laughing mockery, who always thought the worst of me, for all I'd done to help, be part of her life, their lives. Deathbed vows? 'Your Auntie Irminbruga, don't ...' – she'd surely not have been so heavy-footed, the clever-silly bird. Go canny, mix honey with any vinegar. If in his surprise he forgets his manners, makes no offering of food - reproach him gently, pleasantly, for his own sake.

She tried phrases half-aloud as she walked, with a fitting smile; she made small gestures with her hands. A steep section faced her, leading up to a moon-backed skyline. She stopped to get her breath, staring up, preparing herself for the climb.

Then she saw Peterkin, in head and shoulders silhouette at the skyline, seeming to toss something. A faint low whistle came down the wind to her. Then she saw the wolf.

Hunters' word of wolf tracks in the upland had lately come and not raised a fuss, had been met with a shrug or with blunt disbelief – no tracks had been seen on the lower pastures, the few lambs lost were blamed on eagle or lynx. Who says wolf? Someone killed a two-stone fox last year, showed its skin at the fair.

But Irmin hadn't seen a boy and a wolf. She'd seen a young wizard and his demon. Moon and skyline: the fearsome beauty of Darkness in those silhouettes, lithe and silvered, stark and at the same time unreal. Fear took her; she stepped back very quietly the way she'd come, the first stretch walking backwards, feeling out each step, not turning her back till a jink in the path hid the sight from her and she from it and then she took all the speed she could on her heavy tremulous legs. Only when she was back in her world, of rushlight and sullen husband and squabbling children, did Irminbruga settle her breath. She slapped the children to their cots, and sat at the hearth and stared into the small summer fire with happy surmise rising through her astonishment.

The sun was high next morning when they came and took Peterkin. Six men from the village, purposeful, gruff, heavy-faced. He was hoeing and raking the barley field. The sheep were in fold – fed, the lambless ewes milked, the milk curd-skimmed.

He felt sick when he saw them, sick and fumble-headed as they walked him to the village, as if abruptly woken from a drunken sleep. The so-familiar world was suddenly strange. The sun's heat not its usual heat; the now-unfriendly path tried to trip him, jumbled his feet.

We should put him to the torment, said Aylard the Man of Law, but no-one had much stomach for it, nor much idea what to do. So Mulda and two henchmen snapped questions at him, taking it in turns, and Peterkin answered, honestly more or less. He said he wanted to tame the wolf, the way the animal trickster had tamed his fox. He didn't know why he just did. He knew nothing of witchcraft. No – people said his mother was fey but she'd never been a witch. She'd said all that was nonsense. The scry-women she'd seen for spells against the cough had been useless – she'd mimicked their garbled invocations. He wanted to tame the wolf he told them, he didn't know why. Over and over.

It's him that's been bewitched said a henchman when they broke off from their questioning. The others thought the same, had been near to saying the words. *Tame a wolf* – he must be.

They needed to find who could have taken a lock of his hair – sweat, saliva, urine, excrement. Living up there half-wild, his hair grown long. Who last cut his hair? Himself, he answered mystified, honed his knife to its finest edge, little pressing chops against a soft-barked tree. Yes, he left the hair where it fell.

Search for evidence said Aylard, reprising the words of Law. It is prescribed, the penalties severe, that all that is mouth-spoken be set against what's said by the factual world. Is his hair still by the tree? Do the tracks of strangers lead to his latrine trench? And the good Irminbruga swears the wolf is no wolf but a demon – might sharp-eyed huntsmen spy the pad-and-claw impressions of undemonic flesh?

Wolf tracks there were, so many and so low down it was an embarrassment that they'd not been noticed – though in fairness few walked the side-track to Peterkin's hut where they lay thickest.

And none, before the search party, had seen the place where a half-hitched dangle of dried-out rancid intestine was glued to a branch, a turmoiled scraping of wolf-action below it, a braid of prints trotting away. The wolf then was no demon, but a factual beast of heft and appetite – tempted down very close by the boy to a mighty feast on the season's lambs. Was he bewitched – a youth with the wit to run a farm? Knowing the ancient love of villagers for wolves, and the fine welcome they'd always been given? And if bewitched who by? A half-dozen minds or more, on separate paths, found their way to Irminbruga.

Mulda the Headman was in a sweat of discomfort. A thick-bodied, ruddy-faced man, never quite easy in summer heat, and now tugged all ways by this unvillagely flapdoodle. He liked Peterkin, or had till now, sympathetic to his loss and impressed by how he'd managed. So far. His mother Ella, how hard was all that. He took dark witchcraft for granted as most folk did, but although he had no trust in his sister he couldn't think that of her. Worse yet was the surge of energy filling the men and youths of the village. He'd seen it before, maybe thrice in his life, and knew how brainless it was and how unstoppable.

His hope was that killing the wolf would be enough. That it would give a good run, slip through the net of bowmen and have to be cornered two or three times – wear them out so when they carried it back hung from a pole they'd be wanting beer and feasting and then their beds, and not have venom for other indignations. He wanted it believed that Peterkin was bewitched, by persons unknown, not it was certain his sister, who take my word has no yen for the worship of Darkness. If he was forced to a choice of who to protect from the hand of an enjoyingly outraged mob, it had to be Irminbruga. Not that he loved her much but the outcome was unthinkable. Not so for Peterkin – no more, with his age, than a flogging, and of course to lose the farm. And Mulda would clear a space for him somewhere once the dust had settled, and give a quiet hand as he found his way.

Such was the excitement that at first Mulda at first lost control. No-one needed permission to go and kill a wolf, and no-one asked for it – small packs of men and of youths were out on the hill in tacit competition, expecting the wolf not to notice them and wander into bow-shot. But Mulda hived off the best two trackers as soon as he could find them, and – giving a string of names – sent out his go-fors to gather decent bowmen.

And when they set out Mulda led. Lately unused to uphill travel he slowed down his party, and he slowed it down more by hailing smaller posses when they were seen and making them join up, insisting a single dragnet was the only way. Meanwhile the wolf, tabled to die for the second time in his year and a quarter of life, heard the commotion and smelt the men coming and took a long and slinking run towards the high peaks, drawn to a certain outlook with a three-way choice of escape.

Peterkin was held by Mulda's two main stalwarts in the village Meeting House, big bruisers in early middle age who had helped bring to order many an unpleasantness. The larger man cuffed him round the head ten or a dozen times, shouting between the blows about children and lambs and the duty of a villager. The other watched incuriously, eating a pasty he'd brought in, sipping at a cup of milk.

For Peterkin the world was going blurry. The incomprehensible morning had built to a climax – he'd never given a thought to discovery, and what would happen. The shock of concussion and the shock of dismay combined to an unstoppable force. He felt it coming but

could do nothing, in his new world of utter helplessness: he broke down, and paroxysmic sobbing jarred
and jarred him. Somewhere, distant from the bucking
and tearing of his soul, he heard as if it belonged to
someone else his voice trying to apologise.

C'mon big man, said the second stalwart, chewing the
last of his pasty.

Dyah! said the big man, kicking Peterkin's feet from
under him, booting him some more as he curled up on
the floor.

Don't mark him. You know Mulda.

Fuck Mulda, said the big man. The kid deserves to die.

C'mon, take it easy old son.

And fuck you, y'big woman.

But the big man stamped away and sat on the bench
against the wall, staring ahead and muttering.

The second stalwart, keeping a taut but unworried eye
on his comrade, tipped back the last of his milk.

Peterkin, left alone, shuffled to the wall and sat with
his face in his hands, his sobs slowly trailing off. The
word 'die' had entered his blurred awareness. Somewhere deeper a 'no' began to ascend.

Mulda's hunting party didn't come back that night but
stayed out on the hill, making a huge fire and sleeping
under the sky. Their carried provisions didn't stretch to
supper. A late-commissioned posse found the evening
hillside a frugal market, returning – along with two
young marmots, and a near-grown ptarmigan chick –
with a billy goat whose heroic rearguard defence had
cost him his future, a bowman some tumble-cracked

ribs. The goat looked on the small side, slung on a sapling between two weary bearers.

But the men made the best of their meal and their night away from farm and family, singing lewd songs, guffawing at anecdotes, ignoring sprains and contusions gifted by the terrain. Only when a man stepped away from the pack did he sense the vast night rising above him in all its holy dread, and this, adjusting his garment, he kept to himself.

Their wives worried in the village below, until they realized their men couldn't all have fallen off cliffs or been torn apart by the wolf, and they sat by their hearths with the children abed, some with a cautious half-cup from the mead jug, feeling the stillness, sipping with their mead the double-edged nature of widowhood.

The men, sleeping in their clothes, woke shivering in the night, crouched at the fire, tripped over each other, rose cold and hungry. At first light a sheepish group was sent to the village for food, and stumped back when the sun was high with heavy burdens of bread and smoked mutton and oatmeal, and the biggest cooking pot that could reasonably be carried, and the men ate a big midday meal and after discussion set off again after the wolf.

The doings of the men had not dulled the wolf's reserve. The smell of fire with in it the smell of man, the many alarms of birds, threads in the breeze-whispered distance of a lusty chorus or a burst of heavy laughter, kept him close to his lookout. Every now and then he would up and trot out one of the escape routes, as if in rehearsal.

Chapter 6: Sinew

The breakfast-bearers carried news of Peterkin. This is what had happened.

The two stalwarts had taken the boy from the Meeting House to a one-room hut, and forced him onto his side on the floor and tied his feet to a bench with sinew and tied his hands behind his back, and kicked across a straw mat to roll onto if he could. Then they went to the tavern, barring the door from outside, wishing themselves on the hill with the hunters. After each of the first two drinks they went to check on the boy, but then didn't bother till after the sixth and last. They were arguing: the larger and angrier stalwart wanted to give him another kicking; he crashed in with the other behind preparing to drag him back, or try.

But Peterkin was gone.

The first time they leave him he hears them go and knows where they're headed. He squirms his hands down behind him towards his heels, writhing his way to a lying-down squat position. They've tied his wrists too tight, his hands are half numb. He feels out the knots at his ankles. A lump of half-hitches and grannies

– have these thugs ever strung a bow, let alone made a bowstring?

He struggles to a sitting position, pulling his hands up behind his knees and as far to the side as he can, and pushes his head down to press his right cheek on the side of his left knee. He drools as much saliva as he can make into his upward cupped hand, then rubs the saliva with awkward care into the sinew that binds his left ankle, pasting it onto the bonds and kneading it in with his fingertips over and over, hooking and tugging to stretch the sinew, then kneading over and over again. By the stalwarts' first return he has eased the sinew enough to squeeze three fingertips under it, and knead and roll it between them and his thumb.

He hears their voices in the lane and is back in position before the door-bar scrapes and the door creaks back. Fresh air, their grunty breathing, the scuff of their feet. One comes up to look at him and he lies very still and keeps his breath as slow and as quiet as he can, and the guy stomps off and the door thuds shut and the bar thuds down.

He's back to his task, working and working the sinew, kneading in his meagre spittle, stretching the sinew, kneading again. Soon he can work the loop around one ankle, almost to the heel. He levers with both thumbs, the loop biting into the front of his ankle, then kneads again and levers again clenching his teeth against the pain and the sinew works by tiny degrees over his callused heel and then eases, eases, and then his left foot is free.

Now with strain he can draw his left knee up to his chest and inch his bound wrists under, wincing again at the bite. His hands are under his crutch now, the right behind and the left in front. With strain, barely able to take breath, he can get his mouth to the sinew that binds his wrists, and lick it and chew it and work it with his teeth, exploring the knots with his lips and his tongue.

He's got this far when he hears the stalwarts' voices in the lane for the second time. He's barely back in position and hauling on his breath when the bar scrapes up and the hinge creaks open. They see his shape in the light of the moon. One steps in and toes him to make sure.

'Will we get him a blanket?'

'Nah, let the little shit freeze. Our brothers freeze on the hill through him.'

The bar thuds down again, darkness retakes the earth-smelling cell. He hears their voices retreat; some moments later a waft of fainter voices through the open door of the tavern, silence again as it thunks closed. Peterkin's back at his chewing and mouthing, breathing on the sinew to warm it.

His mother taught him to work sinew at five or six years old. He's never had a bowstring snap; his fence-bindings, greased against rain, hold back the impatience of a ram. He knows sinew, sinew is his friend. Sinew dry is sinew strong, wet it and its strength is gone. The heat of his breath and the wet of his saliva and the work-heat of his chewing. The slow filling-out of its sweet-rancid taste as it softens and stretches. He

68

works the widening loop by fractions over the heel and the thumb-base of his left hand: one side the other side, one side the other side – a slow toil, and then out slips the hand all at once. His hands are free.

He's down at the agglomeration of knots that hold his right ankle to the bench. To chew and work the whole mess free would take half the night. He feels the floor for a stone or some kind of shard but there's nothing.

He feels out his attachment to the bench. He's tied to one of the legs, above and below its junction with a stretcher – the stretcher peg-jointed, held by ancient glue or just by closeness of fit. The old bench has creaked under generations of heavy arses and clambering children; there's promising movement in its joints. He shunts in and braces his free left foot on the back leg of the bench and grips the near leg and heaves. He hears and senses the far end of the stretcher pull out of its socket, reaches in and feels – it's dropped a couple of inches. He levers it sideways, works it back and forth till he can tug free the near end. And he presses a knee up under the seat of the bench and lifts it a couple of inches and works the sinew that holds his right ankle down the leg of the bench and he's free.

And now he stands, liberated, wobbly on his feet in the dark of the hut. Fear hits him now he's standing. His exertions have kept him warm but now he's a-shake and a-tremble. It takes all his effort to still himself and tie off round ankle and wrist the loose ends of his bonds. Then he's at the door but he can see no way with it, heavily barred without. Thin slivers of moonlight at the joins – he'd need a blade to lift the bar. The high shuttered window, likewise edged in silver, a size to barely squeeze through, is the only chance – that or try and burst past the heavies on their next return, take them by surprise, sprint for open country. He likes the window better.

It's high, and has no sill. He might have to drag the bench across for a platform; if he does there's no going back to his masquerade of restraint if he hears them coming. The tremor in his limbs intensifies. But he reaches a tentative hand for the wall and feels its untrimmed boulders, and before he knows anything else he's feeling out a route on the pitchblack stone, and his foot finds an inset step for just the purpose of reaching the shutter, and a recessed hand-hold, and another fine step.

Panting he feels out the single shutter and finds the catch and with no thought he's squirreled up and through, arms head and shoulders, nearly too late he thinks of the headfirst drop and twists and grabs the flapping-out shutter and grips for his life as he frees his legs, and one warped leather hinge breaks with his weight and he falls quite sweetly into hump-tussocked grass.

There's no-one in the lane. He makes himself check all ways. His route to open country needs no thought: a few steps towards the tavern, then duck out from the lane and thread between grain-huts and then along by the shadow side of the mill, out of the moonlight. Then by the bean-rows and blaeberry patch of old Colwen's cottage, to the edge of a climbing fallowfield and a twisting steeper path close by the rush of the river, to leave the path and hack away from the river and climb more steeply through boulders to come out on the side path that leads to his hut. And here to sneak very carefully, to see if it's guarded already, or cousin-taken.

With his route at the front of his mind it's as if he's already slipped past Widow Colwen's cottage, Colwen last of the famous goat-girls since Bode and Biddeka died in the same month seven years past. Asleep he's assumed, so old, not knowing her ways.

He's passing the moonlit side of her cottage, using the bean-rows for cover – the beans already shoulder height, he creeps in a low crouch – when Widow Colwen speaks

from her porch. Barely above conversational pitch, but it might be the loudest sound he's ever heard.

Ho, creeping youth ...

She catches him at the point of sprinting ...

Run and I'll scream blue bloody murder. You hear me, sneaking boy? Come here. Come *here*.

Peterkin, at a loss, at a loss, steps closer. She's sitting half hidden in her porch, bundled up in many clothes, watching the moon and the night, a cup of mead on a ledge of the porch beside her.

Why of course – the wolf boy! Fey Ella's fey son. Thought you'd take a stroll in the night – not enjoying your company?

Peterkin is tongue-tied. But it seems he doesn't need to speak. Ah, wolf boy, let me see you.

By the moon her old wry face stares into his, her eyes still quick as a bird's. She takes a sip of her drink.

Your mother was so sweet, everyone loved your mother, except the eaten with envy, and her I shall not name, your virtuous accuser. The devious tub of lard. Everyone, your mother ... I remember her as a child, slinking in at a gap in the circle to hear the old stories, eyes big as an owl's. You'd try and cover up her ears when certain events were mentioned but she'd squirm away, politely mind, she wanted to know everything.

She takes another sip.

Well, bold wolf boy – Peterkin? Peterkin. Run if you can, bold Peterkin, I'll not halt you longer. Hide in the hills till the moon's past the full, they'll kill your wolf and if no fool breaks his neck up there they'll come back very full of themselves. Then show yourself when the mood's still good and you'll get away with a hiding, maybe get branded with some mark or other but that'll intrigue the girls, you'll be the bad boy they dream about.

She gestures him closer, then creaks to her feet and winces and grunts at the pain and then smiles to herself as if it had amused her. She takes on a formality of manner. She hand-wafts him closer still, then reaches up and takes his face in both her hands and stares into his face myopically close, with an almost eerie intent. The sharp sharp eyes in her weathered and deep-lined face, like a crone from the dreamworld.

> Luck go with you, Luck preserve you
> Luck by day and Luck by night
> Luck at risk and Luck in action,
> Luck in hiding, Luck in flight.

I bless you, Ella's son. Go.

Thank you Mother Colwen he says, stepping back and bowing.

She has dropped the formality, turning away with a slight acknowledging raise of the hand. She moves stiffly round her chair and goes into the cottage, lit by a single candle, to fill her cup and find a warmer bonnet.

Peterkin bows again, then hurries into the night.

He steals up on the hut, keeping well off the path, checking behind and around him for watchers. The sheep are bawling in the fold, penned in all day, unfed since morning. There's no sign of presence.

The half moon that shone on Colwen's porch shines on the front of the hut. He sees the door is part open, shifting on its hinges. The windows unshuttered. No light, within, but would there be, this late.

He's on the right of the path, in birch and sallow, working towards the door. The window would be better for squinting in but it's to the left, out in the open moonlight.

But he must let go the fear of an outside spy or be stuck. They wouldn't watch the hut, if they thought him bound and prisoned; and even if they'd sent a guard as soon as the heavies crashed in on the scene of escape the fellow would hardly have got here so quickly.

But if he did, he'll be in the hut.

Peterkin creeps to the gap in the door. It creaks a little on its ox-hide hinges. His mouth is wide open to silence his breath. No sound within, no breathing, no shift of weight.

He listens in frozen attention. His mind's eye sees the watcher, alert as Peterkin himself, sitting hard by the door, waiting to grab.

But then another image, this one a certainty. They'll be coming up the track, very soon. The hut's the first place they'll look.

He glances down the track behind him and crosses to the window. He keeks in aslant. The moonlit patch he can see is a chaos of intrusion – chair tipped over, his mead jug on its side on the table, spilt mead gleaming in the adze-cuts. But whoever it was, they've gone.

He's quickly in at the door. He finds flint and steel in their place by the hearth and fires up a fluff of tinder and lights a candle. There's his best bow cast down on the floor, and his quiver, open-topped, arrows spilling. He clears space with his foot and lets down his crib-bed and sleeping mat and places on it, very quick but holding back from clumsiness, his bow and quiver, the flint and steel, his tinder purse, his cloak, his satchel. He sets up the chair and reaches into the rafter shelf for the bag of two dozen bowstrings he's been pounding and winding of nights for the summer fair.

Whoever's been in has emptied his larder. He's at the door and stares down the path and quick-foots to his smoke-shed at the back for a shoulder and the hide to wrap it in. An explosion of baa-ing from the sheep in their fold alongside; he tries absurdly to shush them. After a second's thought he slips the tie of their pen, so they'll find their way out, but not soon enough to get in the way.

Back in the hut he takes the candle and feels for a loose stone at the side of the hearth and prises it out and feels for a leather purse, small but fat, that makes a slight gravelly crunch in his hand.

And he packs the satchel very full with the tight folded cloak squashed under the flap and takes it and his bow and his quiver of arrows and steps out of the hut. His fear has almost gone: a hundred coming up the path could never catch him now, he could run this hillside blindfold. Beside the hut is an alder tree he climbed a thousand times and fell out of thrice: it's a living signification of mother, childhood, home. He goes to it and presses his forehead against the trunk, a hand against the side. Then he turns and sets off uphill, ignoring the path. With the heel of his free hand he smears off the tears that are wet on his face.

His route passes his mother's shrine to Luck, and last of all he kisses the symbol and whispers a prayer. Composed, now, he climbs. He's gone hardly a mile, with the very first grey of dawn behind, when exhaustion comes suddenly upon him, and he squirms into undergrowth and wraps himself in his cloak and takes his first bedless roofless repose.

It had happened that Irminbruga, as soon as she heard of her nephew's arrest, had sent her two eldest boys Jep and Beri to take squatter's rights to the hut and the farm.

Headman Mulda, as soon as he heard of his sister's ruse, detailed two second-tier heavies to go and turf the boys out. His order was immediate and instinctive. A balance of motives: his fear of what might be made of it, with talk going round that the boy was bewitched; a wish to see things done properly; a chronic distaste for his sister's wiles.

The cousins were half drunk on Peterkin's mead when the heavies burst in. There was a dying fire in the grate, a smell of roasted meat. The older boy had filled their satchels from the larder to take back to their mother. He wanted to take Peterkin's bow as well but was booted out for his cheek. The men encouraged their stumbling progression with hearty threats not to return, and watched them away down the hill to the village.

Then they turned uphill to join the hunt for the wolf.

Peterkin was well on his way to his hut when the two stalwarts came back from the tavern. They blundered around the vicinity, yelling threats and improvised deals, stubbing their toes in the black spaces where outbuildings shadowed the moon.

Colwen listened to their progress, still in her porch, now in her cape and two bonnets. In due course they found their way to her blaeberry patch.

What ails you drunkards on so sweet a night? Don't dare piss on my beans.

Mother Colwen?

Who but?

Not abed, Mother? (She'll have heard something.) What've you heard at all, this last while?

What've I heard? Two oxen broke from their stall, is what I've heard.

I bow, Mother Colwen. Forgive us our intrusion. The boy has run – the friend of wolves, Peterkin son of …

Thessel, murmurs the other.

Thessel.

He nudges his partner as if, out in the moonlight, they're as shadowed to Colwen as she is to them. She smiles to herself as he speaks.

Someone let him out – opened the door and cut his bonds. We were only gone a while, for a bite of bread and curd.

Well if he'd come by I'd have hauled him in, young men have too long been scarce hereabouts. A fine boy too, Peterkin, I knew his mother well. Wolf? – I'll wager it was a fox – don't you know that slant-tongue Irminbruga?

There's evidence, with respect ...

Didn't come *this* way, anyhow. I heard not a thing till you fine fellows began your exertions. He'll have headed down, for the Valley, to find summer work till the fuss dies down. But you'll do well to catch him, and not break your necks in the gorge.

The men bow and give the courtesies, muttering. They slip back to the holding hut, feel for the sinews to slice them off neatly but they're gone. They replace the stretcher of the bench by feel, one gives the other a leg up to fix the skew-whiff shutter well enough to seem untouched to an unsuspicious eye.

Chapter 7: A Passage

eterkin woke up shivering, numb in hand and foot. It was daylight but the sun had not yet found its heat, under-lighting a drawn-out whey of cloud with exceeding fineness of colour, cinnamons and apricots too sweet for the world he knew.

He was up and moving to make some heat. He had a vague plan. First he needed to bypass the hunting party. Then he needed to find the wolf, which he knew without thinking had fled to the highest ground, and with it slip away unseen. Slip away how, slip away where, he didn't yet know.

He guessed where they'd be and they were. He'd taken an ascending route to the right hand side of all paths, catching the remnant odour of their fire, working for a viewpoint past and above them. He peeked out from the scrub at the top of a short cliff; if they spotted him he'd have a long lead by the time they worked their way round it.

They were mostly up, stamping and slapping their arms across their chests for heat, some round the ash of the fire, half the group fanning all ways for wood. The nearest two, no more than a hundred yards from him, were trying to break down a small half-rotten tree, working it back and forth, back and forth.

Peterkin watches. There seems to be no hurry; no-one is heading anywhere bow at the ready. They're more concerned with stirring the fire for warmth than with hunting a wolf. He's bemused, till he gets that they're waiting for food. He's suddenly ravenous at the idea. A day has passed since his last breakfast, with neither a morsel nor a moment's conscious hunger. He backs into cover and, making himself move slowly, extricates the mutton from his satchel and cuts two thumb-thick slices and eases back to his watch-point and chews hard on the uncooked meat as he watches. He's missing bread already. By the time he's worked through the first slice he's almost too dry-mouthed to swallow, and he re-packs the second and wipes his greasy hands on a tussock as best he can and takes a last scan of the hunters and moves on, satchel and quiver and bow.

Once he's covered a distance he starts to make the dusk-owl call, untimeous under the now well-risen sun.

He's guessed that the men will wait till after they've eaten, then take elaborate care in arranging a line of beaters, stretching east to west across the tilted shelf of land to back up the wolf and take it at their leisure. He thinks to find the wolf and somehow lead him around and behind the dragnet line of men.

He heads, calling as he goes, for the north end of the four-mile upland shelf.

Once the men have eaten and stretched the hard ground from their bones and warmed in the sun now high now in the sky, and drunk from a stony stream, and moved their bowels in random half-discreet recesses, they set off at Mulda's direction. Nine have been picked to fan out ahead: the best trackers, the keenest eyes, the agilest legs. The rest, twenty-seven in number, move behind at Mulda's pace, spread out sideways to beat the whole width of the shelf.

But while Peterkin seeks to pre-empt them, in the long and broken-grounded north end of the shelf, the hunters are heading south.

They aim to try the easiest option first. At the south end of the shelf are three cliff-walled corries, the last just beyond the famous Notch. If the wolf is anywhere down that end it'll easily be cornered.

And Luck is with them. The wolf is hid up at the mouth of the middle corrie. A faint smell of man comes up on the north-east breeze; then a distant sliding of scree, a whirr of ptarmigan. The wolf is about to slip from the corrie and travel north when he gets first sight of a man, a half-mile off in the way he wants to go. The wolf stops to watch. The man is making waist-high subtle movements with his arms. And then the wolf sees another man, and another, and climbs a little for a better view. Fear takes him. The upland shelf is narrow here; a line of men a quarter mile long is spaced across its whole width.

His first impulse is to weave through the boulder-field under the corrie wall, slipping unseen past the near end of the line of men. But then yet another clambers into view on that very route, red-faced and seeming enormous.

He turns to go the other way, make for the scrubby woodland below the final and southernmost corrie, take cover, spurt through their line when the time comes. But a louder scrape and tumble of scree and there's a man that way too, apparitioning below him.

To hunt and to be hunted are the same. It might be the oldest game of all, there are stars in the sky that are younger. The game is woven into the tissue of the wolf, woven with great refinement. Its play makes no call on 'thought' or 'decision' – the wolf is a beast, it must go with the moment. Every move is forced.

So there's some exact distance in the lumbering approach of the till-now-unseeing red-faced man at which the wolf will bolt, and when the man starts to bellow and wave his arms about, and the whole line of men takes up the bellowing, along with high whoops and the clapping of hands, the terror catapults him at full sprint, jinking fore-scouts who don't see him till he's by, clean through the scrub woodland that was his last chance of a hideout, into the southernmost corrie the ends the long upland strip like the toe of a stocking.

Now he's trapped.

Peterkin was weary, moving slowly north to south and calling to the wolf, humping satchel and bow with the high sun in his face another burden, too vague-headed to wonder why there'd been no sign of the hunting party, when he heard the great shout a mile ahead.

He hurried on sick to the heart as fast as his breath would let him.

The wolf is at bay, crouched and snarling, every hair on end.

Seven leading bowmen have arrows notched but Mulda, leader of men, has stayed them with a gesture and a bark of command. He's made them hold back till he's puffed up the corrie to join the lead. The men, so close to the climax of events, would mutiny, but Mulda looks sideways and growls individual names and they back down.

He's had a sudden idea.

We'll take it alive, take it back and hang it in the square for sacrifice. Then feast, to Luck and the Huntsman.

The wolf is backed in a crevice, a bowstring loop on a pole will haul it out, barely conscious from the strangulation. Pronged branches, not even stripped of their leaves, will pin it till it's tied. They do this every year with a billy goat, to sacrifice to the Sun. A stick is worked between its teeth and the jaws tied shut. Its feet are tied together, a pole threaded lengthways twixt hindlegs and twixt forelegs, and it's ready to carry, writhe all it likes.

They come back down to the foot of the corrie and stop at a clearing of level ground in the scrubby woodland and lay down the wolf. It lies still, panting, its tongue protruding aslant behind the stick. Mulda has them tidy their bows and gear at the downhill end, and they wash their faces and hands at a stream and drink mountain water and sit together, and share their provisions and take their ease.

They've eaten and the talk has gone round and they're coming to the time to start the long trek home when someone smells smoke, then others. Then in the cease of conversation they hear crackling. Their gear is on fire.

Consternation, a shouting rush. Every man wants to save his bow. How? they shout, and look round for someone to blame. The fire is beaten out, most of their stuff is saved. They come back to purpose shrugging shoulders, shaking heads.

Two men go to take up the wolf but the wolf isn't there.

Peterkin had hurried on, and he saw the pack of men surge up into the corrie. With them out of sight and engrossed he took an open loose-screed route between the final corrie and the Notch. A goat path that contoured and then dropped. Where the path bent left he had a clear view of the mouth of the corrie. He settled to watch, crouched between boulders.

When they brought out the wolf the boy saw straight-away he was still alive. His heart was overwhelmed; he'd take any chance to save the beast. His weariness fell away, as if his soul had been plunged and washed clean; even the heat of the day had a coolness to it, a clarity.

When they stopped and dumped the wolf he thought to sneak down and cut his bonds, but it would have taken too long. Then distraction occurred to him; then fire. He left his gear, but took flint and steel and his knife and easily worked around the excited group, snatching up sun-parched kindling grass as he went. Four years bow-hunting in the woods, he could move with near-perfect silence. The fire flared up briskly; he was back round and crouching not three steps from the wolf.

Here he could see how awkwardly he was tied – knots upon knots. No chance of slicing in time through all of that. And – two legs free – then what? The wolf would be scrabbling frantic while he freed the rest. The men's attention is loosening from the fire. Peterkin moves in and takes the mid-point of the pole and squats deep and shoulders the pole and he's stumping uphill through awkward bouldery scrubwood until he hits the goat-track, the wolf writhing and slamming against him.

The men in their astonishment are blundering close to their halt when Peterkin, gasping, his legs a-tremble and weak as a baby's, eases down his writhing load at his watch-point. Barely a hundred yards from the Notch.

Old Colwen's hint, that Peterkin had run for the Great Valley, had hardened into assumed fact and travelled up with the news of his escape. So no-one thought of him. Surly eyes were turned on notorious pranksters: there were hard words, threats, even a buffet or two. Time was taken, floundering in undergrowth. When a twenty-yard margin had been double and triple-checked a voice shouted 'the *Boy*, it must be the *Boy*', and Mulda called in the men for more rational search.

Again the Notch calls to itself the play of events. It has done so all along, unbeknownst.

As far as he had any notion at all Peterkin's thought had been to gather the wolf and circuit above all trodden paths to the northern end of the upland, then drop down and hide in the woods across the stream from his now forsaken hut. Then sneak the wolf around the village and down through the gorge in dead of night, praying to Luck and the Moon. Once in the Great Valley he didn't know – show him perhaps at the summer fair if he's tame enough by then, for stones and beads and barley corn, to catch a wealthy patron's eye, who knows.

But Luck and the Notch had other ideas, and gathered events towards their fulfilment. Drew the line of play by complex means, a beckoning chance always just ahead.

So Peterkin, while the men still bumble in the scrub, leaves the pole-bound wolf and taking his satchel and bow and quiver he scurries across to the Notch and looks down. A sickness takes him; every muscle in his body goes weak. The skulls in the drystone cairns might be staring down with him. He heaves himself from the lethargy of dread and goes back for the wolf.

His legs and arms feel uselessly weak but they work. He shoulders the pole again. The frantic strength of the wolf in its writhing, thumping against his hip and thigh, throws his balance about as he lurches across. He'd thought to maybe carry it down on a headstrap. He lowers the wolf with care and again he looks down, and he knows they'd both die. A forty foot drop onto boulders. He stares with vacant intensity at the wolf, at his gear, at the green and brown-streaked face of a skull in the right hand cairn, its cranium half collapsed.

But then the clear-mindedness fills him again, as if a second sun has come out. Again given new life, he sees what to do and he's doing it – quickly, decisively, without the stumble and jerk of hurry.

He takes out his package of two dozen bowstrings and reef-knots them end to end, to make a cord of sinew maybe thirty-six yards long, with a breaking strain at least twice the pull of a bow. Double it, the strength maybe half again. When he's done he threads the doubled line through the satchel strap, through the quiver strap, between the string and shaft of the bow. He counts twelve knots through and hefts the load to the edge of the drop. The nearest surface is a flat-topped boulder, he guesses fifteen yards down. But he needs it for the wolf. He checks: satchel tied, quiver lid closed. He lowers his belongings hand over hand, wrapping the doubled line round each hand in turn. The burden is less than three stone, but even at that the bite of the sinew's a torment – the weight of the wolf would pull the skin off his hands.

But this descent, anyway, goes well. A skid and a slither rather than a drop; here and there he swings the load around a projection. A last swing to the left of the flat-topped boulder and he's got enough line to ease the burden two yards more and onto a mess of smaller boulders. He lets go one end of the string and throws it out and down, and shuggles and tugs the other end to free the string of its load. The bow doesn't want to disconnect, a knot trapped where bowstring meets stave – he improvises various swings and jerkings before it drops.

Now the wolf, lying as if dead. but for the deep pulse of his breath.

Peterkin doubles the length of the string once more, and slips the midpoint loop under the balance point of the carrying pole and threads the whole length of the doubled string through the loop. Deadlifts to check the balance; the wolf thrashes.

How to lower, how?

He knots the parallel strings together at points about a yard apart, snakes out the double cord and checks for snags and hitches. How much length in the extra knots? No matter, it's the only way, no matter. Shouts from behind and below – the men have started to fan, have they seen him?

Peterkin heaves the wolf to the very edge, above the flat-topped boulder. Writhing, the sinews he's tied with biting into his legs. The boy holds the pole right-handed, his left hand upraised between the doubled strings. The wolf is side-on to the drop. Peterkin takes three-fourths of the weight of the wolf and nudges him to the balance point. Then the wolf's slipping over – the weight almost takes the boy as well.

Hand by hand he lowers the bucking wolf at a long slow scrape, he in a back-leaning half- squat, looking over as far as he dare, the switch from knot to knot each time more desperate, praying to Luck all the way for the sinews to hold the wolf's writhing five-stone-plus. At least his squirmings help him over the lumps – Peterkin has no strength for steering.

At last the wolf reaches the boulder and the weight eases and he's lying half on one side with his legs at a tilt against the cliff wall, the pole threaded between them.

Peterkin feeds out the last two yards of sinew and lets the line go.

Now he's alone in the Notch, with no possessions but the clothes he wears. Before him, if he gets down, an even deeper aloneness. Another shout – his name – he's been seen now for sure. He knows – most of the village boys know – where the climb-down starts. It's a test of youth to make the first three moves, and risk a fall or the Headman's wrath.

He hears a scrape on the scree below and behind. Now it's time.

He's not before made so much as the very first move. His cousin Jep did, and laughed his braying laugh with just his head above the edge, and then made the next two moves before he came back.

Peterkin knows of only two who've made the move after that. The crux. You must traverse to your right around a projection. Lean way out on a left-hand hold to reach around it, and hand-search unseen rock till you find another hold, then dare to poke your head round for a glimpse, then hold on tight and straddle the lump to get a toehold on nothing very much. And then you take your deepest breath and let go your left hand, and swing out like a shutter in the wind, and then dart the left hand in to join the other, and then you hold on gasping.

The rest is handles and doorsteps they say, handles and doorsteps.

He's frozen at the crux when the first head peers over. His legs are a-shake like a man who's fallen through ice, again he feels that all their strength has gone.

Back up boy, the man above shouts, like a press gang marshal. Get back up.

Another appears, another. He's got to get down before they notice the wolf.

He scouts with his right hand and scrabbles, scrabbles, grips. A split-second glance round the hump and the rest is a piece of logic that his body solves for itself in less time than it takes to think. And then, yes it's easy, he's down, he's down, and rockhopping steps to the wolf and he's up and leaning over him before the first arrow is drawn.

Move boy or we kill you, and the whip and chap of an arrow a yard to the side.

But then he hears Mulda's voice in a growl, and the first voice says no more.

Peterkin, says Mulda.

Peterkin squirms out of his jerkin and half-wraps it round the wolf's head. Then he's drawn his knife and working on the sinews that bind the beast's jaws, sawing with care above and below one side of the stick they've thrust there. The instant the stick is out he wraps the jerkin tight so the wolf is blind and muzzled.

Then he extracts the carrying pole and throws it aside. He pins the wolf legs-up between his feet, and gripping as tight as the writhing demands he saws with great care through the knots that bind his legs, first the front and then with an awkward turn the hindlegs.

And then he wrestles him onto his side, the freed legs thrashing the air, and lies on him to hold him down and cover him from arrows and makes ready to flip off the jerkin. He does and in one movement rolls off the beast and shouts GO, GO, and the wolf has scrabbled up and made an ungainly leap not yet found his legs and skids a landing on the next boulder and down and slaloms through the boulderfield with arrows near-missing, and then he's beyond the boulders and heading down the shaly falling slope and into the trees and gone.

Mulda has been shouting down.

Peterkin says nothing. Silently he gathers his satchel and quiver and bow, retrieves the carry-pole, loosens off his cord of bowstrings, winds the strings and packs them. He takes up his gear and in (it seems) a long bamboozling dream he works his way between and over the boulders, following the wolf.

He senses Mulda feeling the occasion, the need for a formality. Perhaps he does himself. He stops with his back to the Notch and the men of the village above him, and Mulda sings down in his great, rarely heard, ceremonial voice.

PETERKIN son of THESSEL son of BOSE, Peterkin son of ELLA.

COME BACK NOW or COME BACK NEVER.

Peterkin stands some moments more. Then, still not turning, he steps past the last of the boulders and onto the shale, and walks away slowly at first and with composure, and then he quickens his step and then he's running, down towards the trees.

Part 2: The Hermitage

Chapter 8: A Welcome

The sun is falling towards an alien skyline, far across the unknown land.

Peterkin's legs walk him downwards, away from the world he knows. They seem to have some plan of their own – he stares at the broken country around like a child who is being carried. Not once does he turn and look back, towards the cleft in the skyline behind, and the men who might or might not be watching him go. Such is not in the plan of his legs, which have only onwards and downwards in their tendency.

The terrain so far is familiar, almost weirdly so. The same granulation of shale and boulders, the same trees making the best of it, sudden patch meadows stippled with flowers.

He's gone well over a mile and is deep in the shade of a wood, the trees now higher, when he's jolted from his numbness. To his left runs a stream, he finds himself on a track. Big human-looking prints on the edge of a seep but they're not the prints of a man. If they are it's a man with claws. Earlier today by the look, by the near-fresh edging. He knows about bears but they're only a creature of anecdote back in the village. The joke about a traveller led by such humanoid prints into a cave, calling out a greeting. A needle of fear and he starts to wake – to his weariness, to his hunger, to the opening concerns of his predicament.

He slips his bow and reaches behind his shoulder to thumb up the cap of his quiver and tweak an arrow, all very slowly and quietly, listening hard, staring into the trees, rocking left and right to triangulate his view. He's never felt fear in the open before, bar a couple of times with the wolf – the most dangerous beast in his valley would be a cornered lynx or billygoat, and only a fool would arrive in such company. But now the chance of a bear will be with him every step, and of creatures more storytale yet: the boar, the panther, even the lion, believed in by the credulous.

He needs to find somewhere to stop. The sun is very low now, big and sullen and slanting down on little skyline hills way off on the far edge of a plain. He sees – does he? – in fading light, down to the left maybe five miles off, the minuscule wisp of smoke of an evening fire. He tries to landmark it, though whether to find or avoid he doesn't yet know. Beyond and below the wisp of smoke a thick collar of forest runs north-south between him and the plain. Are the people here more dangerous than the beasts? – the tale of the goat-girls says so.

Once he's seen the bear prints he takes the most open route he can for fear of ambush. His hand is moist in its grip on the bow and free arrow. A startled roe crashes through sticks to his right, he just about leaves the ground. His whole idea now is find some cliff or outcrop to back against, with a fire close in front so nothing can sneak up behind him.

The light is low when he finds it – a giant boulder, facing onto a half-acre rocky meadow, open woodland beyond. Abundant dead wood to the sides and the rear, bone dry blades of last year's grass among the new green.

He makes himself at home. He thinks to give the dusk-owl call and now and then he does, with no real hope of response.

In the last of the gloaming, a second round of smoked chunks of mutton braising on sticks, thirst-quenched from a nearby streamlet, eyelids starting to droop, he hears the howling of wolves. He's never heard the sound from his companion wolf. From the wood across the patch of meadow it comes: a thin eerie yodel coiling up through the trees, then three or four others in slow pursuit, weaving their ascent to join the first at the top of its scale, where they hang together above the trees and spread their presence across the darkening world. And then the voices drop in a heap with sudden informality, and then they climb again and climb again.

As the howling lifts through the forest it lifts through the boy, an icy ascent through crotch and solar plexus and throat. Death himself might conduct the sound. He's never felt so small and so alone. But he reaches out to his bow and quiver and touches the haft of his knife.

Then they're silent awhile, and then they howl again at half the distance. A crawling on his neck and scalp, a crawling in his stomach. He thinks they've smelt the mutton but they've smelt the newcomer wolf.

The wolf, the newcomer wolf, has made no sense of what's happened to him, has no way even of wanting to. The present he lives in has eased back from a somersaulting derangement of events to an easier and more usual flow. But his soul is mangled, trauma-punctured. The hunting-pack of men, its bawling and its stench; the abject terror of capture; the searing pain of the ties as he bounced upside-down; and then it's not the men but the boy; and a new surge of terror, scraping down the cliff; and the boy again; and then he's broken free. None of all this is a puzzle to him but a blur, with no idea of sequence or of point.

When he escaped his first propulsion was for cover. He hides up and licks his wounds, two places where the sinews have bitten right through the skin, the pumping of his lungs settling slowly, very slowly. Jerks and quivers make routes through his musculature. Then he's hungry and thirsty, thirsty first.

He can hear a stream, he's up and limping, whitish-green water spread out and plaiting through stones

on a level, as cold as ice. He drinks a mighty portion, the ice-water chilling his wounds and his jangled soul.

Then he is hungry. He hasn't eaten for two days. Luck brings an eagle, swooping on a spring- born mountain hare; he charges it and it can't lift the hare in time but wafts off a yard or so indignant, and then he goes for the trees while it dives on him, a big female, her last hunt of the day, she'll take his neck if she can but he jinks aside and she brakes hard as he makes cover.

He eats every scrap, working the whole head in his mouth, working through the leg bones. He could manage three more but it's something.

Now though, watered and fed, he takes in a smell that has hung in the air all along: the territorial urine of stranger wolves. He's not near any marker tree but the odour's at the back of all other smells, steady but slight, neither fresh nor faded. What little direction he's had – away from men, down into the cover of forest – is re- versed: back, back up into rock country, the lone wolf's retreat to the margins.

But then things happen. Piercing all other odours, smoke – a thin acrid note, re-awakening fear. The men, fire, a terror outweighing all else – he hadn't thought they'd throw him on it, he hadn't thought they wouldn't. Faintly, also, the boy's low whistle. And then, sudden and close, the howl of the pack.

Peterkin, taking with him a brand from the fire, gathers stones. Anything a size to throw. He carries a clumsy load in the crook of his arm, the next trip he takes his cloak. The vanished sun underlights distant clouds a deep and deepening red. The moon is unrisen. It'll be a dark night.

There's movement to his right and he grabs a stone (only in desperation will he shoot his precious arrows into the dark). He takes a step from the fire, trying to see, shielding his eyes from the firelight. A scuff and a movement of shape, a shifting of densities – he lifts his arm to throw. Whatever it is moves again, the firelight touches its outline. A split-second hint of its face. Surely it's his wolf, his wolf come. He whistles, gets it wrong a couple of times, not able to loosen his lips. Then he finds the owl-call and makes it over and over.

His wolf comes entirely into sight, buckled with fear and ingratiation: crouched prawn-like, the rear right down with the tail curled under the belly, ears flat and back-hair crested. The pack has gone silent; there's movement in the meadow but Peterkin doesn't hear it, with the crackle of the fire and his joy and concern for his reappeared wolf. He thinks the wolf's fear is of him, and mixes the owl-call with soothing and clucking words. But then in a moment a great stranger wolf explodes out of the dark, and is on his wolf which prawns snarling right to the ground, and Peterkin shouts out in shock and stamps towards the snarling melee in tiny steps still shouting brainlessly, and only when the great wolf wheels and is gone into the night does he think of throwing the stone in his hand and he miss-throws maybe five yards into noth- ingness.

He's to his heap of stones and snatching them up and dropping them, and with half a dozen crooked in his arm and one in the other hand he sidles a little away from the light of the fire, wary of his own hair-on-end wolf, and stares into the dark. He notices, as if in some sideroom of events, that he's making shouting noises. In front of him, fanned out at twenty-five yards, six pairs of eyes are glowing red with reflected firelight.

He starts to shout in words, and the words he's shout- ing help discipline his throw and the stones fly true, and the wolves out there can't see them coming for one thuds home and yelping and ki-yiking follows and he's back for another armful. Two of the pairs of eyes have wheeled to his right and are sneaking towards his wolf. Peterkin shouts and throws, shouts and throws, and another yelp and the eyes are gone in a shush of retreating movement.

And he's back for more stones, but instead at the fire he snatches up the branch he'd used as a torch and he steps out boldly, shouting, waving his brand in a wide overhead arc, and he sees the sullen beads of eyes now further off but still with foot-dragging hopes of attack- ing his wolf, and forward he stamps and they vanish and he sends in pursuit fierce shouts from his little stock of obscenities.

He goes back triumphant and sets a second small fire to block further wing attacks. Clumsily: he feels very fine but he's shaking like a man pulled from an ice pool. He goes back to the main fire and his gear, giving his own wolf room as he passes. The wolf is backed against the rock wall and panting but has no obvious hurt from the assault.

Peterkin gives a breathless owl call or two as settles back, makes orderly his place by the fire, puts on fresh wood. With twigs he combs the scorched mutton chunks from their sticks and onto a stone to cool. He sits against the sheer wall of the boulder with the fire slantwise in front and to his left and the wolf haunched down three yards to his right, and he stares into the night, seeking the eyes of the enemy pack.

For some time all is still. And then again the pack commences to howl, voices interweaving as they climb, and again the tendrils of living fear climb Peterkin's skin to match them. But the howl comes from half a mile away. The fight is won. He owl-calls to his wolf, and says some words, and tosses across a chunk of half-carbonized mutton.

The sun rises late this side of the mountain range.

It paints a thin layer of heat on rock and tree-bole and skin, deepening only slowly – two yards into a cave or a gorge and the mountain cold will last all day. Peterkin, under his cloak, knees drawn up for warmth, is woken by the light, opens his eyes a second, fingers the sheathed knife beside him, drops back down into deep disarticulate sleep.

It's well up when he wakes again, its now-thicker heat oozing through the cloak, even in the shadow of the boulder. He steps away from the wall of rock and lets it soak into him, bleary-eyed at first, not quite sure that he's awake. That this is really this. The flowers and rocks of the meadow, the acrid smell of the dead fire, the wide and high-lit alien vista before him, have to them a kind of bleakness, desolation almost. Deep in his gut there's a seed of fear, cold and indigestible. In its insidious way it's worse than all the craziness just past, even the wolves. A black bean of fear, ready to sprout in a moment and tendril up and take over.

The wolf is awake, licking his thong-hurt ankles. Peterkin speaks to him quietly, recounting the dramas of yesterday, piecing them out from the single concussive blur; telling him of their predicament, that the mutton's finished, an ill-natured wolf pack jealous of its domain. Bear tracks. The unknown land before them. Then he prays aloud to Luck, thanking him for his help last night – the stones that thunked home in the dark, the big wolf's attack that seems to have found no more than a mouthful of hair. All along – between glances at the wolf, who sometimes looks up and sometimes just licks at his heels – all along the boy eyes the vast land before them and below, seeping fear as it calls them down.

It's easily the broadest view he's ever seen. Across a vast plain the land meets the sky in a moulded line of hills, sharp in the bone-dry air. How far? Forty miles? Fifty? The plain wooded and hillocked in patches but mostly good farm land so far as he can tell, pieced-out fields discernible at the closer edge. Before the plain a long and easy drop of land, most of it thickly wooded. He can't see, but knows from his native induction in the ways of land and water, that somewhere down there's a great river. Down where the land stops falling, surely – nowhere so far as his view permits does it snake out onto the plain. He takes it that the river runs north-south, right-left from where he's placed, like the Great Valley river far behind him. He knows without having to think that it might well be uncrossable, unless some jovial ferryman looks kindly on his wolf.

He tells the wolf what he's thinking. Should they stay up here or travel down? Bears, he points out; the afore-mentioned resident pack. A meat-only diet, give or take a few berries – okay for wolves, less so for bread-yearn-ing youths. But then the route down – to what new dangers? Why?

As he talks the black bean of dread slowly softens. To speak of the new world as he scans it seems to make it a little friendlier. The wolf, watching him as he speaks as if taking in his words, seems to be agreeing. Gone are the drawn-back ears, the lifted hair. That was yesterday; this is today. The thickening late-morning heat is also in agreement.

He's heard it said that you can't make sense of the people here when they speak – not the desperadoes in the goat-girl war, anyway. But surely, howsoever, you could swap a deer-haunch for a couple of loaves, hoping that the wolf keeps out of sight?

He tells the wolf about the wisp of smoke he thinks he saw. Five miles about, south-west. Oblique to the fall of land. Maybe near the invisible river.

He runs through a possible route, with variations, the wolf watching his gestures. They get up almost together.

Chapter 9: Sujata

he old woman, first and last of the Hermit's acolytes, has swept out his cell, dusted and freshly arranged the relics on the relic table, polished with natron and a kidskin square the silver rim of the cranium, scolding herself half-aloud for the oxidation.

Midsummer, she's sure, is just three days away. The Feast of his Enlightenment, its sixtieth year. An alignment of boulder-tops – he showed her – will mark where the Sun swims up from the mountains. She'll open the shutter so the light falls on the relics: on the complete arrow and the four shaftless arrowheads; on the sealed pewter box that holds his heart, pickled in ice-distilled mead; on the roof of his skull. Now she holds the skulltop to her face, closes her eyes, attends to the dry, barely perceptible odour behind the tang of the natron.

Then she looks at the lozenge-shaped puncture on the cranium and then she kisses the puncture, with a ghost of the sensory reverence with which she kissed the scar when the man at last lay dying. And then she lays it with care in its place on the table and takes her staff and walks out slow and crablike into the day.

Two bear-hunters had found him close to death. Friends of the rebel cause, they had dosed him with patient care from a flask of poppy and aquavit, eased out the arrows, smoked out a rock-cleft beehive to honey his wounds. They thought he would die but he didn't. For three-fourths of a month they tended him in their cave encampment, laid on the new-scraped skin of a bear, feeding him on its meat and on honey and twice-baked bread.

When he could speak he told a garbled tale of a land beyond the mountains, of wickedness done and the folly of strife, of the Dancers of the Gods who came as he lay in extremis, of his trek to the edge of Paradise and the voice that said 'Go back and tell them, Go back and tell them'.

They waited till he could walk to bring him down; even so a whole long day it took. They gave what help they could; but with one toting the five-stone skin and head, and the other that weight of smoked meat and grease, along with the gear they'd come in with, they were hardly more mobile than their patient.

It was dusk when they got to the hut of Milus the acorn-gatherer, which with its outgrowth of lean-tos gave roof to the slow-footed patriarch and his four-generation family – two wives, sisters; their mother and his own; his thirteen children; a stray nephew and a stray niece, one from each side; a half-year-old grandson, mother unwedlocked, given to indignation.

The three men made their slow approach, watched by goats from their slit sardonic pupils, so unperturbed they barely stepped out of the way. Milus, shucking last year's acorns along with the older children, with a wife each side at a quern stone, looked up as they came. As he watched, unblinking, his mouth slightly ajar, a slow smile came to his face and a slow left-and-right rotation to his head, and then a deep I-don't-believe-this chuckle. He stood, slowly, hands on hips, and waited till they reached him.

The men heaved down their burdens and Milus embraced them, saying each man's name as they said his. That was all he said at first. But he made a palms-raised shoulder-shrug gesture, muted though theatrical, and half turned with his still-raised hands to show his ramshackle sprawling abode, the gang of children who'd stopped in their doings to gawp, the old woman peering from the porchway, a second come to join her.

To either side his wives sit back on their haunches but feel no obligation to stand, staring at the wounded man who leans against a hurdle post and seems to see only the blur of his exhaustion. He loses balance a moment and catches himself, only just. The younger wife, whose face is less hard than the other's, gets up unhurriedly and goes to him. She puts an arm around the wounded man as informally as if he were her brother. She feels a wetness of blood and her arm jerks away and she pulls a face, but then puts it round him again a little lower, and she looks across at her husband and shrugs a shoulder. Now he's laughing, shaking his big bearded head and laughing.

And so the ex-desperado, the Hermit, comes back into the world.

It was soon clear he'd been touched by the gods. When his wounds allowed he bent and plaited a cell of living hazel a little way off and covered it with turf, and relinquished the pallet of the second- and third-oldest girls, who were now freed from sleeping end-to-end with their sister the single mother, and from an over-closeness to their tiny nephew's displeasures.

The wounded man could be heard in chant and prayer as he worked nearby, addressing tasks with great concentration. He more than paid his way, setting fish traps on the river, bringing fish most nights to add to the evening meal: catfish and trout and eels, sometimes a sturgeon, crayfish, mussels. He'd kill neither bird nor warm-blooded beast and wouldn't eat their meat.

After a year he moved away, built a stream-side stone habitation a mile uphill, where a shelf of the falling land looked out across the river below with its collar of oakwood, to the great plain of farmland beyond. Here he prayed and chanted, prostrated towards the rising sun, spoke with the gods when they visited. Here he kept beehives and goats and a barleyfield.

When a bear came he went over to speak with it; it swung round, baffled, and trotted off. When wolves came raiding in winter he'd out and chant a prayer to the god of night to look after his goats; the wolves would fade away. He lost maybe a beast a year, and wished the thieves well at that.

Many came to hear his words, to take his blessing, to bring him gifts. To be in the presence of an extraordinariness, of a light from another world that was already your own but you hadn't noticed. Word spread and they came from the towns of the plain, from the barley-fields hid in the northern woods, from the western hills, from the twin cities of Lix and Meghara facing where the mile-wide river flows into the sea. Pilgrims came: seekers, tourists of the god-touched, some a mixture of both. Holy men and women came, and he looked into their eyes and took their measure, and two or three he acknowledged and spoke closely with; but he had no thought of fellowship and shrugged off return invitations.

He made a pilgrimage himself, just one, some years after he came from the gate of death. No-one knew where he'd been though rumours were many: he'd been to Meghara, and either turned back in disgust or else taken a ship to the Empire, and there persuaded the Emperor to ease off the tribute in years of drought, and cured his eldest daughter of her unmarriageable squint and himself of a fierce insurgence of the gout; or that he'd sat cross-legg'd in a south-faced cave for a month without food or drink, staring the sun across the sky; or that he'd met in the half-world with twelve other adepts and with them toured invisibly the precincts of the gods to plead for an end to the Empire's claim on Megharan lands. The tales were believed in their saying; but tribute was never forgone, no softening came in the Empire's impertinence, the Hermit blinked in sunlight like anyone else.

One result of his trip was undoubtable though. He came back with a girl.

She was of the age between childhood and marriage, a sombre wee soul of few words which she mumbled

with a northern twang. People were shocked, till even
the sceptical saw that nothing unhermitish went on.
Together they fashioned a tiny hut in view of the Milus
abode, neither far nor near. Each morning in the first
dawn light she would rise and wash her face in the
stream and walk up to the Hermit's hut and together
they would greet the sun, and then they went about
their day: prayers, chanting, call-and-response or in
unison; the work of goats, of beehive and barleyfield,
of other necessities, sometimes together and sometimes
apart, hardly speaking. Between them there was a mysterious devotion, the Hermit for her as much as she
for him – a deep and attentive concern hardly short
of worship.

 The girls of the Milus household tried to befriend her,
and tease out her secrets, but she didn't seem to know
how to get along with anyone but the holy man, mum-
bling one-word answers from her excruciated shyness.
Her name at least they got: Sujata. After a while they
left her alone. She seemed a creature for whom the
world had been poisoned, who carried within her, precariously, a near-mortal woundedness. They took it for
granted, when they shrugged and accepted her secrecy,
that the Hermit had saved her from something, and the
connectivity left in her was forever locked onto him.

With the after-sense of the relics still with her she walks
out into the day and leans on her staff and watches. All
is as it should be, as he so often said. Don't question the
gifts of the world. Wherever it bears you is where you

were meant to go. Whatever it brings, give thanks. Only then are you safe, only then do you see.

She senses something behind her. A hip and both knees pain her as she turns, in staff-assisted stages.

A youth is looking down on her, he raises a hand in greeting. Behind him is a wolf.

Five days had passed since the boy and the wolf had left their first encampment. Peterkin wanted the leg of a roe or somesuch, to offer as a present, but right-sized game was scarce. It seemed that the roe that had shocked him when first he arrived was a fluke: no sign of deer at all, but tracks and spoor of wild ox and of bear, a first encounter with boar. Beasts all of dangerous reputation, and he felt he'd had trouble enough, and no doubt more to come without the seeking.

They lived well enough on hare; grouse; a goose. They camped at a shelter stone a mile above and aslant to the cottage of the curling smoke, and Peterkin found a viewpoint and watched for half a day at a time the old woman's goings and doings. Sometimes she made strange gestures or quavered gobbledygook chants, each night by means of her staff and a helpful boulder she creaked down to her knees and kowtowed to the setting sun as it fell across the plain.

Afterwards Peterkin sometimes looked back on the days that he and the wolf were alone in this near-empty land as among the best of his life. They had a soaring quality, like a stone slung or an arrow shot for distance, when it lofts and hangs at the top of its flight before it commences to fall. A sweet unanchored freedom, where the dramas before and whatever dramas might come were small things far below. The days were long but felt much longer: time did not crush and nip but gave itself open-handed, welcoming their actions, giving them space. A Limbo that when looked back on seems a silhouette of Paradise.

But Peterkin hardly noticed this quiet bliss, thinking his thoughts, trying to plan. His mind was taken with moving on, with trying to see what might happen next; only much later he saw where he'd been. The slow easing-down of his various twists of pain – bruised ribs from the kicking he'd had, thong-bitten wrists, boulder-scraped shins, small tender burns from the night of the wolves. With that bodily easing came easing of his soul's cuts and bruises. That, too, convalesced, in the balmy midsummer Limbo.

In these five long days a growing rapport with the wolf. He keeps by Peterkin now on a hunt, his grasp near perfect of stalking and downwind and silence. This is the core of things, the time they're most as one.

The boy finds – almost as if in a dream – that the wolf picks up his gestures and gets their intent, often first time. He silently wide-arcs a hand right or left, and the wolf wheels. He flat- hands downward, slightly crouching himself, and the wolf drops too. He shoves the air backwards and the wolf holds back. Peterkin gives few owl-calls now, few educative titbits. Sometimes a low, cajoling voice; endearments; nothing more.

They are indeed of one mind – their mind is the terrain and the aim: the marmot strayed thirty yards from the boulderfield; geese on a woodland pond, requiring delicate stalking through the close-shrubbed and boggy margins. The wolf catapults forward when an arrow strikes, seizes the prey, lets Peterkin take over when he comes up.

The time they met with a sounder of boar, a creature neither had ever seen, they both knew straightaway to be wary. Toothsome as the piglets looked. Together they circumnavigated; only later Peterkin realised he'd given no sign. Five sows – their grunting had a weird power, a squalid and graceless aliveness. Two, front-heavy above their dainty feet, must have weighed twelve stone each, the other three almost the size. They'd be better facing a bear. When the boy and the wolf come upwind they trot off with a quick directive grunt or two, the sweet stripey piglets guarded front and rear.

Later the wolf sat with him close by their small fire, and Peterkin, hardly knowing he did it, put out his hand and gently palmed the wolf's coarse-haired back, his hand getting easier and bolder. Above them the uncounted stars confided their blue-white truths, the ageing moon hung yellow.

Next day he shot a second fat goose and thought it was time to approach the old woman. She – a mile from the nearest neighbour, old, arthritic, no stranger in her life to rape and to torture, guarding the precious relics of her saint and guru, guarding the chest of pilgrims' gifts, latterly hearing word of bandits, sworn against the eating of meat – sees the ragged youth with a bow strung on his shoulder holding up a bloody goose and calling out in some coarse tongue, a wolf half-hidden behind him.

Sujata stares up at him, frozen. A surge of terror threatens the vessel of awareness that has rarely been shaken in fifty years, since first the Hermit taught her. Her soul bounces and tilts on the wave; she stares at the apparition until there comes some steadiness.

Then she looks down at the trodden ground before her and murmurs the death prayer.

She recalls his words, the Hermit's words: 'If the Devil comes to your door, greet him with milk and honey'. So she calls out the words of welcome, beckoning with her hand, and turns and goes into the Hermitage.

Chapter 10: Adaptations

eterkin's taken aback by the woman's nonchalance. You'd think that vagabonds with wolves turn up at her door every day. He sees the dung and hoof-slots of goats and thinks, what do I do with him?

He calls to the woman but she's gone inside. There's a fold to one side of the building, and he cuts off a leg of the goose and steps into the fold and calls in the wolf, and leaves him with the leg as he steps out and ties the hurdle gate. He gestures him to crouch down and he does, seeming a little bewildered. The woman hasn't re-appeared, though the tactic seemed to take a long time.

Now he goes to the door and calls again softly and waits.

She calls back, again incomprehensibly. Her voice is very quavery but intent. A back-of-nose tone to it, the words seem to writhe in the saying. He takes a step inside, holding in offering the now-bloodier goose, trying to turn it so it won't drip.

The place is spick and span. He's never been in a room so clean and tidy. There's a table with food.

He's suddenly aware of the stench of sweat and wood-smoke from his body and clothes; he's not thought until this moment what he must look like. The goose is an extra embarrassment; it seems to have grown in size. He bows, mumbles an apology, raises a halting hand, steps back and out with the goose and lays it beside his gear where he's put it down. He breaks off a big furry dockleaf and goes back to the doorway and bows again and makes an effort to wipe up the drops of already tacky blood on the porchstone. He discards the leaf and wipes his hands on his tunic and then he comes in and bows once more.

She's still standing exactly where she was, behind the table. On it are a jug of milk and two beakers, a plate of cheese and dried figs, a pot of honey, a small loaf of unleavened bread. On each side of the table is a stool. She says some more twisty words, a lot of donking Ns and Gs and Ks. Her voice is less quavery than it was. She says the same thing again, whatever it was, and this time gestures to one of the stools. He bows yet again and sits. He can't keep his eyes off the food – seven days of nothing but scorched meat, the smells of fresh-baked bread and newly pressed curd are exquisite. She gestures him to take.

All demonic suggestion has vanished from her guest. But the Hermit's hospitality rules would still have applied, if his pupils had been slits and smoke had come from his nostrils: what's mine is yours, without onus or obligation. For two days and three nights. Only then come the first nudges towards reciprocation, if none has been offered.

She gestures again to take, speaking with exaggerated clarity. He responds, slowly, glancing at her as he does.

She watches him eating, wishing he'd washed his grimy and blood-smeared hands. Bread, cheese, honey, figs – all seem to bring him joy. Sometimes he speaks but it's gibberish. Perhaps he is touched by the gods, a mad boy – but what boy mad enough to befriend a wolf, and sane enough to manage it? He has no manners, breaking the bread not cutting it, squashing the cheese into mouthful-sized lumps with his black-nailed fingers. If it weren't for long-practiced take-as-you-find she'd hardly be able to watch.

She presses food and milk on him till he can't take any more. He holds up both palms and leans back, as if to hold off some falling shape. Then little pecking apologetic bows, for his ingratitude. She holds up the smallest remaining fig, the stalk between finger and thumb, her head tilted to one side, a frown toned by the faintest of smiles; then she gives up.

Her other guest, outside in the fold, has also finished his meal.

For hours he'd sat with the boy watching the place, and its occupant slow and weak in her movements. He smelt no other human stranger. The boy had kept him close by – if he got up to pick off one of the goats the boy would cluck and gesture him down and he'd hunker back, ears cocked and tongue a-loll but accepting for now their forbiddenness.

Mostly a warm south-westerly had played, carrying balmy heat and the odour of goat. The one time the wind turned the goats had plunged and scattered all ways but mostly downhill and away from the wolf in the air, and the little old woman had had great trouble to call them to her. She'd stayed with them all that day, peering about for the danger.

The wolf had been happy with the goose leg, the tricky but saliva-inducing stripping of feathers, tug by tug.

But now he had eaten the leg, foot and bones and all, and had licked the last blood from his muzzle and feet, and he got up to explore and found he was enclosed. He made a yelping, whimpering sound, very breathy, and circuited the small arena bamboozled. But then he crouched and a step and a jump took him over the hurdle with easily and he was out.

With the boy fed and so brought into guest-role Sujata gave thought to her other visitor. She shunted back the stool in three moves, and levered herself up with aid of table and staff and bowed to Peterkin.

'Dokha?' she said, with an elegant gesture of open hand as if offering the door. He assumed it meant 'Would you like to go out?' but it meant 'Wolf?'

They went into the day, the blinding morning light. Flies were buzzing around the goose. He went to the fold to check out the wolf and saw that he was gone.

'Where are your goats?' he burst out, and then kept saying it, piling up the words to break through her in-comprehension. Urgent hands-spread shoulder shrug, pointing to dung and hoofprints, then pointing in all directions and then again the wide-armed shrug.

She watched it seemed impassively, even showed the trace of a smile when he made some approximate bleats. But she'd got it. She shrugged herself, speaking in her tongue with a tone that said 'What can you do?' What, with the goats' vast and fenceless pasturage. Then she shrugged a second time, and pointed an outstretched hand to the well-grooved goat path that ran away north into bouldery scraggy low-canopied woods.

Peterkin ran and was was gone, not even bowing.

The wolf has followed a scent trail as thick with invisible goat as the hoof-slotted path. But a doubt drags on his intent. He has watched these goats from their viewpoint, the boy not letting him hunt them. There's a shadow of the hold-back gesture somewhere.

And the goats are of an ancient breed, still wise to their enemies – to wolf, to lynx, to bear. It's not wild goat country, precipice and rampart, haven for the sure of foot; but it has its opportunities – terraced outcrops, mazes of grown-over trackways. They scatter under threat, so a lucky predator takes only one.

In little time from his leaping the fold the wolf is among the goats. But – recently fed, though with room for much more; wrong-footed by their criss-cross scatter; maybe that wisp of taboo – he makes no kill, chasing a kid that skiddily crosses a boulder face and perches on a finger-wide downsloping ledge, braced and a-tremor like a little quivering soldier. It might be on the moon for all the wolf can do to reach it, so after mooching one side and then the other he sits below, tongue lolling, a yard too low to leap and grab, uttering small whimpers of desire.

Such is the scene when Peterkin runs up. The wolf has heard him coming: his focus on the kid has blurred, a faint unease comes in at the edges.

No! yells Peterkin.

No! No!

He's making the 'come' gesture. He scans about all ways, praying to Luck.

The wolf takes a last look up at the kid, in its virtuoso precariousness. Then he ups and trots halfway to where Peterkin stands, and stops. His tail is curved just slightly between his legs, his haunch just slightly lowered, his ears not flat but a little that way. His breath is audible, his eyes uncertain.

Peterkin turns and gestures him to follow and he trots behind, keeping a distance, the boy glancing to check. Scenes of carnage are in his mind's eye, he wants to go back and search but he can't and manage the wolf. Then it hits him – glances again to confirm – the wolf has no smear of blood on muzzle or pelt. He's seen him often enough at a kill, how he gets besmirched. Peterkin whispers a prayer of provisional thanks.

When he gets back the old woman seems unperturbed. The wolf keeps back from her, ears right down. She takes a long look at him and gives a dry smile, says some play-scolding words, as if the wolf were himself a recalcitrant goat.

Then she points downhill and gestures her guests to follow and sets off step by step. A track runs alongside the stream that runs behind her settlement. Less than a hundred yards down, but hidden from the Hermitage by trees and the lie of the land, is a hamlet of six little huts, various and dilapidated.

She stops above these and points with her staff further down and to the right. Deep between trees, hard to see, is a seventh habitation, well away from the stream and the other huts. The boy has understood. He makes a bow of gratitude.

She motions him to go and look. There isn't much to see. When he comes out she's still standing where she was. 'Dokha-da' she calls, and waves them back up. It means wolf boy.

She turns back up the track, leaning on the staff each laborious step. For a long moment she's skylined to Peterkin's view, inching uphill. He watches, half-tranced by her slowness; her bent figure, backed by the void of the sky, is mirrored somehow in the back of his mind, inching its way.

Once many would come at midsummer, at all the seven festivals. There'd been other huts and hutlets, some just wicker shanties in nooks where a spirit had been sensed.

The near neighbours would come, children babies and all, though households were few indeed: the acorn-gatherer dynasty, now thinned down; a family five miles downriver, who fished and kept some beasts and ran a ferry – the river there easing and pooling to a lake, to gather itself and then hurtle down in a great smoky cataract, the highest of the river's three.

A few years in the Hermit's early days an ancient couple would come. They'd snuck back to the farm where the woman was born and lived all her days till the clearance. The Empire dispersal force had tried to fire the thatch but a spring storm had doused it. The couple dug and re-seeded the terraces, cleansed the befouled cottage, mended what furniture they could, lured back a few of the scattered goats. At first they would make the trip through the backlands together, then just him, then neither.

They alone knew the Hermit as he had been, but nothing of that was said.

The rebellion had stuttered on in the highlands, never quite finally failing. The unenthused and bribe-milking Megharan force promised no conclusion. The once-honourable rebel bands themselves slipped into corruption, became no better than bandits, leeching and extorting from the souls they'd sworn to liberate. The one who became the Hermit had been with them, when the local gang came to the couple's place for a tithe of the harvest and the yearling goats. He'd opened his mouth and said to the captain, if we take too much they'll die in the winter. They're old, said the captain, they'll die some winter soon, why not the next?

But he'd had his men go steady, put some back; the couple went hungry but made it to spring.

Soon afterward an Adviser from the Empire was caught and sent to Hell, unhurriedly and with sportive embellishments.

The Empire responded. A legion of high-grade reliables came from some iron land beyond all ken, with a tongue that no-one had ever heard but making entirely clear their contempt for the Megharan army, appearing without a by-your-leave, while the Megharan government simpered and wrung its hands. The King bowing deeper to their general than the general bowed to him. They scoured the rebel country, refugeed its population, took no prisoners. The last rebel bands fought well with nothing but death before them, the honour of a brave one their only reward. One last gang, driven above the treeline and seemingly doomed, simply disappeared; some spoke of collective suicide.

The long strip of once-rebel land between mountain and river was cleared and declared forever empty of settlement. The alien force entirely without compunction: any soul who didn't run, or couldn't, was put to the sword. Huts fired, fruit trees felled, livestock slain. Only a few of the bold crept back, once the ashes had settled, and traditional Megharan blind-eye-turning restored.

Only the old couple knew who the Hermit had been. They knew his punctures weren't from Empire bows (they'd yearly viewed the arrow and the arrowheads, but then so had many). They knew his band must have found some sacred, guarded realm in the heights of the mountains, and he the single escapee had brought back the secrets he'd stolen, passing through the forelands of Death, cleansed and transfigured. They were right, more or less.

And Sujata leads the boy back up the track for a fuller tour of the Hermitage and estate. She points out her six patch fields much smaller even than his, and weedier: two of barley and one of beans – familiar crops, though of foreign strains; a couple fallow and tangled; one of wheat which the boy had never seen before nor heard of. New to him also were terraces, perched, no more than the size of a room, with straggled vines and skinny fruit trees footed by the browning white and cerise of their fallen blossom.

She shows him the folds and the lean-to of gear, she shows the latrine trench tidily dug, an old half-busted shovel by the pile of earth.

The latrine trench confirms a thought that was already pressing: she can't be doing all this herself. She's still the only human being he's seen this side of the mountains; but the tumbledown but still used bothies, the fields (unkempt as they are), the neat workmanlike edge of the latrine, dug in hard stony soil – all tell of others, of helpers, of visitors. Of likely wolf-plus-vagabond dis-approvers.

She beckons him once more into the cottage, the Her-mitage. He gestures the wolf to crouch so as not to follow, and the wolf obligingly settles down, to his relief and the old woman's wonder, an echo of the thought that the beast is his demon.

She takes him into the shrine room. She shows him the silver-rimmed and punctured skull-dome, the punctur-ing arrow, the other teased-out arrowheads still fixed to stubs of shaft, the stubs brown-mottled with staining of ancient blood. She shows the case with the heart, fingertip-stumping her own chest but he doesn't un-derstand. She shows the spoon of bone which fed him his last meal but the boy doesn't get that either. She shows the one surviving piece of attire, a single clapped-out ankle-strapped sandal, the sole worn thin, the sin-ew-knotted upper a tale of improvised repair.

There are three chests in the room and she opens one, full to the lid with gifts and offerings, each with its meticulous place. End-shelves bearing neat square baskets of carvings of the gods and their totems, of fortune-bringers for furtherance and health, of hand-length clay or soapstone tablets incised with prayers to the spirits of forest and stream and rock. In the central recess a single large basket of robes, of woven wool dyed with many colours, of goatskin figured with symbols and hieroglyphs. The old woman takes out a cloak and spreads it to show, then folds it again with ritual care and presses it to her forehead and replaces it. She does the same with all the things she takes out, a slow pressure to forehead before they are with care returned to place.

Peterkin makes little of the reverential aspects. He sees none of the symbols, the shrine-marks, that are all the religious insignia he knows. He's never before seen script, or heard of it more than vaguely. But the arrow gives him thought, and the arrowheads – they are old-style but familiar, many like them still used in the homeland he's left, a couple indeed are in his own quiver. Familiar too the tiny forge-marks, scratched on each haft-cup. He has heard all the tales of the goat-girl war, of the arrow-hedgehogged escapee; he feels the weight of a troubling secret.

She doesn't show him what's in the other two chests. The Hermit's sacred accoutrements in one, gifts of greater value the other – gold-woven robes, rings and brooches and torques and armlets of silver and gold and electrum, a spring crown of silver inset with malachite cut to the shapes of twigs and leaves, the veined stone mimicking nature. Perhaps it was a foolishness to show what she's shown already, though *he* might have done the same, with the wisdom that lies beyond folly.

Peterkin wonders at all he's seen, pleasantly amazed at the woman's hospitality. He must make some response. He bows to her and points to the nearest field, and goes to it and starts weeding. Soon he comes back and takes a stick from her kindling stack, the ground far too hard to ease up the roots unbroken. A little later the woman creaks up with a pole-handled shovel, a hoe, a thing like a mattock, and he bows to her and she bows back an inch or so and gives perhaps the fourth part of a smile.

The wolf found the goose when the boy and the crone were indoors and has been occupied. Now he comes over and watches, baffled – inching quite close to see what underground prey the boy is hunting. Then in a couple of strides he's on top of a fieldside col where he turns around twice and hunkers down to watch between his paws.

Later Sujata gives the boy a basket with a loaf and cheese and a smoked eel in a bowl and points downhill and smiles, and Peterkin bows deeply and he and the wolf go down to their quarters in the outlier bothy.

Once the boy and the wolf are away she follows the goat-path with care to a flat-topped rock she knows well and sits down with relief and calls her goats. She calls and calls before they start to come, against the grain of the residue odour of wolf.

There's no enticing them into the fold, wolf-pungent and strewn with goose-down. The light has mostly faded before she persuades them to crowd into a smaller pen, with crooning words and honeyed barley-cake. Seeing its fence is a height to keep in goats but not to keep out wolves she goes to a stack of spare hurdles and walks one across a step at a time and heaves it up to improvise half a roof. It takes all her strength.

She's back to the lean-to for bark-twine and ties the hurdle down, taking her time, recovering. Then she goes back for another.

Chapter 11: An Intermission

wo full days went by from the coming of the boy and wolf to the coming of the midsummer celebrants.

Peterkin lay on a pallet wrapped in his cloak on his first night in the little outlier hut. He'd tried to get the wolf to come in but he wouldn't, though he crouched near the door and seemed to settle. He couldn't be hungry anyway – the goose had vanished from where it had been left, all but a wide splash of feathers.

The boy was tired, but with a cool and floating tiredness that left his mind very clear. There were three things he had to think about. Listing them gave him a purchase, a sense of capability, floating above the fears and the worries.

Pushing from behind – he kept it there, never thought it full-on – was knowing he was indentured to this world, body and soul. Knowing he had nowhere else to go. And that it wasn't in him to live with the wolf like two wild beasts on the hill, that he couldn't live without human fellowship. That he had to find some way to work himself, wolf and all, into this world's geography.

Three things.

To handle the wolf. Goats; strangers.

To make sense of the old woman's speech, and anyone else who comes.

To repay her astounding hospitality.

The last is easiest. Fields to hoe, fences to fix, burdens to carry. And flour to grind, dough to knead – women's tasks, but he's done them himself long enough.

Speech, who knows?

He'd heard there are other tongues, but never quite grasped the notion and never much tried to. Word and thing, word and action, had always been one – how else could it be? (He and the crone had been the same – repeating things louder and with fiercer articulation, as if incomprehension were only a kind of deafness.)

Wolf, wolf.

Goats: no possible harmony. The goats are out, the wolf is with him all the time, or else fenced in.

Ah, the wolf. The way he whacks his tail from side to side, panting and slavering, sure of some forthcoming joy in life. His wariness has mostly melted off; now he resounds with physical celebration. He's gotten rather larger since the spring; his smile of chronic exuberance shows the length of his canines, the strap-like tongue lolling out sideways.

This great zest rotates around Peterkin. Wanting to do, wanting to go. The boy his only gravity, with the task of somehow making it all work out.

He takes the wolf out early the following morning, to find the next thing for him to eat and to relieve him a little from the torture of his energy. They cross the stream and head southwards, into a contorted land of scrub-oak and boulder. As they pass below the Hermitage the ancient woman is skylined on a knoll to greet the Sun, facing a skirt of mountains east-north-east, a splayed hand of beams already a-reach from the peaks. She stands as still as a piece of the landscape as she waits.

They work the terrain till the forenoon. The land is rich in game, but all quick and wary: wood-hares zip into labyrinths of brush, a capercaillie explodes into the air as the wolf jumps for it, a full yard short but hopeful. At last he corners a half-grown hare and brings it unbidden and drops it at Peterkin's feet, and the boy strikes up a fire and gives the wolf a back leg to work on and by the time the rest is scorch-cooked he has masticated bones hide and all, and they breakfast on the rest together.

Further south they wander, the wolf making thrice Peterkin's mileage in side-forays. After a while there comes to the air an immense continuous crash, curious at first and then progressively fearsome: the roar of the Third Cataract. The boy has never heard such a thing. They slant uphill for vision, and from a stubby blackstone knoll they see it: the great river, till now invisible, splaying out into a wide onion-shaped lake that slides through a narrow escape-neck, very fast but holding its glass composition, then disappears from sight in a long explosion. No other sound can be heard.

The wolf is up and down, very uneasy. Peterkin breaks out of a kind of trance and turns back. Only then does he see the cottage of the ferryman, across the lake where

the water is still sedate a quarter mile from the fall. A
woman is approaching it, walking heavily, with twin
loads on a carrying pole. A child runs beside her. The
second and third of the people he's seen in this world.

On the way back they come on fresh deer slots, a kind
new to Peterkin. Too big for a roe. Moments later he
sees it descending a gully to drink, bracing its feet on
the skiddy slope with a deer's pragmatic grace.

He gestures back the wolf with movements slow and
smooth and slides out and notches an arrow. He has a
perfect side-on shot from almost forty yards and knows
he'll get nothing better. He draws, focussed on the point
of desired puncture, clearing for his arrow a corridor of
intent. The arrow whaps in a handsbreadth low and the
beast in its sudden anguish spins incoherently, but then
sees the wolf almost on it and scrabbles at the bank but
the wolf dives head a-twist and grips a backleg and it's
sliding as it scrabbles and then slips and crashes down.
Peterkin is there now and takes the shaft of an antler,
but the strength of the twisting neck is ten times the
strength of his hand and there's no moment to offer up
his blade and sink it between the vertebrae. It might be
their first joint hunt again but this time the deer has
twice the weight, twice the heft. It'll any moment surge
back to its feet and throw him off.

But the wolf in an eyeblink hurdles the thrashing legs
and has gotten the stag by the throat. Three faces in dramatic tableau in a space of less than a yard. Peterkin sees
that the wolf's ecstatic purpose matches the strength of
the stag, his canines locked in a grip that is the nub of
his whole being, that the rest of his form and his soul

exist just to serve. His eyes so close to Peterkin's, shining amber and staring at some beautiful nothingness.

Now Peterkin can slip in the blade and the stag's chaotic strength is gone as suddenly as a blown-out flame. Its dead weight is still a problem. He opens it up, tosses the wolf the liver. Even with the carcase gralloched he barely hauls it up the bank. He takes off the head, severs a haunch to take back, still he's at his limit to heave and wedge the remainder in the chest-high fork of a tree.

When they get back he disposes of haunch and gear and strips off his spattered clothing and plunges into a deep smooth-bouldered pool a little below the Hermitage. For all the miles it's run down summer hillside the stream still holds its gasping chill. He washes his hair and body as best he can, then sets about washing his clothes. He departed his previous life without a spare stitch, even with habituation he's been aware of their stench. He tries to knead out the recent spatter of blood, then beats and beats each garment on a big convenient boulder. He wrings them and lays them on brush facing up at the sun, now hot and high, and lies in the sun himself to warm up and to dry.

The wolf has watched his antics with bemusement, pacing and looking worried. Then he settles. When the boy has finished the wolf sniffs at the drying clothes, sniffs at him as he lies. Peterkin shoves the his face away without knowing he's going to. After a second or two the nose is probing again, the boy takes a breath and lifts and shoves the face very deliberately, with a quiet command. The wolf gives up and hunkers down beside him and falls asleep.

Peterkin has been sunburned, badly, doing just what he's doing, and after he's dried off both sides he gets up and puts on the still half-sodden clothes and goes up to meet the old lady.

Sujata had begun looking out for him, more and more concerned. She made her way to where she could see the visitor huts – no sign. She set out the late-morning meal, covered with a light cloth to keep off flies; in the end she put it back in the larder. She let out the goats but kept them in view, hobbling the lead nanny.

Then she hears something down at the stream and pieces her way with laborious care to a viewpoint masked by a willow that frames her view. It's the boy, his back to her, thigh-deep in the pond and naked, beating his rancid jerkin on a rock in a steady unhurried rhythm. You can see he's used to doing it. She scans nervously for the wolf. There it is – hunkered down, watching him intently, as if he enacts some puzzle it needs to unravel.

She waits to get back her breath before she sets off to return, not of an age any more for off-path terrain. It's slow to settle. She watches it; how much of the last fifty years has she spent, watching her breath. There's something happening, something not familiar – as if there's not enough room for her lungs. As if her diaphragm presses into her ribcage. When she gets what's going on she is almost thrown, for the second time in two days,

from the poise of soul that's been her whole life's work. She watches into herself, holds herself steady.

The boy. The boy at his task, bizarre and beautiful cameo framed by the long-leaved willow, his skinny nakedness, his self-enclosed diligence, work she's never before seen done by a male.

Not sexual, or not to speak of. But a terrible tenderness, for the skinny bare orphan out of nowhere. Not a truant from one of the higher hells, with his wolf-familiar; not a godling come to test her. Just a boy lost and alone, arrived at her porchstone with his stuttering courtesy, washing his stinking clothes.

A terrible tenderness. The pain of blood in dried-out veins, of the insurrective swelling of her heart. She turns and picks her way back, by the time she reaches the path she's gasping. She goes straight to the shrine room and prays intensely, prays to keep her soul in balance. Easing back from her recollection: the boy, the watching wolf, the slow slap of wet cloth against the rock.

The boy and the wolf must learn all they can. Sujata has tried to get it across that in two days time other people will come. Peterkin needs a few words, and a knowledge of customs; the wolf must learn to be contained, to not kill goats or trouble strangers.

The boy's a keen student. As he eats his belated fore-noon meal Sujata names each item of food, each utensil. He tries to say it back and she gives the name again and again, emphasising the alien consonants, trying to massage them into his attunement. He wants to know the colours, the numbers, the names of everything – with every word this world gathers closer about him, like a garment. He goes round naming everything aloud.

Ah, but the wolf.

Sujata has chivvied the goats back into the fold. His massive early meal has slackened the law of the wolf to kill where you can, but still a joy lights in him at their sight. Full-bellied as he is his eyes are filled with something like love, his tongue lolls and his long teeth show and a cord of saliva droops from his jaw. Peterkin knows he must be restrained, there must be a way of restraining him. Otherwise they will have no life, down among people in the farmlands.

Peterkin gets him to lie in the shade on the far side of the building from the goat pen. He knows the wolf will be sleepy, well fed as he is in the heat of the day.

He feels a sliminess of guilt, an ugliness in the adjustments. But if one of them must live in the other's world then the wolf must live in his. He can't think of a life without bread or cheese, with never a roof to keep off the rain, without idle talk and a feast to come. If one must defer to the other in the end, then the wolf must defer to him. Whatever way cramps his soul the least, that must be the way.

Guilt will always nag the boy – that he took a wolf, a being so of itself, so singular in the tumble of beings, that stalks through the stories and dreams of humans, who loathe it with a fervour that has a whiff of the sacred, a hatred from the depths. That he took a wolf and so inveigled its soul that it slid by his contrivance into the human world. That he made it so much less than it should have been. A sense of treachery, too deep for excuses. (But what could I do? Slip away and leave him on the hill, to die when the home pack catches his scent? Live my days alone to all company but his, while girls dance at the solstice fair and taverns roar with laughter and with crack, a mighty fire in the hearth?) The guilt nags on, quietly, its wry and sceptical voice untouched by reason.

What he has to do is, he has to restrain the wolf. He can't trust to Luck. Luck has been good: great thanks, great praise; but Luck turns sour on the over-importunate. Everybody knows this. Give thanks and plead no more.

Peterkin tries to tell Sujata to let her goats out, he'll look after the wolf. At least he knows the words now. Then he goes and lies with the wolf in the shade. Later he'll sickle hay from the fallowfields, chop some logs, the wolf kept close. Later still they'll go back to their outlier bothy; this time the wolf will join him, not whimpering to get out till grey light keeks round the door.

Next morning they go back to their kill. Seven bold ravens are at work on the innards – the wolf charges and they loft up begrudgingly, corvine satire in their minimal flaps and flops.

Peterkin severs the second haunch as the wolf drags at the intestines. Flies hum in the morning heat in a ticklish multitude. The carcase is too awkwardly wedged to take back to the ground, so he ups and half-hangs off a branch to cut free a shoulder and foreleg. He cuts and trims a carry-pole with flies zoning around his perspiring head. He swats one-handed, distracting from the tiresomeness by chanting under his breath an old song of gratitude for the service of his knife.

He gets back with the burden of meat and hangs it beside the previous haunch which swings among zigzagging flies from the roofbeam of a tumbledown bothy, and then again he bathes in in the grateful chill of the stream. Sujata, with gestures and their handful of nouns, tells him she's done as he asked and let out the goats, keep the wolf close. More hay is sickled, new words learned, help given to wiping and dusting the clean-already Hermitage.

They take the evening meal outside in the last of the sun. Tomorrow the pilgrims arrive. The boy knows something of this, but he has no idea what a pilgrim is nor why they should come.

The sun blinks down at the north-of-west skyline. Stars are prickling out, a big round moon has nudged up. The boy carries the dishes and plates, carries in the table, carries in the stools. Bows to the old woman and gives thanks, then tongue-clicks the wolf and they head down to their accommodation.

On the next day there came in the forenoon a man of late middle age but limber, eyes very clear and sharp and a tidy beard, bearing by headstrap his blanket roll and gear up the jinking streamside path with a kind of attentive ease. The second inhabitant of this world to meet with the boy and the wolf.

Kuzak the Errant, Sujata waiting his approach, unhurriedly lays down his pack and they caress, forehead to forehead, hands on the other's back a little below the shoulder, an angled and precise connection like two devoted mantises. By this time Peterkin, watching, knows maybe forty words of the Megharan tongue. He knows the words of greeting, knows it's all to do with the sun and the longest day. Somehow also to do with the Hermit, owner of the cranium, punctured by an arrow that is so like one of his own.

He watches a little way off, trying to keep the wolf crouched close, but the wolf fears the man and slips into cover. The boy makes the *crouch* move towards where the wolf disappeared, although he can't see him. Then he goes to meet the man.

He bows to him, to Kuzak the Errant.

I Peterkin he says, aiming for a friendly and confident tone. Mine is wolf.

Chapter 12: Kuzak the Errant

Kuzak took his Oath of Errancy back in the days of the Hermit's great fame. He was a young man then.

He'd earlier been a merchant out of Lix. A seventh share he'd had of a neat two-master, back and forth to the Empire; a fine house at the better end of the waterfront; a pretty wife to keep eye on trade and the servants when he was gone; a firstborn son, another child coming.

But all to nothing, all to nothing. The boat's four-sevenths holder was skilled in making enemies, preferring the powerful and ruthless; the docklands welcomed exotic pestilence. The nullifying winds of Fate blew away his life. He left it by rooftop as the sheriff's men pounded the door, his last possessions in a grab-bag satchel, all the stones and trinkets gone in bribes.

From family man to vagabond in a few disastrous months. A big cold moon stared down at him as he soft-footed a tangle of alleys, not even knowing where he was going. What friend's life could he pandemoniumize? The same moon had watched them across the water with infinite geniality, he and his wife and child, they watching back from their balcony – gigantic at the horizon, silhouetting a hundred masts. She handed him the tiny one and he said no, feeling his hands were the hands of an ape, but she insisted, and he cradled the child with his elbows jutted for fear he might suddenly fling himself sideways, and smelt in the smell of the baby's head what a gift of the gods he'd been given, and had no spare hand to palm off the tears that came to his eyes.

No home, no harbour – no harbour, no home. The words belonged to a song he'd thought ludicrous, often sung in taverns late on, lurching out of key the way the singers will lurch off-line on their journey home – *home*, yes, safe to sentimentalize when you've got one. Now the song took vengeance for his disdain, sticking in his mind. He'd catch himself singing it half aloud as if to slip his own scrutiny.

In Lix the ancient laws of hospitality were forgotten. A needy stranger was shunned, was a leech, was a thief. And so he was, more than once, out of hunger, and pretty good at it. His life had been in the city and on the sea, with short sojourns in Empire harbours where the aim was to turn around fast, unrobbed and unmurdered, above all uncheated. A life with his back to the country, facing south across the sea. But now it seemed the city was done with him. He'd seen them whipped through the streets – thieves, vagabonds, chancers. People like him.

Lix is tucked under cliffs by a natural harbour, where the Maker of the World has left a city-sized apron of land. The cliffs are the end-stubs of a mountain chain that forms the eastern boundary of the Megharan vassalage. There's no easy landward access: a great river estuaries out on the town's western side, but only after crashing down a cataract, the first of the river's three. An ox-track zigzags up to meet with river trade from the north, but after it reaches the wharf above the cataract it dwindles to almost nothing.

All other Lixian trade is by boat – from the Empire across the sea to the south, or by barge across the mile-wide estuary. The sister city of Meghara has no deep harbour – the flat-bottomed barges make a daylong relay from city to city and back like an ant-trail curved by the tides, the stevedores too like ants half-jogging with their loads, or side-to-side spiralling massive oil jars up ramps on their circular bases, appropriating their world with curse-heavy ruffian zest.

Kuzak, Lix born and bred, has hardly looked behind him in all his young days – at the loom of the mountains, at the other side of life. But the city has no place for him any more. This isn't just bad luck, this is an expulsion. No way back to what he was, and nothing else is bearable. He's got friends who would help him out, but he'd rather starve. The trouble with being the nobody he's become is that too many people knew him when he was somebody. Go, says the city, this is over.

He trawls the docksides with the last barges unloading, scanning for any fallen edible, but gulls and rats and vagabonds have taken all. He asks at any door with a lamp still burning if there's a task to be done for a mouthful of bread. One says kiss my arse, one says go to Hell, one gives him half a loaf and a hunk of cheese for a quick sweep of the floor. He thinks he'll go take a look at the house he once lived in but then he thinks he won't, and he walks up through the steepening labyrinth streets and where the city ends in scrubland and boulder he turns and looks at the moonlit roofscape, the moonglade on the sea, most of the shutters drawn and hardly a human light to be seen. He eats his fill and curls up to sleep beneath a low-branched pine, and wakes at first light with ants all around him and isn't slow to rise.

He drops the ants some morsels of bread, and with the same now-battered satchel he snatched up when he fled his past life he contours a short way to the cataract track and climbs till it levels out above the cliffs and the crashing fall of the river. There's an ox-train loading up. He wishes the drivers and bargees well and they him but he doesn't stop.

From just past dawn till early afternoon he walks the hard path to the north. The least-bad route through near-impossible country: vertigo-sick where it crosses the face of a cliff, new to such situations; sweating over passes in the bleakest terrain he's ever seen; rock-hopping side-streams that want to carry him with them on their twisty rampage down. He walks twelve miles to travel eight, before the great river bends away and farmland spreads below him. He's met no other traveller; he's never in his life been so long entirely alone.

At the first steading he calls a greeting. A man comes out with a stave; another is crossing a field.

Begone, calls the stave-holder evenly, as if the scene is well-practised.

I'm looking for work, calls Kuzak.

I've no use for you says the man.

Close now: a swarthy, physical man; his voice is contained, matter-of-fact; his eyes are fixed on Kuzak's with steady intent.

The other man comes up. He's bigger, younger, glaring.

City rat, city rat, get back down where you belong, he half-sings, weirdly, with puerile malice. It might be a line of a song.

Heesh says the first man to the young one, with a slight almost dainty waft of his fingers. Not taking his eyes off Kuzak's.

He's right. There's nothing for you here. Don't tell me there's no work in Lix, the docks, the barges.

Kuzak replies, meeting the farmer's stare as best he can.

Nothing in Lix for the luck-fallen. The stevedore gangs and the boatman gangs keep the work to themselves – only scraps for outsiders. I've trailed through the docks every dawn for the last three months, I've not worked twenty days. Working hungry, hefting twelve-stone grain sacks, the overseer's boot if your legs give way. Most nights no gift for the flophouse wife – sleeping in ruins, in alley-backs, hiding from the Night Guard.

As he speaks his voice and his eye become more assured. Hearing his story from his own mouth reminds him that his life's at stake.

The farmer, leaning on his stave, half-smiles and spits into the sun-scorched pasturage.

Good story. Now get off my land.

Kuzak makes to walk forward. The farmer grips his stave and faces him. The younger man positions himself a little to the side, very keen.

Are you deaf?

Where does your land end? I'll soon be across it.

I say go back the way you came.

I'll go round it then. D'you own that mountain? I'll go over it. D'you own the river? I'll wade north in the shallows.

You need to listen my friend, you need to listen ...

His feet are at shoulder width, he holds the stave horizontal, ready for action.

I'll keep off your land. Where's the margin?

Kuzak's shoulders are shrugged, his hands raised in question. He looks towards the mountains, towards the river, all the time watching for the blow.

Is it a secret?

This is the last time of telling ...

The farmer is bouncing the stave in his hands. Kuzak can hear the younger man's breath a yard from his ear, almost behind him.

I'll go round your land, I'll not trespass. But you'll have to kill me to stop me. No-one knows I'm here or cares, you'll not need to fear the gallows. Just a body to hide, or dig a hole for. And a weight of murder on your soul – they say the first one's heaviest, after that it gets lighter.

The farmer's body lets go its torsion. He backs the young man off with another flick of his hand, he makes a teeth-clenched sound and a slow both-ways rotation of his head.

Okay my friend okay o fucking kay. Y'see yonder big old oak a mile upwater? That's my boundary. My neighbour's a meaner bastard than me, let him bury you. We'll watch you all the way and don't you fucking dare turn about.

He stands off and with a sarcastic gesture he offers Kuzak the track through his land.

Kuzak bows to the man, in contrast with no show of irony, and raises both hands in a gesture of appeasement, and says the word of thanks very quietly and shifts has satchel strap as he walks on.

He works up and down the wide east bank, the fifty-mile coverlet of land before the hills bend in at the Second Cataract. He makes himself useful and quits before he's told; at the harvest he works the sun across the sky. He holds himself compressed and balanced, keeping his secrets, an orphan of the city making good. He slips all company when he can. His situation of choice at the end of a day is solitude, a bivouac or a shelter stone, a fire to stare into until his eyelids droop.

The first winter he's offered an outhouse floor for the season with bare rations but he demurs. He wanders, picking up this and that, bearing an extra satchel of salted mutton and biscuit, but the pain and the iron unmercy of the cold are breaking him down. He'd limp back and plead for the outhouse with all the humility needed but now he can't. Snow has fallen, all lesser tracks have vanished, to walk them would be to wade. He'd die.

He's taking a path for no directional reason, just that it's not too snow-choked to walk. He puts his feet into predecessors' ice-skinned footprints, sometimes high-stepping, his sandals bound loosely with skins. It's the best he could do; even so his feet are as dead as stone. A side-valley climbs to a stark stone building with a snow-capped roof, the only two-storey building he's seen up here. Chimneys both ends send scarves of smoke into the very clear air, bending only slowly to vanish sideways. Their reek comes to him in small deliveries, exquisite.

He has a plan; not something he'd have thought he'd ever do, but the torture of cold and the fear of death carry great persuasion. He hasn't known till now how much he doesn't want to die. The one thing he has left of any worth is his marriage chain – electrum, heavy-wrought, he's never from the first day taken it off. Maybe now though, maybe now.

As he nears the shuttered face of the building it seems to grow, looming up almost black against the snow. Another thinly trodden track joins his, and then another. A frontage of trampled snow spreading out from the central door. No sound, no sign of life except the trampled snow and the woodsmoke.

No entry bell, and he has no staff to thud on the nail-studded boards. He knocks with his knuckles – the sound is barely audible even to him. He calls a greet-ing – his voice is a puny thing, it juts into the silence and vanishes. He calls again and beats between the nail-heads with the bottom of his fist – it's like hitting granite with a pillow. The snow begins to fall again. He tries the protruding latch-grip with no expectation, but it easily lifts and the great door creaks open half a yard, and he pushes it wider and calls again.

Come in and close the door, says a voice. The air in the hall is balmy. He can't work out how the latch goes, his hands flop and fumble. He wants to give some account of himself to the man who has appeared but he hears his voice – is it his? – speak in disconnected phrases, vibrato'd by his shuddering jaw.

The man has come up. Welcome, he says, in a warm offhand way, as if Kuzak is expected. His hand takes the latch, very warm as it touches Kuzak's, and slots it quietly into place.

Come, he says, gesturing. Something about the brethren being at prayer. Corridors, very dim; a high lucerne window unshuttered, snowflakes meander like dust-motes in its beam of light. Twice Kuzak stumbles, though the floor is smooth. The man opens a door. Heat booms out, and a dense odour of baking bread. A bench against the wall, facing a great central range inset with ovens. Two busy youths. The man sends one out; he comes back no time later with a heavy felt blanket.

The man is down on one knee, untrammelling the ragged skin around Kuzak's foot. Kuzak tries to help but the man pushes his hand away. He works off the sandal and checks the soiled insensate foot with the care of a connoisseur. Then he checks the other. He helps Kuzak to stand and winds the blanket around him arms and all and then sits him down again. As he does he says some words over his shoulder, with authority but no sharpness, and the boy disappears again and comes back with a pair of huge felt boots into which with care the man slips Kuzak's feet.

And he sits, still woozy. Still shuddering. Squirming and wincing with pain as his blood works back into fingers and feet like the gnawing of iron teeth.

Before the day is over he's out clearing snow with the others.

It turns out he's not in the chance-charity kitchen of some lordly house, but that Hakan the cook is Master of an Errant House, and that seventeen inductees had been in the prayer hall at silent observation, a door's thickness from the scene of his entrance.

Hakan walks in the deep-grooved persona of a Master Errant – toughness and kindliness, on a steel frame of honour. Nested within that frame, contained but fully acknowledged: egotism and anger, tinder and spark to the fires of action. He unvowed after twenty-six home-less years, freeing the last Master, Eren the Wise, to take back the vow for his final years, to die on the road and not in the false indulgence of some bed.

Hakan the Master tells Kuzak his options: stay three full days as a guest and then leave; stay longer as a servant; become an inductee. The last will take three days and three months and three years. Kuzak doesn't have to think. His life at twenty-six a pointless blank; grown up on tales of the Errants, their goodness and their edge; seen the machinations of the Lix priesthood to have them barred from the city, put to shame by their work with the abjects and desperadoes of the waterfront. A future opens; a different air fills his lungs. For the fourth time in his adult life his eyes fill with tears.

Twenty-six years was Hakan on the endless way; twenty-six of age was Kuzak at the start of his induction; twenty-six years he has in turn walked the road as an Errant. He liked the number, the comely awkwardness of twice thirteen, like two loads on a carry-pole, lumpish but well-balanced. Maybe he should unvow, give service in a House till it's time to take the final road. One more task, perhaps, before that. One more piece of work.

Chapter 13: Other Arrivals

fter Kuzak the Errant come eight more arrivals, twenty-seven visitors in all. Twice the kind of number Sujata expected. The long afternoon is repeatedly surprised as a collage of humanity takes form. Each party is greeted and offered food and drink in the Megharan way; goatskins and bearskins and cushions are brought out, the visitors settled in sun or in shade as they choose.

First come two ancient sisters of the acorn-gatherer clan. They alone of the company recall the Hermit's arrival – one was twelve years old and the other ten. The stumbling, drunk-looking man seeping blood; the bear-hunter with the skin had the bear's great head as if peering over his shoulder.

Crablike on the final climb with their headstrapped offerings, halting every dozen steps to lean on their staffs and pant, they arrive with wry remarks on their fitness and the heat, and each grounds her burden and wipes her face on a sleeve and presses her cheek to Sujata's with modest grace.

Soon after there follows another senior Errant with four fine inductees. One of them is his son. Youths a couple of years past Peterkin's age, leggy and muted and watchful, at first not that easy to tell apart.

The older man's name is Kan. He and Kuzak know each other well; when the introductions are over they touch faces and sit in the shade to talk. Kan speaks and Kuzak scans the boys as they are made known to him. Then Kuzak speaks and Kan stares at Peterkin who is bringing a platter of food. Kan shakes his head and pulls a frowning, sceptical face; Kuzak shrugs his shoulders, spreads his hands.

Kan and the boys have walked three days from a House way out on the plain across the river, a land of manorial farms, of fat sheep and ten-acre wheatfields, of temptingly lively villages. Kan has a word with Sujata, the group goes off to the pool below the Hermitage, soon whoops and splashing ride up on the westerly breeze.

The third arrival is also from the acorn clan: a senior man with a fervent adolescent girl, daughter of his nephew, he the unenthused chaperone. He greets Sujata cool-eyed and thin- smiled, and she reads the situation and presses her face to his a second time and whispers a word of commiseration.

With Kuzak's arrival the wolf had slipped into hiding. When more came he stopped watching and turned and trotted north, first of all country he knew already and then to newer ground, tall pinewood, sniffing the air and the underbrush and the boles of trees. He has often caught old scent of other wolves without concern, cocking his leg automatically, the fadedness of the odour reassuring. But then a tang of fresh urine comes at him all of a sudden, fronting layers of older smell on a marker tree, and every hair on his back is alive with the nearness of stranger wolf.

They must be upwind, he can't smell them. That means that they can smell him. As if he walks in an open field before a hidden enemy. They might be stalking, this side that side, any moment to catapult out of cover. He trots downwind quick and sleekit, weaving the least-bad path through shambolic terrain, listening hard for followers.

He scents boar very close and aims to circuit the sounder but he shoots past a strayed piglet that squeals blue murder, and the sows pick up his odour and set up a cacophony that must carry a solid mile and the wolf breaks into a run.

Terror of wolves that aren't of his long-gone pack, terror of men who aren't the boy, at the same time sucked towards the boy with all the force of an animal's will to live. He makes no calculation: he runs the path from greater terror to less, with neither hope nor despair.

Meanwhile five more typical pilgrims arrive at the Hermitage. They are from a Meghara cityfellowship, devotees at a stage of life when the prosperous might deputize their duties for a half-month or a month. Each has a pilgrim satchel embroidered with insignia of devotional journeys. Most prominent are from voyages to the temples and miracle sites on the Empire coast; next come visits to the few remaining hermits and hermitesses, cave-dwellers or sky-roofed wanderers, god-taken declaimers spilling half-comprehensible messages in voices not theirs. The Hermitage at Solstice, though now a little second-tier, is due at least one visit.

The five know each other well, their talk is all of pilgrimage past and desired. How this wonder-haunted spring was a muddy trickle, lost among the pasty stalls and charm-barterers. How that god-taken declaimer bumbled his words or fell into dialect. Ah, but how worth all the toil was the setting of the sun – you should have seen it – into the sea from the Temple of the Cape, a thousand voices chanting its descent. When one describes a circumstance another comes in with a better or a worse, like turnabout dancers scuffing each other to take centre-ring. Three women and two men, but their gender is somehow irrelevant.

They're hardly settled in, and remarking on the excellence of the mead, how welcome after their hike the figs and cheese (... ex*hausted*! – next time hire a se*dan* ...), when who comes but a holy man, a hermit, his approach unnoticed in the buzz, suddenly in every eye. Forest Penitent Kadri of Maul, half-naked and unsightly, sleeper under winter stars, eater only of what is given unasked, by folk or by nature – berries, roots, acorns, honey; freshwater mussels, a nest of fledglings; but often half a loaf, or a roast pigeon, or a bowl of broth and dumplings, from shy-giggling children watched from the cottage door – to adult and child he bows somewhat curtly but later for whom he prays, chanting verses into the night, blessing child and hearth and field.

He has no human connection, no-one knows how anyone knows his name. He's not from the town of Maul but from the forest beyond it, a great half-waste where the northern plain rises into the hills, a region that ranges from tiny but permanent patch-farms, to swidden terrain on which nomad slash-and-burn farmers eke a precarious crop, to virgin unfarmable woodland hunted and gathered-in, to forest so hidden or so bulwarked by terrain that it might go a hundred years unvisited. And Kadri has the look of a forest spirit, matted-haired, naked in summer when not in company, silent when not declaiming, his arms often weaving slow and inscrutable gestures, his face often taking intense expressions whose meaning is unknowable.

He comes for every festival of the Sun. He must wade the river at one of the upstream fords and pick his way through, he's never seen at the ferry. Sujata shows him discretion and kindness to which he seems impervious, listens with careful attention to his rants, sometimes with small gestures guides his conduct – when his loin-cloth is coming loose, when he mutters when others are talking, when he takes food from the wrong plate. He always responds, without hurry or embarrassment.

Kuzak knows him too, and Kan. Last of the Maul Forest Penitents, all the Errants know him. Twenty years before he'd been just a boy, runaway or orphan, youngest by far of a penitent band. A group of seven, then five, then two. No-one knows where the others went – died, or wandered off still hermits, or slipped back into a life left somewhere on hold. Kadri, touched by the gods – you might think a tiresome, misbegotten entity, and yet the wise will hearken to his rants, whisper passages over and over to fix them in their minds.

The pilgrims from Meghara are taken with him. They'd been unsure of the trip – so long now since the Hermit's death – but Kadri has already made it worthwhile. They too will repeat his phrases in debate; the youngest, a freelance scribe with old and wealthy parents, writes the best ones down, promising fair copies to the others. The holy man's exclamations become more frequent, his gestures broader. Kuzak and Kan exchange a glance when he shouts in his trance a sentence they've heard before, word for word. The scribe snatches up his slate and awl.

The wolf's dread eases now he's nearer to the boy. The odours of the Hermitage are thick in the lazy breeze, no home pack component since that single tang of urine.

He's slowed to a trot when he half-hears something, and takes a knoll in a couple of bounds and looks back. Nothing to see; nothing to hear but the rinsing song of a wood thrush and the sough of summer leaves. But then that under-sound again, thin-textured as a wisp of the air itself: the two-mile howl of the pack, seeping through the woods.

They've caught his scent, they're coming.

The sun has slanted lower and the mead has softened edges in the diverse assemblage. Conversation breaks out from familiar couples and groups, starts to cross the front-of-Hermitage clearing where all are seated, every speck of goat dung removed by the boy that morning, the visitors cross-legg'd or reclined on skins, felted blankets, cushions, the last declined by the men. The clustered distribution becomes a circumference; across it Errants and pilgrims exchange words.

Lale a Megharan widow, flaunty and bold, calls questions to the Errants, who answer with slow care but without condescension; she soon loses interest in their guarded replies and launches into an anecdote, recruiting fellow pilgrims to fill it out. As her tale meanders Tolga and Tutku, a married couple with six grown children, start a *sotto voce* side-conversation with Zeki the acorn uncle, their manner shy and only slightly patronising. He answers with congenial dry humour. When they hear that the elderly sisters witnessed the Hermit's coming they break into Lale's narration, their shyness suddenly gone.

Meanwhile Zeki's great-niece Yeta excitedly questions Kadri who sits cross-legg'd on stony bare ground close by. Sujata has twice gestured him down when he seemed about to get up and wander off. He stares into mid-air as she persists, muttering obscurely, as if he hasn't noticed her.

Peterkin has attended to the company, topping up mead cups, trying to save Sujata work. But half of his mind is elsewhere. The Errants see it and are watching him: he stares into the surrounding bouldery scrub, now and then vanishing into it, once reappearing on top of a knoll, staring all ways.

He has given each arrival the greeting he gave Kuzak, declaring himself the owner of a wolf. All at first assume that he's touched by the gods; but Sujata confirms his assertion to Kuzak, who can't believe it, thinking the beast a jackal or even a fox. But Kuzak passes on her words to Kan, Kan to the inductees.

The goats have been penned all day and are making their feelings known, impeding conversation. Sujata decides to let them out. The boy is instantly troubled in word and gesture, shaking his head as if pleading, saying *no no wolf wolf no.* When he draws a finger across his throat Kuzak almost starts up, thinking it might be a threat. But Sujata is smiling, shrugging her shoulders. She draws a finger across her own throat, then raises it – just one, he'll get no more than one she says. And she opens the pen and the goats mob out and skedaddle round the blandly intrigued and laughing party in wide circumvention and head for their usual grounds. The boy is on the knoll again, staring after them, Sujata smiling and shaking her head.

A noble couple arrive, their approach not heard in the fuss and noise of the goats. Suddenly a swordsman is crying the name and titles of Tark, the Baron Tark, and stands to the side as a large perspiring man appears where the streamside path meets the clearing. Improbably large he seems, with slabby chops clean-plucked and the chest of an ox, a great sleek belly below, smug in its fine-woven travel smock. He carries a staff of blackwood carved to a twisting design and topped with a silver boss. He's stopped till his wife the Third Baroness comes up, and to get his breath back: a square-on stance, feet spraddled, unhurriedly eyeing the company. Each morsel of his presence tells of immense self-importance: the pose, the lovingly chosen attire, the insolent unhurried

stare, the way he already imposes his physical mass. The Lady Damla comes to his side. She has almost his height but only a fraction his mass. In contrast with her husband's expressionless stare she beams with great generosity, as if she is a present she has brought them. She is much younger than him, her long-necked elegance set off by her fluid tunic and dangling silver.

A surge of movement as the company lifts to its feet, in contrast with the aristocrats' fine stasis.

The pilgrims bow like puppets hinged at the waist, the others less extravagantly – least so the senior Errants, who never bow till the other has met their eye, and then at only a terse and minimal depth. Sujata creaks up from her stool without hurry and wades forward to greet them, speaking the formalities with easy amiability – Tark came once before, with another wife. Sujata makes a point of greeting the servants too – the loud-voiced guard bowing punctiliously; another dipping from the waist still headstrapped to his burden; then a composed and alert-eyed personal maid; last an enormous man, a specimen bruiser who dwarfs even Tark, an ill-disposed pudding of a face nodding down offhand as he slips his pannier and eases it to the ground.

The names go round. Sujata has the pilgrims give their own for fear of misremembering, with a light apology. Kan names the inductees and they bow in turn – Tark is avuncular and jestful, Damla oozes her smile.

Kuzak somewhat jars the harmonious flow: he meets Tark's gaze very coolly, and gives short answer to his in-quiries. They knew each other once, though only Kuzak recognises, remembers. Back when the Baron was plain

Serkan of Lix and was making his way, treading down friend and enemy alike. Back when a treacherous run of events undid Kuzak's world, just as he scrabbled to move wife and child upcountry away from the plague – Tark then a drinking buddy to many, with a flattering interest in others' plans, a gift for steering a mead-warmed exchange in a confidence-sharing direction.

Tark's eye darkens. The giant is behind him – this is Ruslan he says, you might get to know each other, and turns abruptly as Kuzak stone-faces up and makes his minimal bow. The big man stares down and nods a half-inch with a grin of sardonic amusement.

Tark ignores Kadri the penitent. His nod to the acorn people is barely perceptible.

Sujata has whispered to Peterkin.

Hail O Baron Dammela Targ. I name Peterkin. Mine is wolf.

He hardly spares the boy a glance, assuming as do the others he's a piece of the flotsam that washes to the holy, taken in by Sujata for want of other harbour in the world. She says the wolf's a shy guest, daunted by company, off somewhere eating her goats. Tark takes this as a jest on the boy's delusion and deigns a smile. The ramshackle assembly becomes his court: a rug has been laid out, the female servant makes a round requesting extra cushions, with a breezy mix of directiveness and deference, persisting till Tark and Damla have three each.

The wolf makes a long zig-zag detour, twice crossing the stream to throw the pack off his scent. The guile is intrinsic to his fear, requires no coolness.

And the odours of smoke and humanity impede the pack's purpose. But they catch more and more in the thick stench of man thin wisps of the intruder. Like a half-hid creature in a landscape – such is the scent of the stranger wolf, hiding in the mix.

The afternoon rides on, in the beauty of early summer. A mother of the acorn people wanders up with her daughter, a girl of five or six years old who gapes up at the storytale crowd, dumb when Lale of the pilgrims dotingly asks her name, a cuff from her mother not lifting her out of her trance.

Sujata and Peterkin are preparing the evening meal. The acorn niece assists, but she alone; she tells the boy her name and fires at him questions, undaunted by his embarrassed shrugs. At any pause in the work he is out and climbing the knoll, looking all ways and giving a low owlish whistle. The assembled glance, make a smiling remark to a neighbour.

And now the evening meal is almost ready, the sun has slanted low across the plain. The last guests arrive: the ferry wife, a woman of barely thirty years, with daughters of maybe five and fifteen. She is taciturn and shy but with a density of confidence, a readiness to snap. The younger girl is the one who skipped beside her as Peterkin watched in the distance, in the silencing roar of the cataract. The older is as hard-faced and as silent as her mother. Between them a sullen tension. They are hot from the five-mile walk; before that words between ferryman and wife, he not letting her leave until his meal was on the stove. Sujata greets them, gently smiling, surmising the context.

The table is carried out. Only four can sit at it; any more and their backs would be turned to the ones who eat cross-legged. Kuzak and Kan both disclaim the fourth place with Sujata and the nobles. The oldest male pilgrim is next in status; Lale gives sarcastic congratulation.

The pack has approached the feast with care, outrunners scouting to left and to right. They pick up a clearer scent, then one sees a shape in cover a quarter mile off, the scout's sudden directiveness tells the others.

They've found the intruder, skulking halfway between them and the humans. They're covering ground now, eating the distance, forking left and right to scissor their prey. Suddenly goats to one side of the chase are bolting in panic; the wolves in their focus ignore them.

Sujata has a sporadic gift from her life of meditation. She sees beyond the here and now – sometimes a stab of vision, sometimes a steady awareness. But fitfully, unreliably.

This time she senses the coming pandemonium, but only by seconds.

The visitors are all seated on ground or at table. Peterkin and Yeta bring out the main course – a big sturgeon, headstrapped up with great effort by a youth of the acorn clan, divided into four on four heavy platters, served with bread and a pottage of sorrel and pine nuts. Cups are being filled for the hailing toast: Tark who will deliver it glances about unhurriedly, makes an aside to his bonny wife. Her responding smile is now thinner, with a sardonic asymmetry. The heat of the day has pleasantly eased, the afternoon has slipped into evening.

Chaos chooses this pause to make his entry. Sujata feels his approach and is suddenly on her feet, shouting to Peterkin. Wolves, she cries, your wolf brings many. As if on cue the eerie rope of a pack howl climbs upwards, goats as if flung come scuttering round the clearing-edge

or swerving through the company. Sujata cranks over to their pen, calling them, calling them – they're milling and bucking too panicked to enter until, yawking in pain at the move, she grips the alpha nanny by ear and tail and skids and slaps her into the pen and the rest follow, one and then two and then a rush.

The wolves howl again, no more than a hundred yards off. Tutku the pilgrim wife is wailing in counterpoint, the Baron's men are on their feet, a sword is in the giant's hand. The Errant party is up and heading towards the sound, shouting as they go.

The wailing of the pilgrim wife tightens into a scream as Peterkin's wolf bolts into the clearing, skids round the circle of participants, swerves behind the Hermitage and is gone. All are on their feet, surging forward, pressing back, shouting incoherent advice or calling on the gods.

Peterkin instantly follows the wolf, the big man close behind him with his sword.

Chapter 14: Arrangements

he big man with the sword is well apprenticed for his place in life. Ruslan of Tannak, unwanted eighth child of inebriates now long dead; a half-renegade gang of brothers, cousins, comrades now also far past. Courageous, with a sour pride, naturally cruel, he indentured five years to a troop of Empire occasionals, then sought the eye of the Megharan nobility.

'Mine is wolf' – he heard the boy say it. He thinks he'll follow him.

The wolf's terror has logic.

To slip behind the noisy and odorous wall of newly arrived humanity. To find the boy, his only refuge in the world. He circuits behind the little hamlet of bothies, takes cover behind the outlier shack where they spent the last two nights, with its smells of deer meat and the boy.

The pack is no fool. When the fervent men and youths appear from the odour-wall of fire and mankind the wolves let go their purpose instantly, soft-foot into cover and away. The frontmost inductee alone catches a glimpse of one, and he's not sure. The pursuers stomp around in the tangled scrub, the wolves are soon a mile away. They group and rub sidelong and take in each other's defining smell, all with a certain intent, a formality. And then they howl – not for the men, for whom their enmity is a fact of life, indifferent as the weather, but for the stranger wolf, the traitor wolf, folded into the world of the ancient enemy, of the foe whose stench creeps across the world. All that a beast can know of abomination they feel for Peterkin's wolf, and they howl their hope and intent for his destruction.

The Errants have worked uphill, fanned out and picked up rocks to throw, but they shrug and gesture when the howl goes up, eerie but very thin against the breeze. And the seniors call to two inductees who have crashed ahead with great keenness, as if overplaying a game of chasing wolves.

The others – pilgrims, locals – assume that Peterkin's wolf is leader in an assault, a failed attack on Sujata. Demon-possessed they suppose the beast, to slay the Hermit's acolyte in the sight of nobles and devotees at the feast on Midsummer Eve.

Tark meanwhile looks about him, stung to have the attention abruptly diverted. A fuss about not very much. And where's Ruslan gone?

Peterkin has the gift of rapid thought in the swirl of chaos. Or is it that Fate lays out a single path for him, however twisty and narrow, and lights it up as he goes? Or is that the same thing?

He feels the mass of the giant at his back, the heavy-footed purpose. He knows the wolf is thrown by a mixture of terrors. He knows that he is the beast's only refuge. He might make for the shack or he might run on, into the deep-wooded downhill terrain, maybe to vanish entirely.

Peterkin slips the big man by heading through the backstage region of outhouses, slanting left as if meaning to turn upstream and then dropping sharp to the right when a shed hides him from view. He squirms through a sallow thicket and picks up the streamside path below sight of the compound, then cuts through the bothies to their solitary shack.

He makes a staccato owlcall through the gasping of his breath when he hears a whimper behind him. The wolf is here already, ears flat and hackled hair and buckled like a crayfish, tail hooked far between his legs. Peterkin goes no closer but speaks to him, in breathless phrases at first but then in a low incessant murmur, drawing out the vowels of reassurance. The same half-chanted register his mother used when he fell out of the tree, when the muster gang took his father away, preserved in his soul for such times as this.

The wolf approaches the boy prawned-up and almost sidelong, still bristled along the back and hackles, whimpering in plea and ingratiation. Peterkin wants to hug him in his arms but doesn't. He closes the distance slowly, play-scolding as if with a child; he drifts his hand and strokes the neck, taut and hard to the touch. And the long tongue slaps up against his face, and he winces and laughs in shock.

He sits awhile, talking, letting time pass, letting him settle. But then there's movement nearby – the crack and shush of foliage, a woman's voice, a man's, very deep. Where to put the wolf, and no time to think. He lifts the cross-latch of the shanty door and makes a hissing whisper and urgent gesture and to his relief the wolf slinks into the hut. He thinks to drop the latch and return insouciant to the disturbed assembly but they've seen him. An odd couple – Asli the maid, a face of sharp but fearful inquiry; Ruslan enormous behind her keen to use the sword that juts from his paw.

Sujata had called out not to worry, the wolf that ran through belongs to the boy, it means no harm, the boy will manage it. She guessed the back-country pack were pursuing it, enemies of her livelihood not seen for years.

Tark asked some questions. He sent Asli to investigate. Pick up Ruslan, keep him from undue mayhem.

Tame wolf, he said to Sujata, as if trying out the phrase. Not a demon. You're sure?

No demon said Sujata. I think not even a miracle. A wonder, not a miracle.

I will see this, said Tark.

Asli is as rare a find as Ruslan the giant. She is Tark's creature, his eyes and ears, doubling as Damla's maid, twin-roled in the demands of pilgrimage.

She has construed, along with much else: that the Errants and Sujata are sound, not the usual half-frauds; that the pilgrims on the other hand are very much the usual; that Kuzak the Errant's ill-will towards Tark is more than mere disdain for the worldly and proud, that there must be a story to it; that Kadri the Renouncer is playing a part from a basis of true derangement, a tiresome but intriguing phenomenon. And that Sujata's boy is no idiot but surely a foreigner, not long arrived from his handful of mispronounced words. And has she heard that tongue before? Empire slaves in the harbour at Lix? The complexion fits, the hair, though the boy's deceivingly sun-baked. She'd suspected the wolf was neither delusion nor jest before its materialization.

When Tark sends her off she quickly found Ruslan and gestured him to her, not needing to say they're on the Baron's orders. Asli and the big man have worked together before: situations where a certain impression needs to be made. The way she handles him comes easily to her. Flattery; give him an overall view of what they're about, pretending he has a say in it; then establish a breezy and amiable leadership as soon as action is called for.

She leads to where the streamside path drops steeply below the Hermitage. She has guessed the boy might head for the bothies.

You scared of wolves, Big One? Silly question, you could wring its neck. Me, I'll be lucky to keep my water in. The thing here is that the Baron is curious. So soft touch unless the circumstances require. Yeah? I'll be the negotiator, you keep back unless I yell. But if that thing goes for me, chop off its head. M-hm? Great. Here goes then. Keep ten steps back, stop if I signal, let's both stay wide awake.

Then, in a grateful tone:

Thank the gods you're behind me Ruslan.

The gabble behind them quietened as they footed the steep and loose-pebbled path. All was still in the hamlet of bothies. Silence but for an ousel, singing from a lone black spruce.

At the bothies Asli looks about and listens. She's no tracker, but quick of eye and mind – she sees pushed-through vegetation in the wall of scrub on the far side of the hamlet. She raises a hand to shoulder height for Ruslan behind her and points, not turning her head. She crosses and eases forward and through, stepping quietly. There's a soft, cajoling voice somewhere ahead. Scuffling sounds, a creak and clonk of wood. Her water does indeed threaten mutiny.

Peterkin has nowhere to go, and anyway they've found the shack, or will in a moment. Hello, he says, ridiculously. Hello, with a would-be-easy smile.

Peterkin, says Asli. Aha.

Ruslan has lumped into view, she palms him to stop. She hears something and points to the door of the shack.

Wolf? she says. Your wolf, in there?

At the interrupted supper they're saying the wolf is huge, a freak in size – they saw it so in their fear. Some believe Sujata that the boy has tamed it; some still think it's a demon, and that its size is proof.

Then Asli and the giant come back, and she tells the Baron that the boy has it penned in his shack. Tark beckons her closer and they speak quietly, intently. Damla twists to hear, gives up, twiddles with plate and spoon.

Her gift of persuasion bought her a glimpse. Peterkin was anyway off balance, in the chaos of events. He understood few of her words, but she got him to prise a slot in the random and ill-tied shingles, the shack having no window: mime-pulling at the shingles, looping finger and thumb and peeking through, the steady melodic push of her incomprehensible speech, her amiably persuasive gaze, give resistance no purchase. She first sang out to the giant to sheath his sword; he squats sullenly twenty yards back.

Peterkin finds a shingle to shift, an easy task. Asli peers in one-eyed but she sees almost nothing. She doesn't need to: the wolf, hackling at the new voice and the rummaging, then the beam of light and the stranger's eye, snarls as if truly a demon. She hasn't seen much – a shift of movement, near-black on near-black – but that sound is enough. Fear bolts through her, she jerks back from her squinting.

Wah, she says, *wah*. You tamed *that*? He doesn't understand.

She asks him by word and gesture to come back up to the feast.

He puts her off, trying to say he'll come in a while, he needs to see to the wolf. She shrugs and moves away, then turns to try again. But then she hears him speaking in his own tongue. Sing-song cajoling, ending each phrase on a drop-tone vowel. Now he's unlatching the door; she quicksteps towards Ruslan, who heaves to his feet. The boy is crouched in the four-foot-high doorway of the shack, carrying on his hushing monologue. Then he goes in, easing in slowly. Asli's stomach turns over, her mouth is open. *Ahhh?* she says very quietly, as if it's a question to herself. Then he closes the door, the muffled monologue continues.

Peterkin keeps back from the wolf, so recently made fearful again, now with no retreat. As far back as the little shack allows. While his eyes adapt to the dark he tells him that everything is fine, the other wolves have gone, the people here won't do him any harm. The tone of his voice does not betray the unease he feels at his words. A promise you'd like to keep but mightn't, they say where he comes from, is worse than one unmeant: the second's at least an honest lie.

These people won't hurt you, I'll see to it, all's good, his voice goes on.

Now with his eye dark-adapted he can see the wolf unbristle, the tail to lift and the ears to rise. Outside hang strips of deer meat he's trying to sun-dry for want of a smoke house. Slowly and with detailed explanation Peterkin eases out and closes the door and fetches a strip and comes back half-crooning reassurances. He doubles the end of the strip round the blade of his knife, a piece just long enough to grip and no more, and slices it off and places it down for the wolf, and the wolf comes forward and takes it and hunkers down to chew, and then gulps down the softened chunk and looks for more. Peterkin beckons him close and moving slowly reaches a hand and touches and strokes behind his ear, and the wolf licks his face and the boy half-laughs and gives a second chunk and leaves two more when he heads back to the company.

When Peterkin reappears Sujata waves him over.
  He's bowing apologetically. Wolf good he says. Wolf – hut. Wolf good.
  But she smiles and gestures away his conciliation. Come and see Baron Tark, she says.

Sujata is a saint but also a pragmatist.
  The pack has kept away five years, since a winter when they took half her flock. But now they've been brought back, by the boy's tame wolf. And she can't now get out with the flock, even in summer. A saint but also a pragmatist. When Tark asks about the boy and the wolf she tells him what she can. She knows the man's character, but she knows too that he takes an easy way

with valued servants – Asli, Ruslan – and the boy with his grateful diligence will please him. And she guesses a tame wolf would be a wonder and an envy to his peers in the nobility.

The world is a dirty place, the Hermit used to say. Seek the path least soiled, but don't expect clean feet.

Come and see Baron Tark she says.

Asli meanwhile has thought to tour the company group by group, to see who knows any foreign tongue apart from the two that she herself can get by in. No-one – but one of the female pilgrims can sing a chant she heard sung over and over, by galley slaves on a crossing to a spirit-haunted island off the Empire's north-west corner. She sings it to Asli and Asli presses her, blushing and a-tremble, into the Baron's presence, and she quavers the song with a Megharan twang but close pronunciation, and Asli glances sidewards to see Peterkin listening open-mouthed and astounded.

> South wind blow and melt the snow
> For the people of the Valley
> Seed is sown and barley grown
> By the people of the Valley
> Sun by day shine Moon at night shine
> On the people of the Valley
> We the people we the people
> We the people of the Valley
> We the people we the people
> We the people of the Valley

The pilgrim said they sang it in time with their rowing, over and over and over. The words so simple and sung so clearly, how could she forget. She was seasick, the song still makes her queasy.

Mine people this, announces Peterkin, with some generality but mainly to Sujata. Mine people this.

The woman doesn't know where the slaves were from.

Mine people, says Peterkin. Over mountains. He waves an arm in direction.

Perhaps we help you find your people, says Tark. Or maybe we can help your wolf – bring it somewhere safe.

Standing a little off, Ruslan spits on the ground. Abomination he mutters, almost too loud, thumbing the pommel of his sword.

Don't trouble, O Ruslan the Large, says Asli from the corner of her mouth. What the Baron wants the Baron gets.

Tark beckons Asli closer. He enjoys her quickness of mind, she is one of the very few whom he trusts. Their offhand rapport disconcerts his wives, but their spies report no greater indecorum.

I want the boy and his wolf to come back with us. Help things along if you would, Asli daughter of Arda. Teach him to speak Megharan for a start. Yes?

Love to, O Baron. Which, the boy or the wolf?

The wolf, if you show off your impudence he says, sidling his eye towards his ignored and sullen third wife.

Sorry. I'm scared of it though.

You'll make friends in no time.

Mm.

Tark is from Lix but now has a mansion not twenty miles downstream, in parkland by the quiet waters below the Third Cataract, with his three wives and the manifold staff and a varying entourage.

He is lowborn, a rich man at twenty-five, awarded a barony for funding the king's summer palace. His first two wives were daughters of straitened noble houses; only the third was chosen for her looks. He agreed the outrageous bride-price for the second with slightly raised eyebrows, a quarter-smile, a hands-open shrug of the shoulders as if such a sum was of no great concern. The matchmaker bowed deeply, containing a sigh of astonished relief.

His wealth is from trading, the land rents are merely a bonus. Fractions of many enterprises, in the tangled transactional networks of the twin cities and their north-coast-of-Empire connections. A trinket here, a trinket there, an easy smile, confiding advice good or false. The delicate removal of obstruction. Larger gifts where the power is, verging on over-generous but rarely disdained at that. Lately more venturous trade for the gold and stones of the half-mythical southlands, though now through agents – pulling strings at a dignified distance.

He's down by sedan to Meghara thrice a year, hardly ever to Lix; his agents must make quarter-year upriver trips by foot or by oar. His gifts dress the mayors of both cities in satin, and thicken the soup of the watchmen; his many spies sniff out sinners, his heavies chastise them. All goes well enough it seems, despite his rustic retreat.

He'd been riskily indebted by the palace and the bride-price, but his wealth was greatly boosted by the Empire's war with the outer nations. Slaves, so many slaves – unenthused conscripts who took captivity rather than death, dropping their swords and kneeling in surrender. What bribes it took, to curb the sanguinary lust of the Empire's army, long customed to free all enemy souls from the prison of flesh. What bribes, to persuade them to gather and herd the supine hordes, to keep them in decent condition. Ah, but what profit! Each cowed head diminished the squawk for repayment; by the end of the war it was silenced entirely.

Now in his late middle age he tries to ease the boredom of success by seeking the sublime. With no greater prize to reach for, it seems, than the one he already has: the power and creature comforts of a new-wealth aristo-crat. He wants it – sublimity – in the way he always wants anything: with careful attention to what he finds pleasing, selection of targets, the planning of their at-tainment.

His desires have two levels: the wish for a certain pleas-ure, the wish to get what he wants because he wants it. He takes a tacit pride in his many skills. The careful un-dermining of others' grounds for resistance. An almost hypnotic persuasiveness, where his version of reality takes on such light and colour that the other's life-world fades to a shadow. Shows of warmth, of esteem, of finding the other remarkably shrewd or likeable, their story all-absorbing. The many and layered stages of threat, from the first faux-innocent noting of relevant facts of life to persuasive visits by henchmen, livened by token assaults and the non-consensual borrowing of trinkets. A child's first curls tied with ribbon; a marriage chain. And at last, when natural if not formal justice warrants – planned with care, and a little discreet salivation – a message that gets through to even the hardest of hearing. Ruslan, for instance, might be one to convey such a message.

Tark doesn't recognise Kuzak. If the events of thirty years before were spoken of he'd have little recall, of just another nonentity walked over on his way up. Now the world is more dangerous than the docklands he knew then, where the worst you had to fear was a knife in an alley, and sense would always tell you which alley to miss. Now survival trumps ambition. He's seen the overly power-hungry walk to their executions, or else be dragged on hurdles, when close interrogation had taken the spring from their stride. A paranoid king, of an upstart line with ancient enemies, consolidating his power. Tark's policy is keep distance, hedge bets, risk malice from only the weak.

A quiet life on a country estate, with visits to court bearing gifts and praise, neither too frequent nor too rare. Keep the widest possible range of alliances. Play the rustic noble, content with his place in life, counting his flocks and enjoying his wives, musicians in his court and a poet-scribe, a reputation for the good life – fine things, food, tours to see grand vistas and holy sites.

But an inner Tark still squirms with boredom, with frustrated self-expansion. His life might be a fine life for someone he hasn't become yet, for someone he might be in maybe ten years. Fifteen. Twenty. Sometimes he feels he can't breathe, for the press of the inner Tark in his chest, wanting more. More of the game, of the upward reach, of the wins and more wins and the great euphoric balm to his soul that each one gives, for a while.

But every way he looks at the court he sees a fifty-fifty game with no way of choosing and loss unthinkable. Even picking the winning side would give tense and perilous play with no stable outcome, until and unless a strong and knowing and wholesomely merciless monarch comes to the fore. Which person he might himself be, were it not for the sure ganging-up of ancient houses against new blood.

His dreams go all to the Empire. The Empire, not this tattered half-province that thinks itself a kingdom, because some fool sits in a certain chair and wears on his head a certain unusual hat, till the next fool sends in thugs to cut his throat. How much more salutary, fitting, to be at the right hand of the Emperor, of whose house there's no whisper of dislodgement, from whose side can be seen horizons inviting the late expansion of a great and storied life. A vizier perhaps; or lord of a new-conquered province – victories, consolidation, planning the Empire's next step. The Empire. He has a name there, of course, if a small one – gifts, self-disfavouring deals with longer-term goals: a guileful mollusc sucking itself forward. He uses the very word, in his inner voice, in the private archive taken by his scribe: with the mighty suck, don't push. Suck your way forward, then contrariety's relocated behind you, not lurking ahead to plot ambush.

The Emperor has a favourite daughter, beautiful lissom and utterly spoilt. She comes of age three days before the equinox. They say she loves beasts more than people: one fruit of her father's indulgence is a menagerie, the finest in the world. What a birthday gift it would be, a slave boy with a hand-tame wolf.

Chapter 15: Midsummer

The feast regains its momentum. The sturgeon isn't even cold.

But Sujata has felt the reach of anger and needs to head it off. Wolves, back, brought by the boy's half tame one.

A hard winter five years ago and it wasn't just the goats at risk. Too old already to watch them all day in that cruelty of cold, the ground as hard as bone and the whipping, bone-grinding wind. And when the wind dropped there came to the world a silence so perfect it might be the silence of Death himself, and through the silence would rise, like an ascent of thin-layered smoke or like a ruffian congregation singing a prayer to Death, the howl of the wolves, conjoining their intent.

One evening bringing the flock back in, the sky dark and heavy, chilled and half-brainless with the cold, her hands almost useless in big fumbling mitts, the pack came and took a nanny right in front of her. She ungloved and tried to sling a stone and the sling flew off with the stone from her jointless hand, and the two wolves in view backed off hardly a yard. Then one went back to its work; but the other, surmiseful from the feebleness of assault, stayed up on its toes and looked at her straight on, a hunter assessing prey. That very awake stare, so vacant of pity. She threw a stone by hand and it skidded luckily off a boulder and almost hit, and the wolf shrank down and joined its partner at the still vaguely kicking goat, watching her. She doesn't want to die in a blur of fear and body-shock, the agony within a terrible numbness. She wants to die a measured death, to give her full attention to the task.

From the goodness of their hearts and the promise of a cask of apple spirit, the fathers and sons of the acorn clan came up and tracked them in the snow and found their lair and there killed two, and another as it bolted past a rearguard, and the rest had relearned their place in the world of human lethality and afterwards kept away.

The reach of anger, most troublesome of the nine emotions. Anger, enemy of solace, enemy of wisdom. She has to head it off, to baulk it at source. That the pack should be brought near again, to trample the serenity of her last few months or years, to befoul the peace of whatever winter she's due to die in. After all she has done, to serve and to hold her balance.

Yes, she feels it coming, the surge of indignation, like seeing a storm moving in on the wind with just time to bring in the flock and latch the door. Skill has no rules said the Hermit, when Chaos comes by with his old friend Anger. Worse than Lust, for kicking over a jar of many-year-filled wisdom, to soak into the dust like the urine of goats. This he was shown when he came to the Gates of Death.

So Sujata speaks with Baron Tark and then with Peterkin, praising in mime and gesture the grace and safety of Tark's estate. She leads the boy to meet him.

Ah, wolf boy! says Tark, smiling like an uncle.

I keep you safe, you and wolf. Yes?

As he mimes 'safe' his arms embrace some invisible content. The manicured hands oddly small for the big puddingy body, the thickness of the arms under their silks. The odour of a floral perfume mixes with the sweat of his journey. His smile, the gleam of his weasel-bright eyes, baffles contradiction.

Peterkin has never met such a person. He has no idea how to weigh up the grandiosity of presence, the mannered benignity, the larger-than-lifeness. He'd thought to be an outcast now, with the wolf bringing such kerfuffle – but once again Luck's found a way forward. He mutters a prayer of gratitude.

Food is eaten, drink taken, the prototypal anecdotes of this strange and remarkable evening are laid down. The excitements have energised companionship; talk is free, there is much laughter. Once the dishes are cleared the boy is gestured back to sit at Sujata's left hand. The Baron on her right beams across at him now and again, with smiles of great goodwill, sometimes with a wink or an up-flick of eyebrows.

It was no feast for drinkers for all its excitements. When the falling sun was a little shy of north-west and easing into slats of roseate cloud the vesperbell rang – handed by Sujata to the younger ferry daughter, who swung it two-handed in fear and excitement. The final cups were emptied, the company took positions to view the last of the sun of the rising year. The elder male of the acorn clan had prepared for this early end to the flow of drink, with a piglet-skin of applejack waiting in his cabin.

The company disperses, to the downhill hamlet of cabins and shacks, Tark and Damla to the one guest-room in the Hermitage. Peterkin unlatches his shack and the wolf scoots out immediately and after a dozen yards he turns round twice and squats and defecates, and then quite willingly trots back in to Peterkin's call and gesture, and the two settle down for the hours of darkness. Outside the Hermitage door when all is finally still the sack-bodied form of Ruslan sinks to one knee and rolls out a felted bedroll, and he lies huge and silent as the stars appear show in their multitudes.

It's Sujata herself who swings the bell where the path crests above the bothies, a considerate spell of time before dawn with the mountain skyline behind her, a driftaway of peaks jagged up into yellows and pinks. The residents emerge in the grey light, uncomposed and grey themselves, and make gruff half-word greetings, check a comrade's presentation, dither at the counter-positioned latrines.

When Sujata rings the second bell most are already in place in the Hermitage clearing. Peterkin trots up late and anxious; last of all is the acorn uncle, smelling of liquor and unchanged clothing; his fervent niece sighs with embarrassed relief.

The third bell sounds. The company processes to the knoll above the compound: Sujata gestures Peterkin to take her arm and help her with the climb, her staff in the other hand; behind come the Errants, privileged by calling; next the Baron and Damla followed by their entourage; then the pilgrims; then the commoners of acorn clan and ferry. Finally comes Kadri the Renouncer, as ever taking lowest place. The knoll-top barely fits them all.

Sujata whispers to Asli to reposition Ruslan at the back of the crowd; she gestures the children and the acorn crones to the front. Tark and Damla are just behind her, the commoners torsioned and craning to see round them. The Errants make an orderly line to one side, arranged by height. Kadri perches on a thorn-circumfurenced boulder, precariously.

All is ready.

The streaked yellows intensify in a deep cut between two massifs. Not the Notch, but in Peterkin's awareness. He's taken in the lie of the peaks from this the western side, not thinking why – whether a part of him thinks he'll ever return. Where he comes from the sun is already well up, his people are singing the chants of greeting and thanks, the first cups are poured. His mind jerks back from the vision the way a hand jerks back from a flame.

Sujata points with her staff, casual and *sotto voce*, telling the children where to watch. Then she raises her left arm, angled as an ancient branch, and calls out a stark command in a very different voice, a voice that starches the air of all unsacramental blemish. The congregation holds very still, even the little ones; only the speckling of birdsong edges the silence. Then the rim of the sun shows, first an incandescent wire, soon a blinding bulge that grows moment by moment into the U between the massifs, heaving up and aslant, gigantic.

The congregation crinkles eyes or squints between fingers. A trickster after-image will dance through their morning, tiresome as a fly. The silence holds till the tail of the disc lets go its sucker grip on the mountain and the sun lofts free ... then Sujata calls again, with the same intensity: a long measured line of praise, subservience, gratitude. The others respond in a single huge voice, so timed and coherent you'd think it rehearsed. They have done this all their lives; they learn the words, the demeanour, from parents, grandparents, elders, checked and approved by Errants and the priesthood.

The shock of the sudden voice hits Peterkin like an unexpected blow. It's all very different where he comes from, loose and happily shambolic. He's shaken, somehow furtive, the bewildered outsider.

Then over and over the chant goes back and forth, Sujata calling in that voice out of nowhere, weird in its density and power, the congregation's bursts of open-throated antiphon. The giant sun processes up and across, its carpet of yellow-gold fallout thick on the skyline and pouring between its peaks.

In the ten long days he's been in this country the boy's never felt so displaced. Over those mountains his cousins and his comrades and the girls he was starting to notice are singing, laughing. For them he is gone, perhaps, as if he'd never been. Here this incomprehensible world yells out again and again in its incomprehensible tongue, shaking his bones, dwindling him to a nothing. He worries about the wolf, still in the shack. He wishes he were with the wolf.

But after a few more stretched-out calls and replies Sujata cries a single phrase and the rest answer with a single word. Then the same again, and then again. And then the company suddenly relaxes, as if a cable has been cut; sighs, speech, laughter; hands on comrades' shoulders and the rubbing of face on face. And all in unhurried twos and threes piece their way back to the compound.

When the Holy Crone and the boy are past the last tricky step she squeezes his arm. Go see to your wolf she says, as if she has read his mind.

There's a dispersal of the assembly, fingering out into small unhurried missions.

The inductees are detailed to help by Kan their director, and stomp around keenly setting the clearing aright, pouncing on ever-smaller detritus from last night's feast. One tries to help Sujata milk but he's soon sent off; the young acorn mother steps in, watched by her daughter who soon skips away, an over-shoulder warning to stay in view.

The ferry wife wants to get back, back to the man who bites his lip and mutters. A drip-drip of anxiety somewhere behind her smile-proof face. Her daughters aren't wanting to go yet, the little one starting to grizzle; the mother hisses a threat.

The acorn uncle, telling the elder acorn sisters to tell young Yeta to come down and wake him when the food's laid out, picks his way back to his bothy to catch some more sleep. The crones wave him off sarcastically, lower themselves onto rugs in the early bone-warming sun and face it eyes closed, watching the slow vermillion drift – it had been a cold cloudless night, necessary excursions lit by the stars.

The pilgrims also return to their bothies, to pick up the food and the gifts they have brought. Small rinded cheeses, some of notable name and cost; smoked meats of many kinds – partridge, marmot, beaver, ring dove, roe; pickled eel, pickled mussels; a dozen vellum-wrapped spices from the Empire. The gifts: lapis, malachite, amethyst; a four-stumped silk-smooth nugget of electrum like a tiny embryo in its caul; the tooth of an ancient saint, the scrumpled-up ear of another. This is more than usual generosity: hobbyists they may be, a touch poseur, but there's nothing fake in their reverence for Sujata – the decades she served the Hermit, the decades since his death. Her years are few now – who then will keep the Hermitage and its practices? Will its store of treasures interest the priesthood? The Errants – more worthy of trust, but they wouldn't do it themselves – might they supervise a manager from the laity? A retired pilgrim perhaps?

Tark and Damla return to the guest room. For a while they remain there.

Ruslan takes a seat where the knoll rises steeply from the clearing, his back against a boulder, half-watching the Hermitage door. His scowl eases slowly in the sun. The two other guardsmen join him, their talk muted and sceptical. Ruslan smiles once or twice but says little.

Kadri the forest Renouncer is drifting away on the northward goat path. Sujata calls him, insisting he eat with them. He seems not to hear but before long he wanders back.

In the kitchen an unlikely pairing, Kuzak and Yeta the acorn niece, are pulling globes of unleavened dough from a saggy pile kneaded the day before, and slapping them into flatbreads and piling them till the just-lit stove picks up heat. Yeta shoots questions, most of them carefully sidestepped.

I'd love to be an Errant. Could *I* be an Errant? Is there a rule?

It has never occurred to anyone that a rule needed making. He tells her of the priestess role, of the sisterhoods of female Renouncers. She seems unenthused.

Peterkin is absent. He has let out the wolf and straightaway headed north through trackless wood, bending twigs to make a trail. His instinct is to get them back to their settled duality, its mutual understanding, its quality of an offhand conversation, its dual thereness and dual seeing.

If it weren't for the pack they could live like this forever, half wild and half helpmeet to Sujata, work in exchange for bread and cheese. If it weren't for the pack, for which both keep a sharp ear. The wolf stays close to Peterkin. He has about him a diffidence – watchful, uncharacteristic.

Chapter 16: Aftermath

t the centre of the day comes the showing of the relics. When the sun will never be higher and the shadows never shorter. Walk north and each step lands in a hard-edged plunk of yourself as wide as it is long.

The relics are brought out under the sun, offered to the Sun. The table, that has sat out all night beneath the stars, and bears a thin gauze of dust and two chalky splats from crumb-seeking birds, is washed by Sujata with murmured incantation. It's dry in no time.

Sujata leads, precarious without her staff, holding in front of her the arrow that punctured the Hermit's head. Then comes Kuzak, bearing the upper skull; then Kan with the heavy pewter case that holds the heart. Then – a nice touch – the four Errant inductees, each bearing an arrowhead on doubled palms. Last comes Kadri the Renouncer, bearing nothing but chanting with surprising poise and correctness the Midsummer hymn.

The relics are laid out, the bearers stand at ease in attendance. The worshippers file past in order of worldly prestige, the Baron first. All seems well enough – the nobles, the pilgrims, the servants, the locals, in natural order. Asli would be tricky to place were she not entirely free of presumption: she slots in behind the pilgrims, Ruslan's dour mass behind her. Last come the sisters of the acorn clan, standing long to look down on these fragments of that day when the stranger – ragged, stinking, leaking blood – leant half-collapsed against the fence of their goat-pen. Their father's dry smile at this new and unneeded dependent, as if his apparition were no special thing. Pulses of the realness of that day rise into the dried-out memories, as they stare down on these vestiges.

The relics are returned, there's an easing towards dispersal. A last small informal meal; embraces are exchanged, people are leaving. The locals to their ordinary lives. The pilgrims to stay a night with the acorn folk, as they did the night before last, rejoining their three bearers and most of their gear. Their *de facto* leader will press rich stones and a finely wrought brooch on their hosts, the gifts with reluctance accepted on the third persuasion as is the way.

The Baron has a loquacity in his parting, warm and easy. His third wife ducks with fluid grace to embrace Sujata, smiling brightly, her voice a little husky in the sincerity of its gratitude.

But Tark has something else to consider. (His party, like the pilgrims, in keeping with traditions of humility and penitence, was reduced to its necessary core for the final stage of the expedition: sedan chairs and their bearers await them at the ferry, along with two more swordsmen and a baggage ox.) The Baron asides with Sujata and speaks with intent, though keeping all along his bonhomious smile, his well-judged deference. Sujata is replying with her usual slow care, once or twice shrugging her shoulders, lifting a hand to the Fates as they float in the midsummer air. Then Tark gestures Asli over – she seems discomposed, even troubled. When the Baron's party leaves she stays behind.

She will manage the journey of boy and wolf.

The Baron will send up one of the extra guards, a staunch and taciturn man, but he never arrives. He takes the opportunity to return to his true employer the Megharan king, with an account of Tark's doings over the year of his detail, being a spy. So he'll be of no help to Asli, left with no protection for her journey with boy and wolf.

When the swordsman doesn't appear she makes enquiries. Before the day's out she finds that he'd set off on the ferry to head for the Hermitage as Tark's party gathered to travel south. But then as the ferry neared the eastern shore the man loudly exclaimed and demanded, cursing, to be taken back over the water. He said he had forgotten something, needed to catch the now-departed company. When he got back he hurried off on the road they'd taken and wasn't seen again.

Asli sends a message to Tark in her clumsy but adequate hand, asking for a replacement for the absconder. Sujata has the wherewithal: a birchwood slat, a fibrous twig, ink from walnut boiled with rust. She well rewards an acorn youth for running it to the ferry. But next day she sends him again, with a birchslat saying not to trouble: Kuzak has offered to go with them. She, the boy, the wolf and the Errant will set off in the morning, three days after Tark's departure.

She spends the hiatus studying Peterkin – trying to teach him Megharan, quizzing Sujata, watching him with the wolf from a careful distance, trying to piece out his story.

Where in the hills? Why leave your people? Why tame a wolf?

Kuzak has stayed awhile to help Sujata clear up, to grind flour, make running repairs to hurdles and shutters and bothy roofs, to talk with her and chant with her at the day's transitions. He has no home but the journey; he'll move on anyway soon enough, to keep to the rule of his Errancy. And he wants to be sure that Sujata is safe with the boy and the wolf.

When he hears of Tark's offer to take them in he's immediately suspicious. He'd have followed their journey anyway, if the guard had turned up. He can see that Asli's not sure of him, but she has no choice – word sent by the kingdom's village-to-village transmission system can take ten days to go twenty miles, she could find herself stuck up here for a month. And she can't go unprotected – no sensible woman would, on the open road, wolf or no wolf.

The night before they leave Sujata has a dream. The Hermit comes to her, as he often does, but this time he's biting down anger, disappointment. Only twice in all their years was he angry with her, and each time she felt scoured, empty. Now it's three times. He says

194

almost nothing, doesn't mention the boy, the wolf, Tark, but stands back and shows her a scene. Look, he says, gesturing in the way that he did, didactically, with a touch of irony.

The boy is washing his clothes at the pond. The wolf is hunkered down and idle, watching him. It's the scene of a few days ago, but at the same time not: there are dislocations of object and of depth; some entities loom preternaturally, others soften backwards into blur. Over all there is a sense of dread, of soft but all-pervading dread. Someone else is watching too – behind her perhaps. She sees without seeing a face like the moon when just lifted above the horizon, enormous and sinister. Its smile is as soft as the scene's insinuations.

The boy's skin is lambent, smooth, unmarked by his adventures. The face of the wolf is innocent – she can see every hair on its muzzle, it watches half tranced and half puzzled. Then the boy has finished, he leaves the water to carry the clothes up the bank. But he can't: his feet slither, he slips to his knees, trying to hold up the clothes. The wolf is up and troubled, trotting left and right. It tries to climb but now the banks are steepening, rising into walls. The boy falls again, drops the clothes, tries to crawl. The wolf is frantic, running across the face of the bank, skidding down and down. The pond below them is dropping away.

The great face behind is close now, almost at her shoulder. It whispers her name, oozing geniality, so close it might be inside her. She wakes in a surge of fear.

The sun is still below the mountain skyline but the grey of dawn has thickened into colour. Sujata swings a cloak over her nightgown, takes her staff and heads for the path to the bothies and the river. When she reaches the overlook point she knows straightaway that they've gone.

They'd made their farewells the night before but Sujata thought she'd be up to wave them off. Kuzak had been asking questions, intent on practicalities. What exactly had Tark proposed. Asli on parting was formal but warm, appreciative, a little sentimental. The boy stiffened a touch at Sujata's embrace, but then bowed very low and pressed her hand against his forehead and held it there a long moment before he rose. Then he turned quickly away, as if to hide his face.

Now she stares down on the still and silent bothies. She picks her way down, sees Kuzak's particularity in the neat disposal of his and Asli's huts. She makes herself struggle through the scrub to see Peterkin's shack and finds that also neat, though flies zigzag over nearby excrement. She has to stop herself from calling out his name, from indulging a last speck of hope.

She works her way back in discomfort, stopping at points to find her breath. At the Hermitage she stands her staff by the door, with slow ceremony goes to the stove cold and long burnt out, and leans a hand on it and kneels with effort and opens the iron grate and reaches both hands into the charcoal and ashes and rubs the soot and ashes into her face and into her hair. She does it again and then does it again. Then she creaks up, pushing into the pain of the effort, and sits on her stoveside stool, her mouth in a pressed line and her eyes almost closed in her humiliated face, and her hair sprouting all ways and sifting down its dandruff of ash onto the cloak she still wears, and she rocks back and forth in her anguish.

Part 3: Down the River

Chapter 17: Journeyings

The sun has swung south of east when Sujata sets off on her journey. It jinks in and out of her left eye with the twisting descent of the path.

She had sat, rocking, silent, masked in the defacement of abjection, waiting for a word to come. Trapped in nonexistence till it does.

Time passes. The word that comes is, You must go.

The youth from the acorn clan comes up to help as he does each quarter-month. When he tops the rise she is sitting with a satchel packed, her face and hair doused clean at the stream, her cloak shaken out. She tells the bewildered boy that she's going on a journey, she'll speak to his great-uncle the head of the clan about managing the Hermitage and the flock, would he please stand in till someone else turns up. The goats will find their own way home in the evening, will pen with titbit inducements, are never trouble to milk.

Then she embraces him, again to his surprise, and sets off at a slow but decisive pace, angled and tuneless in her movements. He offers to carry her bag at least down the slope but she says no. Then she has gone.

The boy feels uneasy, hollow in this sudden isolation, a vast silence behind the chirping of birds in the scrub all around. He feels he shouldn't watch Sujata go but then he does. When he comes to the point that looks down on the steep descent she's barely fifty yards away, picking her footfalls with minute care. He can see, alien as the notion is to his own loose joints and vigour, that every step hurts. He turns back, a little guilty for watching.

She comes in time to the acorn people's now-sprawling hamlet and speaks with the Headman, inviting in also his wife from her loom and his brother and nephew out front, to his surprise and swallowed indignation. She asks them for help, tells them what she has told the youngster. She takes out a drawstring purse of stones and sits it on the table. For anything you need, she says, and in gratitude for your trouble. The Headman takes up the purse and looks in and tries to argue but she is set. He guesses the stones are worth twice the produce the clan will bring to the autumn fair; he'd bargain her down if he could but he knows she won't move.

They all go with her to the stepping stones that cross the stream to the track that leads to the ferry. The ever-encroaching undergrowth stepped down by recent traffic. Youngsters and children have followed in curiosity; a small crowd sees her off. She won't let them cross with her, or even help. They hold their breath at precarious steps, the staff a third leg planted deep in the stream, the glassy water rearing and veeing around it. But all goes well; she turns and calls out a blessing once she is over, and bows to them and turns and makes her laborious way.

Sujata had hoped for news of the four other travellers, but the acorn people hadn't seen them.

They'd cut right on a vestigial path a little above the acorn hamlet, heading for a summer ford six awkward miles upriver. Kuzak had won a dispute with Asli who wanted to take the ferry, thinking the wolf could swim behind it. He knows how well wolves can swim, but also the lie of the current and how the beast could be dragged, if it tried to short-cut the looping route of the ferry, into the faster water and on down the roaring falls. Asli would have liked to win the point but saw the risk and quickly conceded.

Kuzak mused as he walked ahead on how sweet it would be, if the wolf were indeed destroyed in the cataract. Tark must want it badly, to have given his smartest minion to its acquiring. The boy would lose his wolf, but be saved from the subjection that must surely be part of Tark's plan.

The boy – his open soul, his self-reliance, his native honour – a rare enough creature wherever he's from, even without the wolf. A future Errant? Would that, too, spoil him? Asli though – losing the beast on the very first morning: how that dumb wife would love to see her whipped.

For the feelings of the wolf he has no concern. Boy and wolf? A freak, a picturesque abomination. He once saw the scattered remains of an old couple, caught out by a pack on a winter's night. The flashback saves him from any temptation to wolf-love.

So, thinks Kuzak – what am I doing, and why? He doesn't seem to know himself, why he volunteered. He examines what he can see of his motives (an Errant practice, thoroughly instilled): a sneaky wish for revenge on Tark; the fascination with foreigner boy and wolf (perhaps where he comes from they all have such comrades); the draw of a woman at risk and out of her depth. The draw of a woman anyway? Maybe. These inclinations don't fade off as quickly as you'd like. And – come *on*, what a tale! With mystery, boggling practical awkwardness, no clear sense of a suitable ending, extraordinary characters. So many reasons. Let it run as it runs; you'll see, at the end, whatever the end might be, that it all went as it was bound to, and your part was as laid out by the Fates as any and all of the others.

Your part. What, though?

He pieces it out, from a thought-sketch that comes up more or less immediately. Keep off the main track, away from the populous country, the river. Excitable youths – gawping villagers – tempting sheep and indignant farmers. Would-be pelt hunters. The ford; then a south-westerly route, curving back in south-east to pick up the road just north of Tark's estate. With the six-mile wrong-way start and the long curve of the route they'll be walking forty miles to travel twenty. He could be there himself by tomorrow noon and so he's sure could the boy, but with Asli and the stretches of trackless terrain he thinks to give it three days.

Asli confirms his judgement before they even reach the ford – she struggles without a path, and has no feel for an elusive one. Also she's gut-scared of the wolf, and insists on keeping close to Kuzak, the boy well to the rear. She'd rather go in front but that would be hopeless.

The ford, high-banked and nearly two hundred yards wide, belly-deep in the middle and pulling hard, has only just become crossable. Kuzak has often come this way. He strips to loin cloth and jerkin, packs his other clothes into his satchel and ties his boots to the straps. But he must get Asli over first, or leave her with the boy and the wolf. He eases barefoot down the bank. He's straightaway in to mid-thigh, glassy lianas of water round legs and staff. The water's no longer the turquoise snow-melt of spring but still gasp-cold, though nothing in Kuzak's unhurried demeanour would show it.

He and Asli snap back and forth a little, she still on the bank – where to draw the line between exposure and practicality; whether she should keep on her sandals – he advises yes, doubting the toughness of her foot-soles, the river running on pebbles and shale. She goes in barefoot, and is driven straight out by the pierce of the shingle, the bite of the cold.

Keep trying, you'll get used to it. But put on the sandals. Please. Then after a pause, in a kindlier voice – *please*.

All goes well enough. He carries her satchel, she grips his arm – tighter where the water drives hard in its wide middle channel, wailing a curse as the cold bites higher.

Kuzak goes back for his own pack. By the time he re-crosses to Asli she has magicked another skirt from her satchel and slipped it on. The wet one, rung out, is spread on a bush in the sun.

They step back from the shore to watch. The wolf is wary; it isn't to be seen. Peterkin eases into the water and stands thigh-deep and gestures and makes his owl-call. When it appears Asli backs off another half step, as if that would make a difference.

The boy turns towards them and is crossing, the wolf plunges in and follows. He's very soon out of his depth and swimming aslant to the pull of the water with great optimistic effort, but it's clear the force of the middle current will be too much for him not to be dragged downstream. Peterkin, who has found the section hard enough himself, crosses back through it and gets downstream of the wolf with some desperate threshing and slippage, and buttresses the wolf against the drag and somehow they get through. And then the wolf's feet are down and he makes for the shore in bucking, galloping leaps, and then he's hock deep and then he's out and shaking with explosive vigour, aureoled by droplets.

Asli gasps as the boy caresses the wolf in relief, then yelps in shock and astoundedness as it licks his face with its long prehensile tongue and the boy pulls away laughing.

Kuzak watches too, intently but with no expression.

It takes Sujata most of the rest of the day to get to the ferry, stopping each few hundred yards to ease her joints, always alert for a rock or a fallen tree she'll be able to rise from without too mighty a struggle. The lowering sun is in her face when she squints across the wide-ponded river. She sees no movement.

Where the path ends there's a small roofed shrine to the god of travellers, by the boulders that form a natural jetty. In it is an ancient clappered handbell, incised with the deity's symbols, oxidised almost to black, She lifts its uncomfortable weight and rings it two-handed a length of time, facing across the water. The sound punctures the ambient roar of the cataract; but nothing, no response. She sits on a boulder and lets some time pass and then rings again. A figure has appeared and is at some desultory task. She knows he has heard, is ignoring her – or ignoring the bell, he can't know or even guess who's ringing it. When his small theatrical show has gone on long enough she rings a third time and doesn't stop till he throws down whatever it is and heaves his upturned boat aright and down its cross-logged slipway into the lake. Even from here she can sense that he is cursing.

They scull back in falling light, she in her silence and he in his. Sujata in the upcurved prow of the vessel, watching the east bank slowly recede, the ragged wood-land climbing steeply to stark heights lit by the western sun. Ancient trees on minimal ledges, as crabbed and knuckled as herself, perch solitarily like small unlucky gods.

The ferry wife, flustered and reverent, is tidying hair and apron and hisses an aside to her daughter. They're clumsily offering food and drink when the man shouts from outside and they hurry out, the wife with ducking apologies, to help him drag up the boat.

But when he hears Sujata's away to see Tark he turns suddenly oily, concerned for her comfort, side-of-mouthing the women to bring her aquavit, cushions, honey cake, to ease the pains of travel. The Baron has no jurisdiction here but a word from him could eject the ferryman, wife girls and all, from his sound lodging and undemanding duties. Sujata takes the cake and cushions but not the alcohol. She asks for news of the foursome – boy, Errant, maid and wolf – but they have none.

Soon after she stretches out in the best of the three regulation guestrooms and watches the various pains in ankles, back, knees, hips, treating them as meditation objects, each long breath inquiring of them. Then she is asleep.

The wolf has been trotting a little behind the boy who keeps a distance behind the other two. He fears the one with the hairy face, he knows in his thoughtless way that the one with the hairless face fears him. Often, bored with the languid pace, he scoots off sideways to trace the course of an intriguing smell, to inquire into the country. There's no scent of other wolves, not even ancient.

Peterkin has but a dim sense of what's going on. He guesses they're on a three-day journey (he'd momentarily thought that Kuzak was miming three months, but the fat Baron had hardly made a three-month trek to the Hermitage – and anyway surely there's nowhere in the world so far that it takes three months to get to). And why this way, off any path? Just after the river they came on a wide and well-used north-south track, but crossed it and continued in rough terrain on a dubious path, negligible and playfully self-concealing. Ahead Asli's voice is whiney, she's picking twigs from her clothing. Kuzak carries both satchels.

They eat a midday meal by a wide and indolent feeder stream in the shade of a slabby outcrop. Peterkin sits five yards off, tossing the wolf chunks of odorous half-smoked meat, trying to draw him nearer. Asli, unused to an early rise and rough trekking, falls asleep. When it's time to go the Errant says her name, says it again, then takes her shoulder and shakes it with delicate caution. Peterkin watches. Where he comes from no patience is shown to inopportune sleepers. When she opens her eyes Kuzak is back to formality, distant and directive.

He's set on a bivouac site seven miles on. Asli is clumsy with fatigue by the time they get there. She hadn't fully grasped that they'd sleep in the open – Kuzak said 'rough', she thought he meant the taverns. The thin and elegant cloak in her pack won't keep out the cold of the night once the fire burns down. She ends up sharing the Errant's thick and wide all-season cloak, her own still also wrapped tightly around her. She thinks she'll have to fend him off but he keeps his back towards her. Her feeling is of relief with a touch of insult.

She wakes to the crackle and reek of the rekindled fire. Peterkin is up before the sun and broiling his dubious meat. The wolf frisks panting a little way off, as the boy lobs morsels of meat for it to catch with a snap of its teeth. Stiff from the bony ground, waking from her chilled sleep pressed to the jerkin-clad back of the Errant, the boy and the fire and the scrubby thorny terrain and there like a dream the exuberant childlike wolf – she's had strange awakenings before but none to match this.

Kuzak is up and immediately composed, as if he'd been awake already not wanting to disturb her. He persuades her to try the meat, insisting it's safe – once she does she's chewing with great vim. He outlines the planned route, with simultaneous pointing and miming for Peterkin, promising her a tavern at the day's end. He will sleep beneath the Milky Way with the boy and the wolf – but good people, the tavern, with his word she'll be safe.

Then they set out, Asli stiff and a touch tender-footed. The boy a little closer to her and Kuzak, the wolf a little closer to the boy. By late morning it's circling the whole group in its explorations.

The unctuous ferryman wants to arrange a sedan, to send the older girl to the village downstream, but Sujata declines. She covers her pains as they watch her go with great effort of concentration, then permits herself to limp and to sag, to heave on her staff as if punting a barge. She thought she'd walk the fifteen miles to Tark's gate in a day, but when she gets to the village three miles down she knows that she's done. She toils to the little inn, just a cottage with a tiny public room, a lean-to dormitory with a shack for overspill.

The big-faced seen-it-all innkeeper widow insists that she rest up, that she take a sedan tomorrow, two strong men will get her there by noon or not long after. Sujata has nothing left with which to argue. She takes both applejack and willowbark tincture, agrees to the sedan. As soon after dawn as the mentioned strong men can manage. She asks again about the other travellers, but again they haven't been seen. *Wolf? A wolf?*

She's the only guest and no more expected. The widow makes her up an early bed, with an extra mattress and a noggin to help her sleep. Do what's needed, the Hermit always said – rules are to help, don't let them hinder. When she closes her eyes there's a dust-padded track, endlessly unwinding.

The bearers are two locals in the years of early manhood. They have the excess geniality of scoundrels. The most they can do, she supposes, is rob her on the sly. She goes to meet the Baron; they dare not harm her. She takes their bumptious, covertly jeering care as part of her penance.

They declare she'll be at the Baron's door with the sun barely favouring right eye over left, with the midday meal still at table. But they travel at a crawl, stopping at a couple of miles and then again before the fourth to take their ease and drink from a skin of mead and bray foolish songs.

What in the world are you playing at, says Sujata. I go to meet the Baron; if you plan to harm me you plan yourselves a grave.

But they carry on the pantomime, louder and more absurd with the mead, assuring her with glazed unreachable eyes that they'll soon arrive. It's noon and they're still eight miles off. They've left the track for the shade of a gully, with a level beside the bed of a bone-dry stream.

Then Sujata hears other voices. The bearers throw up their arms in histrionic dread. Three other men have arrived out of nowhere, and these are by no means theatricals.

The bandits go through a rigmarole of tying the bearers' hands behind their backs and making them kneel. Two have war bows and blackthorn clubs; the leader has no more than an ancient Imperial half-sword. But he has a look of settled derangement, a stare of exuberant malice. There are comic elements in his attire – a ribboned jerkin, a felt hat with high stork-wing feathers – but his visage deflates any impulse to laugh.

The bearers are bleating in their pantomime dismay. Shut up, says the leader. When one carries on he kicks him in the gut with immoderate force and the youngster buckles and slumps on his side badly winded, fighting for breath wide-eyed like a man in his death throes.

What's your business with Tark asks the leader, turning to Sujata as if the kick had been nothing.

She doesn't answer. Her eyes are closed, she is whispering a prayer.

I can't hear you, Crone.

Sujata continues to pray, ignoring him.

He cuffs the side of her head with his half-closed fist. The blow is neither light nor heavy; it has a fluency, an accustomed practicality.

For Sujata, closing herself in the prayer she recites, the blow is nothing, not even a surprise.

Speak to me, Old One, the bandit says. His voice has dropped lower, almost a whisper itself. His face is close to hers. He mimics pained appeal with a rubbery, jeering sarcasm.

Speak, Grandmother, speak. You will soon enough I think, so why not now, and save us both some labour? Address me as Golo, Golo. My name is Golo son of Kell: many have I sent to Hell.

Sujata ends her prayer and gathers all the strength she has, the strength that she has been asking for. She opens her eyes and his face is a foot and a half from hers with its vast force of will, clever and berserk and utterly intent. This is the world the Hermit took her from. She holds his stare, reaching into it, looking for his soul. She senses a tiny astounded retreat in him, and he knows she's seen it and she knows he knows she's seen it. Her own eyes have sloughed off their blurred-focus weariness, they're bright as an animal's.

What kind of two-legged jackal are *you*, Golo son of Kell, that you strike an old woman?

Her gaze is unfaltering, her voice is entirely calm, with the balance won by fifty years of toil.

The other bandits jeer sarcastic applause. Golo's eyes hold Sujata's, having shuttered whatever depths he felt her reaching for, but his rubber face pulls into a grin of astonished joy so wide it's almost grotesque.

Woo-oo, he says, on a long out-breath. Woo, I like this one. Woo. Treat her well boys, she's worth ten of youse.

What do you want with me? says Sujata.

Gold and stones from that fat Tark.

Why would he give you anything for me?

You're a Holy Crone, you travel as his guest, he'd be shamed to the world if he let you die for the sake of a few of his trinkets.

You've heard a little about me. But how well d'you trust your informants? Her eyes start to drift towards the bearers, but she checks herself. This man would cut their throats in the blink of an eye if he guessed how badly they'd played their part.

Which bit did I get wrong then? And don't play games with me, wise and holy Crone.

Guest. I'm not his guest yet, he hasn't invited me. I've invited myself.

The man shrugs his shoulders, with sarcastic exaggeration.

Makes no difference, he says. How will the *world* see it, that's the thing. Like a drink?

Chapter 18: Doruk the Spy

oruk the spy had left the road a quarter mile south of the ferry, where a zedbending track leads down to the foot of the fall. Here come travellers, to wonder and to worship. Here in season come the salmon-gatherers, netting from the underfall pools the fish which, unable to go beyond, spill milt and roe to seed the bed with their next generation; they're lifted before they begin their living decay, each opened like a two-page book and pegged on a guild-concessioned trellis and smoked, the trellises now stacked on a ledge above the highest water for autumn. Lashed to the trellises are the fishers' skin canoes, one of which is now untethered by Doruk the spy, such liberties falling under his Royal Warrant.

No-one is around. He lets the current take him for the first two easy miles of the gorge, the paddle mostly just steering and fending off rocks, then beaches the canoe at the start of white water and makes good time on the ancient gorgeside path that snakes a long descent above the river.

Another mile and the cliff to his right has eased to a bouldery slope and then a lower slope of thorn scrub, dwarfish trees, and then the slope is suddenly gone and he's out on the level, his path joining the main north-south road not fifty yards ahead. He guesses he's well in front of the Baron's party but checks with care for any sight of them.

Down here it's farmland, black-soiled and rich-cropped and populous. He has no easy cover, and anyone seeing him might take word to Tark, who'll guess his business and send out runners to prime his famed network to watch for the renegade (so he'll call him) and manage his disappearance. For a generous fee; and they'll never talk, once they know they've killed a kingsman.

He crosses the road with undignified haste and heads due west, by the edges of wheatfields, berryfields, orchards footed with smudged-white fallen blossom, stone-walled fields of sun-languid milk cows or sheep still skinny from shearing. Only when he hits the track from the northerly town of Maul does he turn again to his left. The track drifts south-south-east, to join the main road far enough past Tark's estate for Doruk to think himself safe. And a dozen easy miles will land him at a discreet house where he'll show an escutcheoned stone, and the hospitality will ask no questions with a pack of fine provisions made ready for his departure. They'll give him the clothes of the region and he'll lose all visible sign of service, travelling as a peasant.

Next day he regrets his languid start with a hundred miles still to go, and puts in a decent thirty on easy footing, bedding under the stars. He needs to be sure he can keep ahead of any word from Tark. He's no skin-and-bone message-runner, but Tark has none such either.

Two nights more and he'll wake to see the castle on the skyline, the castle of the king. By mid-afternoon he'll be sounding the wicket gate bell, to be next morning at court in service attire to make his report.

Errants have even greater skill than spies in travelling unseen. Each through training and practice, and trail-marks hid to the common eye, has grasp of a net of gully-tracks, lost roads, ridgeways, little-known fords both safe and chancy, that webs the whole kingdom and beyond. An Errant can pass in daylight from any place to any other as if a creature invisible. Safe houses node this network: secret lodges, discreet taverns, trustworthy farmers. The web of paths in continuous change and yet always the same: through coppices and spinneys, two-year fallows, shaggy heaths and commons; beds of streams diminished or dry; field-edges hid from the farmhouse; scrub hillsides, gullies and gorges, tussock-steps through marsh. Fine ways to pass a wolf through farming country.

They've gone five miles on the second day and are passing through a stand of pines when the wolf shoots to one side and there's crashing, and the boy follows in the sure-footed way that he has. Kuzak too more slowly, guardedly; and he sees the wolf with a roebuck pinned and threshing and the boy with his knife and one deft dip of the blade and the deer is suddenly still. The wolf stares at Kuzak while keeping its hold, a menacing growl arising as if from the earth.

The boy gestures *back off*, toned down by a wry expression. Kuzak re-joins Asli who's looking uneasy. Sounds from the site of the kill. In a while the boy appears with the whole gralloched buck slung over one shoulder, the great abdominal gape skewed for minimal leakage.

He has given the wolf the liver as has become their practice, and now it lies hunkered with head between forelegs as if in contemplation and watches the boy. Peterkin cleans the knife on a tussock and then whets the edge, then strips the skin from the carcase as one who first skinned and butchered a lamb unaided at nine years of age. Boning as he goes and tossing a bone to the waiting wolf who lunges to catch it and gives himself to concentrated gnawing. Shoulders then backstraps, sirloins, quarters, laying the pieces on the hair-down skin at the side of the carcase; then when all is done hefting aside the bonework and remaining flesh for the jackals and the crows, and piling the cuts of meat neatly and rolling them up in the skin, and tying the rolled skin with sinews he drew at the kill site before he disposed of the lower legs.

The hefty little pack weighs maybe twenty pounds. Kuzak whistles in appreciation, shakes his head. Peterkin, taken aback and with a slight glow, tells in articulate mime and mysterious words of himself at chest height doing this – he motions the gore-flecked scene.

He hasn't an understanding of Kuzak: he's never met anyone like him, he doesn't know why he's taking so strange a route, curved as a basket handle if the sun and stars aren't lying. But he doesn't much understand anyone here, except for maybe the ferry wife and the acorn folk, who could be from his village but for the clothes and tongue. His only understanding is that the wolfpack incursion brought shame and dismay, and that he and the wolf are heading for some safe and welcoming place. Why anyone would offer such is beyond him – but so strange is this world of Barons, Errants, pilgrims, that why not? And Asli – a woman alone with a man and a boy and a wolf, the man not husband or brother. *Why?*

But he felt a glow of trust in the smiling Baron, a generous concern that somehow went with his bigness. And so far so good – this journey. So far.

That night Asli takes bed in the promised house while the three males rough it in a copse a half mile off, gorging on tough delicious venison, bread and watered aquavit. Hardly a word between them but those that Kuzak speaks and the boy repeats, with a questioning upturn of tone at the end at which Kuzak okays the pronunciation or not. In all of this a slow but steady easing of rigidities. Even the wolf has softened a little to Kuzak, taking morsels of meat that he throws, sniffing them first.

But later he growls at Kuzak again. The Errant is up when the first grey of dawn lets the world come back to itself, spacing itself as yet without colour, a few birds shrilling early. He comes back to the burnt-out fire, and then for no special reason takes a step nearer the boy where he sleeps and looks down on him. A growl arises as if from nowhere, again as if the very earth had growled. He sees now the wolf, just behind the boy, with lip sneered up and back to show the long canines, the ears half back, the neck-hair half bristled. Its eyes are somehow more visible than all else in the grey of the world. The eyes of a demon, the purity in their intent – he's never seen a demon for sure, except in the possessed, but how can you mistake one when it faces you.

He backs away, smoothly. The scene has lasted hardly more than a moment. He squats and checks the fire for a remnant glow, keeping his knife to hand.

At the court of King Karaman the places have been taken. The Grand Vizier has called the day's business.

A formal invitation from Emperor Sargon (following numerous whispers) to a month-long feast at the autumn equinox, for the coming of age of his daughter and only first-wife child the Princess Ashurina, who will thence take the dexter throne at the Emperor's side. A disappointing midsummer tax declaration – let us not say suspiciously so – from the rich-soiled Midland Province. Worsening banditry, upriver and in the far Westland. And the return of our noble King Karaman's Second Discreet Informant, from the court of the esteemed Baron Tark.

Karaman sits sidelong in his well cushioned throne, his face inexpressive. He has enjoyed the Solstice, with a new chef from the Empire and a bold new courtesan, tumblers and dancers, a rare defeat of a travelling Empire wrestler by a Megharan (now rich in stones, and recruited to the Chamber Guard). Loud (if obsequious) cheering when he took his place for the sunrise. Now back to the irritations of kingship – to energize a sluggardly nobility, to smell out the myriad liars and schemers, to work some shifty compromise between Empire and Megharan pride.

He lets a long silence run. Then he speaks.

With humble gratitude King Karaman accepts, etcetera. The Viziers to work out the details. Not a whole month, Grand V, insist, for the plotters to run free.

Tax cheats? Dish out some marketplace whippings, tell the Headmen, and make the helpings generous, even if it's your brother-in-law.

Bandits? Why do the gibbets swing empty? If the army goes in the locals to pay, and keep the lads in apple-jack and whores. And what's Tark doing? Tangled up in his wife's long legs, while wolves run the countryside, and the sheep come bleating to me? (Tark has no such authority, by his own firmly stated wish. To Karaman this shying from power is troubling, because incomprehensible.)

Which brings us to Item Four. Call in the Second Discreet, if you would. I'm in need of humouring.

Doruk the spy enters and bows deeply, though his steady eye shows no subservience. This partly by nature and partly strategic – he has seen much and heard more of the King's disgust at squirm and the wringing of hands. But any course is dangerous.

Well then, trusted one, what of the Baron Tark?

(The open-ended question is designed to disconcert, by habit and with no special aim.)

He is well, your majesty, and would I am sure have sent greetings had I not left so abruptly.

And why, bold Doruk, with no word from us, did you scuttle back like this?

I'd seen all I needed to see, Sir, of Baron Tark's mind and intent, and wanted only the chance to slip away. There was, besides, a prodigy that might interest Your Majesty.

So what did you see?

That he fears you. He will speak of the folly of plotters in any company, in or out of his cups. Which do I want, I heard him say – a herb-scented feather bed and the torments of concupiscence, or a piss-scented dungeon flagstone and the soft words of the Enquirer? I've got as far as I'm going, one more step could land me in Hell.

And how did you hear all this, a lowly guard?

He always kept one of us close when he entertained. Twice he had guests from the House of Utku and once from the House of the Bear – to each he said such things. It was as if he set a warning, not to make sly hints of discontent, for fear of later embarrassment.

Embarrassment how?

That he might be pressed, or even unpressed think it safer, to report on any such.

And what of Utku and the Bear? Pick up any waft of treason?

None Sir, none at all. Whether because they took the hint, or my presence kept tongue behind teeth, or because their loyalty's sound, I know not.

You know not, Second Discreet, but what do you think?

With all respect, Your Majesty, I have no opinion. All men want greatness, and all but a very few want more than they've got, and surely the old houses still have that yearning: but whether either has any plan greater than daydream – maybe or maybe not, but I've seen no hint.

That bold young Ender – nothing?

Nothing Sir, not a curl of the lip when your health was drunk, nothing.

They must be thorough in their plans, to hide all sign so thoroughly.

Well hidden something or well hidden nothing, I cannot help decide.

So what help *are* you?

Tark, Sir, was the main task.

And he's happy with his lot. How tedious. And always speaks well of me ... you pull a face, fine Doruk, why?

When with nobles, always. Yes.

Be not discreet with *me*, Second Discreet.

Might we speak in private, Your Majesty?

(Doruk knows that men's lives could depend on whether he says what he's going to say in front of the court or to the King alone. That there's even a chance that his own might be one of those lives.)

We might but we won't.

I mean no reticence Sir, it's just that I fear, if I render Tark's play of tongue with his lesser cronies, the repetition might draw a warmth more due to the original.

Warmth you'll get if you don't start telling.

Doruk bows and begins before he's quite upright.

Tark has made many friends among local worthies – merchants, priests, headmen, the wealthier farmers – and holds well-attended feasts, sometimes with wives and consorts invited, sometimes just for the menfolk – though with female company, hussies from the towns and pretty up-country wenches tempted by promised favours. At these feasts he sports with mimicry and jests, sparing no-one and gendering much laughter and applause. But it's only when the feast has thinned out, and a privy band remains, that his jests grow bolder, and extend – it can't be denied – to the very throne.

Examples.

'Shadow-jumper.' He says you think every shadow carries a dagger, plays you having a ten- year-old servant girl searched for weapons. Watching the food-taster's complexion, while the meal goes cold. Taking an army when you go to hunt rabbits.

What else?

'Kingsnake.' That rules the squirmers and schemers by outdoing them all. Also 'Strutter at the Spring Fair' – mocking your robes and accoutrements, though he is perhaps no paragon.

And? I sense more.

(An intake of breath, a slight pause.)

He said, when a bandit was apprehended: 'No need for us to behead the rogue, just tell the King he's his long-lost brother.'

(All freeze – counsellors, guards, train-bearers. As if they've committed some dangerous crime themselves in hearing the words. The King's face tautens its integument.)

And you, did you laugh at the Baron's jokes?

(Doruk expected this.)

No Sir. None of them. He has a droll manner at drink, but I saw early on that if I laughed at some jests I'd have to laugh at all or else be suspect, so I kept my face straight throughout.

What about the rest?

All laughed, or nearly all. Somewhat at the drollery; somewhat for fear on not being invited back.

Who are these host-pleasing laughers?

The privy clan are these, in particular. The landowner Turgas of Bursa, three farms to his name and a fortressed tower house; two merchants, Tolga of Mink and his nephew Haluk; Ferit, also of Mink, a brothel-keeper; and Aydin of Turgutlu, a priest of the Third Ascendancy.

All matched for hilarity?

Loudest is young Haluk, partly for his youth and partly I think to please Tark. His uncle Tolga is the least fervent, watching the others, mostly keeping to a snuffle and a thin-lipped smile. Ferit and priest Aydin – manning opposed temples of worship but fine friends offstage – both guffaw keenly. But three-farm Turgas, who envies all nobility, laughs with the greatest venom, with a fine indignation.

Well, my fine Discreet, you have a sound nerve, and a cold heart, to tell such tales unblinking.

(Doruk, who has just lain the hand of Death on at least one man, and not an especially bad one, bows without expression.)

I do my duty, Your Majesty, as well as I can.

I hope so, bold Doruk, I hope so. And something about a prodigy?

A boy, near full grown, with a tame wolf. I laid no eye on the pair myself but was detailed to bring them to

Tark, from the holy site where he'd seen them. To guard his stewardess, and to see the boy didn't bolt, and the peasantry didn't murder the beast. I took the chance to slip away.

It was you that bolted.

Indeed, Sir. I travelled with some alacrity, for fear the ever-guileful Tark would realize my role and try and hunt me.

Hah. Fine Doruk – you play the hare as well as you play the jackal. But so what? Boy and wolf, eh ... d'you fear Tark'll use them to take the throne?

Two things occurred to me. Tark has no interest in prodigies, or only when they serve some purpose – you've seen his giant swordsman I believe, Sir – no hunchback or dwarf in his retinue, someone gave him a leopard cub once and when it was grown it became a winter cloak for his second wife, young then and sweet to the eye ...

Get *on* with it, Second Discreet ...

... but does he want the boy and wolf as a gift, to gain favour with the mighty? With one, dare I say Sir, however absurdly so fated, still mightier than yourself?

(Hah! says the King again as he takes the meaning. He gives a chuckle and a rictus smile, in scepticism or in approbation.)

The second thing – the boy spoke little of our tongue. Some thought he was an idiot, others a foreigner somehow wandered in – from beyond the mountains, the Holy Crone of the place was heard to say. The mountains? Sung of as walls and battlements of the gods, that only birds ever pass – but might there be a way through? To unsuspecting, peopled lands?

The King shakes his head very slowly, staring downwards.

I think I will see this boy and his wolf, and the humorous Baron Tark.

Chapter 19: Arrivals

Tark hadn't gone straight home.

He'd crossed on the ferry, he and Damla the boat to themselves; Tark for sport coercing strained smiles from the ferryman, then yawning in the sun as the ferrywife curtsied and flustered, watching the man scull back for Ruslan and the other waiting stalwarts.

A restlessness was in him, for all his yawning. The last few days had brought on a kind of arousal: the walk from ferry to hermitage – awkward footing, the climb – more exercise than he's had in years; the ceremony itself, taking him to a locus he rarely visits, returning with a sense of a greater world, that degrades rather quickly to fit his propensities. His plans for the boy and the wolf, yes – but that's underway; he needs a thing more immediate, more here-and-now.

His cushioned and escutcheoned four-bearer sedan, waiting to carry him home, beams out a prospect of day-long boredom – if it weren't for sore feet, and a nagging pain in one knee from the descent, he'd even think about walking. And when he's back, what? The sullen faces of senior wives, the boringly well-run estate, the yawning days ahead till he sails for the Empire, getting there the day before the little madam's birthday, to keep the present secret.

He thinks he'll make a detour, drop in on Turgas the farmer his good friend. A turn of the tide, after all those years of settling for what he's got? He knows the man is over-reached, owing many favours for the building of his house, unduly large and battlemented, sited for visibility above the hamlet of Bursa. Tark knows how weak he is in extracting rents from the peasantry, how he milks ingratiation with feasts, how he postures connoisseurship with over-priced Empire wines.

Tark thinks to make him an offer: stewardship of the farms in perpetuity, with no visible change in his position; all debts cleared; a one-off earnest in grain and fleece to buy him a half-year pilgrimage to the Empire, or the bride-price of the prettiest girl in town. He'll make the offer half as jest, and Turgas will likely refuse. Or maybe not; but if he does Tark will pay his creditors on the sly and have the debts transferred by law to himself, depicting it as a happy surprise, a favour. And then the court takes on the dirty work, and bailiffs away most of the fool's domain, Tark displaying helplessness and anguished regret all along. He thinks to steer the court towards the biggest farm of the three, with an entirely unpayable mortgage on the house.

From there – survey the lands between Bursa and his estate, lay weight upon any smallholders who won't sell at his price: bribe bailiffs and the nightwatch, have Ruslan wander by and stare in windows. Work on the landlords: make a derisory offer, then make it again with a list of their prior-detected sins against King and law.

Ah. *Yes.* This is like old times.

Appropriate common land, block opposition with bribes to the courts, blackmail or other chastisement for the whiners. Aim for a continuous, expanded estate. All from commoner lands or legal purchase, so drawing no noble attention. Wait the moment to pay the King some special devotion, then hint (by way of gift-encouraged Vizier) at the uplift of faithful estate-holder (unmatched in generosity) to (whisper it) landed nobleman.

Then what? Karaman will go, sooner or later. If not an old-house coup his twitchy paranoia will turn the Royal Guard itself. In the deep hours of some black night they'll come by torch to murder him, then light every lamp in the castle and drink the late King's wine as they throw dice for his courtesans. Then let the old houses fight out a replacement; while he, with gifts, quietly reminds the Guard of his credentials: a friend of the fighting man, a new-landed Lord untainted by history, a man who can get things done.

Dreams, dreams. But something like that, the summer fizz in his blood is telling him. Something like that.

The wolf knows nothing about himself. He doesn't know that he's bigger and stronger than when he arrived in Peterkin's world. That he's lost some of his fear of men, the terror from his capture and binding. He doesn't know that if the man had come any nearer the boy he'd have attacked; his growl was neither surprising nor expected, just another part of what was happening. For him as well as for Kuzak, it might have been the earth itself that growled.

The boy is like no other human, but this is no cause for wonder or surprise. The wolf just lives within their simpatico, to which – without knowing it – he gives his immense instinct for co-operation, devotion. The boy is now his pack, but this he knows no more than anything else.

His wisdom, if so we should call it, has no place for any such knowing but lies in the flow of action. Behind it countless generations of packlife, of many-as-one, of the endless hunt, of the fear of those who'd hunt you. Inheritances with no being outside the blink of their manifestation, the ever-slipping moment of wolf being wolf.

Now for instance, on a long strip of worn flattened ground, everywhere the stench of humans, the sweeter odours of sheep and of goats, the deep-voiced one and the high-voiced making the sounds they make to each other, turning now and then towards him and his boy, his boy cajoling him but there's no pant and tail-wag in response in the open terrain and the thick human smell. He wants to drag back, turn off into cover; the boy murmurs and gestures him on.

Ahead the strip of ground is blocked on one side by a long low cliff. The two have stopped where it begins. They make louder sounds now, the high voice and the deep voice. Sounds louder still come from a human who can't be seen. The wolf skips back a way, his boy is calling and clucking him on. The high-voiced one is making the gesture the boy makes, to urge them to come.

His body is one piece of unease, though he doesn't know he's hackled up, that his ears are pressed flat and his tail tucked under. The deep-voiced, hairy-faced one has disappeared through a gap, the other stands loose-bodied and leaning, the high voice stretched out in a long invitatory fall. His boy is cajoling too. He lives within his trust in the boy, he has no other place to live. When the high-voiced one goes through the gap his boy goes through as well, calling and waving him to follow. He comes close and looks.

Grass, trees, thick cover of shrubs; the boy is there; further off a third human stands with their two companions. The boy is cajoling, gesturing. Hackled all along his back, rear end dropped halfway to the ground, he enters.

Tark sent word ahead when he turned off the road, of who and what would be coming. That Asli has authority on the handling of their novel guests, if they turn up before he gets back. No coercion or restraint to be applied except at her bidding.

But the Baron has misjudged. He has taken for granted a competitive repulsion that keeps his first two wives from making common cause. When they hear they're to play hostess to an urchin and a wolf, with the upstart maid-come-advisor to be in charge of arrangements, their eyes meet in rare solidarity.

I think there must be some mistake, says first wife Eren. She speaks as if to the messenger but holds the gaze of second wife Bayza. Some misunderstanding, perhaps an over-emphasis. *In charge?* But authority lies with the First and Second Baroness in the absence of our master. Everybody knows this. A misunder*standing*, yes.

But his lordship the Baron was very clear ...

The First Baroness turns her face to the messenger, eyes and voice very cold.

No sir, a misunderstanding. Go.

In her face the messenger sees the whipping post, and holds his tongue, bows deeply, departs with what dignity is left him.

When word comes to Eren and Bayza the party has entered the gate they call for the forewarned company – of the remnant Guard with swords and war bows, servants and field hands with cudgels and pitchforks, a woodsman with his axe, a smith with his hammer. The Captain of the Guard, a grizzled ex-soldier long used to free drink and light duties, has planned a gauntleted route to a half-empty barn that might serve as a hold-pen. Bayza, dour-faced, gave a nod; he had the wit to glance towards Eren who raised her chin an inch to confirm.

The gate has closed behind Peterkin and the wolf. The Captain, with a glazed sardonic eye and a faint tang of drink on his breath, pulling in his belly in out-of-practice dignity, is in close conference with Kuzak and Asli, who've waved the boy and the wolf to stay back. Beyond the conference armed men are taking scattered positions, in a mixture as improbable as a dream. Now and again the Captain breaks off to look about him, to gesture and snap out an order – the men he looks at shift a little, forward or back or sideways. They don't seem to have much idea.

Every time he waves and shouts the wolf shrinks, hair all a-bristle now, ears flat back. Peterkin keeps up an okaying gabble, and pats the wolf in ginger reassurance, but the small hairs on either side of his own spine are likewise standing on end.

Then Kuzak is raising his voice, and the Captain turns and gestures at two guardsmen who step forward. One has an arrow drawn, one fingers his sword hilt. Asli's voice rises as well, the Baron's name is pronounced with emphasis.

Lifted by the sense of event and by the sight of the wolf the ramshackle occasionals shift forward, not waiting for order. More voices. Louder.

Then the wolf bolts.

He runs through parkland, zig-zagging for cover, keeping the line of the boundary wall but not thinking to jump it. Somewhere behind the Captain is bawling to hold back the rag-tag force which has lurched in

pursuit, shouting incoherently, axes and pitchforks readied.

Peterkin's quicker of foot. He drops bow and quiver and gear but might be standing still against the speed of the wolf, who vanishes over a rise – moments later come the screams of maids, weeding with hoes as he hurtles through the kitchen garden, then rounds the big house and heads downhill for the river.

At this same time King Karaman walks in his castle grounds alone, though a bowman keeps constant watch for a sudden assassin. A vizier also skulks discreetly – the king waves him over. He'd like to destroy Tark, but there are whole bouldery provinces that bring less intaxation than he does in gifts. He'd try to seize Tark's wealth but he knows its sources would shrink back and disappear, such is the Baron's network of trade and usury – so tightly and discreetly manned that it runs on its own, the wealth flows in invisibly.

But I'll grant his young wife the favour of serving a month at court, says the King, as my close advisor and helpmeet. Longer, if I find her company pleasing. Yes, and I shall relieve him from the care of this boy and wolf we hear of. Send word at speed that Tark come to me at Kamnos. Tell him I'll be there at the full of the month, that should give him time. Just. Say to bring his long-legged wife, and the boy and the wolf. Oh yes, and arrest these fine jest-laughers. Spy Doruk will give you name and locality. I'll hang the farmer and behead the priest, toy with the others a little, take their footling ownings in payment for their cheek.

Tark himself is on his way back home, no more than three miles off. He'd said for a runner to bring him word when the boy and wolf arrived – none has, but Tark has faith in Doruk and Asli to slip past bandits and surly livestock farmers. And if the wolf runs off or gets killed he can solace himself with the deal he's just made with landowner Turgas, soon to be ex-landowner Turgas, whose steward has been foretelling ruin a year or more and whose token resistance dissolved in cups of mead.

Tark's sedan bearers, and Damla's, have sweated day after day. Visiting Turgas's properties, detours to take in boundaries, noting who owns what beyond them – who to displace, what commons to encircle and appropriate.

As Tark smiles to himself in his sedan the wolf, jinking at the screams of the girls who drop their hoes and flee, veers from the line he was taking towards a picturesque copse and catapults rightward and downward past shrines and shrubby bowers, onto the broad grassy riverside where willows drowse and a hawsered barque lolls above fish-boats in a flower-edged harbour.

  Peterkin, way behind, calls 'Wolf?' to the girls who have turned at the grounds-workers' hostel door at sight of him, and they point wide-eyed. They take him for a hunter, they gasp with an ancient thrill.

From across the river, wide and lazy this far down, comes the thunk of a woodsman's axe, dragging a half-moment behind the visible swing. Four oxen are hauling a long bole, trimmed of all branches. Out on the river, tethered like a beast itself on a short thick chain, a great half-made raft of similar boles, which the woodsmen will ride down to the Second Cataract. Where two will go to the pool below for the boles which the others will send down the roaring chute, to be apprehended and the raft remade, with luck near enough whole.

Sujata has just arrived at the cave of the bandits. She sees straight away it's a grave-hall of the Old Ones, long cleared out – part natural cave, part hewn, later further extended. The natural approach is stoppered by thorn-scrub and creeper; the only way in is by a long traverse across the lie of the outcrop, the rock leaving no trail. Don't drop me she says to the hefty rogue who carries her by head-strap, as the route takes a narrow ledge on almost-sheer cliff – don't drop me, I can't leave this world just yet.

Once inside she senses the Old Ones' presence, a faint whisper at back of the chaos of banditry. She chants a formal greeting to the spirit of the place. The feather-hatted bandit leader cackles, the others follow. She ignores them and starts on a longer prayer, on a drone that volumes and blurs in the cavern acoustics.

The wolf runs downriver. Ahead a noble cedar lifts in layers against the sky; below it a shrubbery gathers as if trying to climb its trunk. He aims for its cover. The tree marks the end of Tark's estate; the shrubbery conceals the boundary wall; the southward road runs the other side. If he's found he'll be cornered.

Peterkin catches a split-second glance as the wolf vanishes into the shrubs three hundred yards ahead. Two young swains are pounding up behind him, one with a pitchfork and one with a cudgel. He points to the nearby copse where the wolf was heading before it swerved at the girls' screams, a good quarter-mile from where it truly lies.

'Wolf!' he says, 'there … wolf!'

They plunge forward, weapons readied. Peterkin runs with them.

'No hurt wolf' he says, 'No hurt wolf!'

But the youth with the pitchfork has a look of smirking self-will, of smirkily ducking the formal rights and wrongs. The other pursuer, with meaty-faced intent and a tranced blankness of eye, seems beyond the reach of language altogether. Peterkin plays up the anxious restraint, giving strength to the misdirection.

Kuzak is near the front of the following pack. He's not used to such a sprint, fit though he is for his years. He shouts staccato and hoarse between gasping breaths, toiling for a grip on the gormless chaos: 'Don't harm the wolf … the Baron commands … he'll have your skins if you harm the wolf …'. He slaps a big youngster to get his attention, sends him to call the forerunners back, or else … Then he's levered his way to the front and he tries to herd the mob two-armed as if herding beasts at a fair, bending and gasping with hands on thighs when at last there's some order. Only then does the Captain arrive, very winded. Asli is beside him, in no better shape; the mob of irregulars gives her space, the only woman on the scene, in gallantry and also a kind of revulsion, at a wrongness to their mannish enterprise.

The first two have sloped back reluctantly, cudgel and pitchfork drooping. When the Captain at last gets his breath a plan is conveyed: Asli has whispered to him of the nets, a good fifty yards of them in ten-yard lengths, that bring fish to the Baron's table all season. The Captain perks up, waving his arms and shouting orders. The copse is surrounded, a party of beaters will work it through, driving the hidden wolf into a long nipple of pole-raised net which will close behind its captive.

Asli, via Kuzak for credibility, suggests that Peterkin goes in first and tries his owl call. Unable to quibble and feeling somehow disloyal, even though it strengthens his ruse, the boy works the copse thoroughly, wasting all the time he can, the call as quiet as he dare for fear

239

the actual wolf will pick it up from the other end of the meadow and show himself.

When he emerges and shrugs, and gestures towards the river and the steep woods beyond, they go crashing in, deflated by now but shouting and banging away with bogus conviction, to prove with empty nets the absence of the wolf.

For Peterkin any belief in a haven vanished at sight of the party that met them. When the wolf ran and he slung down his gear and ran behind they ran together, fellow would-be escapees.

Asli is now fearful. She curses herself for not checking up on arrangements before they cajoled the wolf through the gate. As if she'd thought the Captain was anything but a fool. A hollow in her stomach – to fail Tark in this, after all her long and wary work of inveigling. One bad slip, one bad slip. How Damla will nag him to have her thrown out, her eyes half closed in rectitudinous passion. She needs to check stories with Kuzak, to be sure the Captain carries the weight of the blame, with inexplicit hints towards the First and Second Baronesses.

The light has begun to fade. She and Kuzak, gesturing the boy who drags behind, are heading towards the sprawling mansion, its half-mock battlements in silhouette, when she sees two figures stroll out from its shadow. One is head and shoulders taller than the other, who but for his martial demeanour would seem a child beside the massive torso.

Asli's stomach sinks again: Ruslan. Tark is back.

Chapter 20: Escape Plans

he King's Premier Runner has left the impregnable palace. He'll cover forty miles before dark, then display his royal seal wherever candlelight shows for the best bed and the best food in the house. Then sixty miles the next day. The system modelled on that of the Empire: from every twenty-mile node on the highway under-runners fan out with the news, veining the whole country. The King will meet with Baron Tark; where; when. The purpose is not given, but none suppose the Baron has cause for delight.

On the morning of the third day he will come to the Baron's estate. He's a gaunt man, past forty, a thin-lipped face entirely closed. The Seal of Karaman renders him untouchable. From here he will go to Turgas of Bursa and Aydin priest of Turgutlu, and the mild-worded invitation he brings will tell them of their deaths.

But now he is at Tark's great door which he strikes with the token bossed rod of his dignity, and is bowed into the lofty hall and soon the Second Baroness Bayza approaches, her face as stony as his own.

Tark has gone, she says.

The royal messenger needs to know more. No duty is of greater importance than his, to carry the word and the wish of the King across his lands. Without that all falls into chaos.

Where has the Baron gone the messenger asks, in a voice as dry as bone and as smooth.

He didn't tell me.

I speak for the King, Madam. I ask you where the Baron is.

She makes a sound of exasperation too heartfelt to be suspect.

Why would he tell me? What am I, but his wife of twenty-eight years, mother of three of his children? He left by barque early the day before last. He was fretting to go but wanted a wolf caught and caged, and loaded along with a half-wild boy who they say has tamed it. He'll be most of the way to Lix by now, so keen was he for the journey.

The King's desire will be in Lix before him, and greet him there.

So be it. Me, I have wronged the King never in word or in deed, and trust myself to his goodness.

Your words will be told him. I bow farewell, Madam, and leave to send word downriver to follow your lord and bid him rest from his travels, and meet with his good friend the King.

Runner, a moment – be plain with me. What's he supposed to have done? By my mother's womb I've never heard him speak ill of the King, and I still share his cups and his bed every second month or third.

I know not, Baroness. It's not my place to know. I am merely the tongue, the mind is not given me. With this I am content.

And the Premier Runner bows, not too deeply, and turns abruptly and true to his calling runs out through the open great door and is gone.

Three days before, in the dusk of Baron Tark's belated return, much is taking place.

Asli and Kuzak step aside and confer in a storehouse angle. Fear does not constrict her vision – the chances stand stark but in full muster. Her first concern is for Tark's good opinion, her only real strength in the world. Without his favour she's back where she started, a piece of flotsam with only her wits to feed and to roof her. She thinks the boy a wonder, and her heart is not untouched by him, but she'll play him without conscience for her advantage.

We must send the pitchfork warriors back to their duties and let the boy and the wolf find each other she says, if it hasn't swum the river and gotten lost in the mountains. Give them a while to feel at home. Then find out what the Baron wants next.

Kuzak shrugs. He doesn't quite see why he's still involved but knows that somehow he is. That his oath by some uncharted course encompasses these events.

You're right. Give the mess a chance to settle itself. The wolf might just come back to him, or he'll search out the wolf. Though they now have little reason to stay around, if they find each other.

I mean for an eye to be kept on the boy, so we'll know if they do.

I wish you good luck. Is my task then finished, albeit in farce?

Please stay if you will. Someone sane in this mayhem. D'you need to be away?

Not that I know about. But maybe I've done too much already – helping Tark and his schemes. Whyever he wants the boy and the wolf it won't be for their betterment.

No indeed, but betterment they'll have from what I've picked up. He wants the wolf as a present for the Imperial Princess, who they say loves beasts more than people. If it works out there'll be betterment all round – the boy will sleep on cushions instead of rocks and wear silk every day, the wolf will feed on spring lamb and princessly caresses. And the Baron, of course, will be greatly in favour. And I'll maybe not do so bad, if I save my skin through the next bit.

I'll speak with my conscience and see what it says. How long do you suppose – I'll need to be around?

A couple of days should clinch it. And thanks, so far. Mother of All knows what I'd have done without you.

Thank *you*, it's been one to remember. Were the wives behind the mess, d'you think?

Not a doubt.

Will Tark blame you?

Maybe. Maybe he'd be right to.

How?

I should have kept them outside till I was sure what we'd meet. With me and the Baron away there's no-one left in the place with the wit of a jaybird, sorry if that's boastful.

What next then?

Make excuses, promise to mend the damage.

Peterkin's hanging back but still in sight. He doesn't want to cause alarm by vanishing just yet.

Kuzak and Asli call him. He acts rather concussed, directionless. They tell him, in gesture and fragmentary Megharan, that they're mortified at how it all went, to please stay around, coax back the wolf, there'll be no more nonsense with cudgel-happy fools.

He thinks to play along. Use the cover of night, call the wolf to him. That hillside across the river looked tempting, maybe there's no home pack down here. Cross in one of those boats maybe, he's never been in a boat but it can't be that hard. *Ach*, he could live without bread and cheese – could he?

The palaver with the wolf is secondary to the Baron.

Why is that Errant here? he asks. What happened with Doruk?

When Asli's messages came a runner was sent to enquire. The man picked up on Doruk's abscondence, but also that Asli was anyway in transit, and when he brought back the information the Vizier didn't think it of much importance.

The runner is quickly brought to the Baron's presence to say again what he heard. Tark's in a stamping and roaring mood.

Used some ruse to double back on the ferry? Then disappeared? A Spy! A Spy!

A spy – Tark beats his fists on furniture, calling for Asli. The servant, running, meets her in the great hall, Kuzak a little behind.

What do you know about Doruk?

He didn't turn up. I waited, sent two messages, heard nothing. Kuzak the Errant volunteered, we made the journey with no mishap, till we passed the gate and into a wolf-hunting frenzy. The swains seemed to think the wolf had been brought for their sport; the Captain had as good a grip as a blind man on a hive of wasps.

None of it your fault then?

My lord must be the judge of that, she says bowing.

He comes disconcertingly close, red-faced and massive.

I will be, Madam, I will be.

She bows again, less coolly, but he's back to roaring, eyes bulgy:

Clear the room, clear the room – just you Madam Asli – you – what's the name? – *Kuzak,* Kuzak – who else? Vizier. The rest out. *Out!*

Tark seems to shrink in size as the room empties.

Doruk, spy Doruk – oh gods what have I said, in front of this reptile?

The Vizier answers.

Nothing that I've heard, Sir. But he was often by you when the party wore on and only the closer friends remained. Them and Doruk ...

Tark clears his throat as if disgusted.

May I propose we consider the worst Sir? says Asli. She has braced into a professional formality.

The worst?

Any plotting? Assassination plans, however playful? Curses calling on gods or demons?

No plots, many curses I think – light-hearted mostly. But can we rely on the mighty one's sense of humour?

Jokes? – jokes about Karaman?

Tark finds it hard to speak, then does.

Brother-slayer. Brother-slayer jokes. Oh Mother save us. Paranoid friendless snake, keen to attend prolonged executions, all that. But the fratricide jests will damn me past hope. Oh Great One, help I cry, this sinner etcetera ... I hear myself jest – why do I *jest*?

The Vizier winces in silence; Kuzak watches and listens without expression. But Asli has slipped into command:

What is the worst he might do?

Kill me of course. Ignominiously.

Any reason he wouldn't?

The wealth I bring. He knows it would all run dry, without me to keep it flowing. All of my private fractions – my debtors: how they'd love not to pay. They'd vanish like smoke – no army of Enquirers could bring them back to the light.

What do you think are the odds?

Depends what jokes Doruk heard, and which he recalls. Fifty-fifty. Maybe. But even at that he's got me, I owe him a gallows, as soon as the income falters he calls in the debt.

If I speak over-directly Sir, forgive me – this is a time for plain words. There seems to be a straightforward choice. Throw yourself on Karaman's mercy (Tark ho-ho's sarcastically) – or run.

Don't go dumb on me, Asli knife-wit. *Run?* I'm ageing and fat and long given to indolence. *Run?*

The way the river runs past your back door. We must think how much of a start we've got. Sorry Sir, I presume – *you've* got. Your barque with valuables, two or three swordsmen, bearers – down to the Second Cataract. Send a runner ahead to charter a barge to the First. A final switch in Lix, to one of your cutters … and then to the Empire, as fast as the wind will take you. Bringing gifts, and much Megharan intelligence. The welcome might be cool but not over-cold. And most of your interests will run as well from that side of the water as this.

You seem keen, Madam Asli – too keen? You fancy the adventure?

I am at your disposal, Sir, either way. If you stay, or go and don't take me, I run anyway – otherwise I'll surely be put to the question. Then enslaved. If I'm lucky. What's left of me.

How soon do you think they'll come for me?

I don't see how Doruk makes it to the palace sooner than today. Then two days and three nights till even the best runner gets here. I'd say prepare tonight, be away tomorrow morning – two days start. Word has to get back to the King. With luck we're out of Lix by then.

Tomorrow morning. But the wolf, I want this wolf. What a difference it could make: 'Ho Sargon, here's a fat old chancer on the run – sanctuary please. Here are some trinkets, my very best, good enough for your trainee dancing girls. And a holdful of barley and oil, best Megharan quality. Oh, I nearly forgot – here's a hand-tame wolf for your daughter, with a bold pretty boy to go with it, and teach her its ways.' What can you give, to he with the world's riches already in his hand? The wolf, bring me the wolf.

In the consternation of facing Tark the wolf and boy had fallen from Asli's mind. Before she and Kuzak entered the house he was with them, drawn along by their conciliations; but when the Keeper of the Door had greeted them and they stepped in, thinking him still behind, he side-slipped and found his way back into the late dusk of the gardens. He soft-footed to where he'd slung his satchel and bow, landmarked by a statue that gleamed ghost-white beneath the risen moon.

Now, after scanning as best he can for late-lurking Baron's men, he wades the thigh-deep meadowgrass to where he glimpsed the wolf at the boundary shrubs. He guesses he has lain low, hackled in fear, deeply secreted. No-one went that way in all the kerfuffle; there's no reason he'd have moved, except to maybe leap the boundary wall and vanish.

As he comes close Peterkin gives the dusk-owl whistle, softly and repeatedly. The shrub-rim is jet black against the grey of the meadow. He works along a faltering margin path, owl-calling. Nothing. Then, suddenly, thirty yards at least from where he'd seen the wolf go in, a thin breathy high-throat whimper. A faint wheesh of movement through vegetation – then the wolf is there, wary, watching him, whimpering thinly. Peterkin kneels on the sun-hard earth of the path, down to the height of the wolf, and speaks to him a little above a whisper, and the wolf comes, tentative and wary, and Peterkin reaches a hand very carefully speaking all along, and the wolf nuzzles him, breathing emphatically, rear a little ducked and the muscular tail flip-flapping side to side.

They creep into cover and settle to sleep as often before, the night velvet and warm. Then they hear footsteps and freeze, a male voice crooning without location, as if a permeation of the air. But the sounds pass. They come from the road, which runs barely ten yards from them, on the other side of the fringe of shrub and the boundary wall behind it – from a guard sent to man the southern gate, to halt absconding boys and wolves, check the road on the way.

Peterkin wakes at the first grey of dawn with the idea of taking a boat and escaping across the river, the wolf swimming behind if it won't come aboard. He supposes a slant route across and down the current. He's even picked out a little headland and pebbly shore to aim for, behind it an unbroken forest that overlies foothills, then scatters and thins as it reaches up to the wall of gigantic peaks. But already there are voices, the sounds of thumping and grunting action. The barque is being loaded – trunks, hampers, hefty jars of oil or wine, small heavy caskets of valuables, the caskets themselves bejewelled. Also five large rectangles, of three different sizes, the space each surrounds barred with metal rods. These when conjoined make a cage that once held a leopard.

As is on task. She quickly ensures that guards are posted at all three gates of the estate, that others are detailed to take positions in trees and in turrets at first pre-dawn light, to give bird-call signals if wolf or boy are seen.

The Vizier and the housekeeper, with underlings from kitchen and from chamber, are up all night preparing for the journey. The Vizier, a man of law, raises the question of the senior Baronesses, who won't fit into the barque nor any better into Tark's planned future. He suggests (with a loyalty to Tark and no great regard for any of his wives) that he order them a month in hodden grey as punishment for the shambles with the wolf, and when they refuse divorce them on the spot as unbiddable. Tark demurs, fearing to over-excite all those old-house brothers and cousins in case they find a way to snare him before he gets out of Lix. Well, says the Vizier, let them keep and run the estate, you Sir to rejoin them (you might say) when the spy's false accusations have been refuted.

(Eren and Bayza will also flee after the Premier Runner's visit, back to their families. The Vizier, left to run things, going with the Second Baroness. The elder wives fear the King, but guess he wouldn't dare capture them in their birth estates – Eren's, though small, is respectable, with many connections – so handing the ancient houses common cause, when he's long worked to keep them at each other's throats.

By their flight they miss by a bare half-day the arrival of yet more visitors.)

Catching the wolf was surprisingly easy.

Asli nudged the Captain towards a stratagem, then gave it wide-eyed praise.

Watchers were in place early. A keen-eyed boy in a tree fork saw Peterkin and the wolf as they snuck from cover to cover to see what went on at the harbour. He whistled an oriole whistle very plausibly, to catch the attention of watchers on the castellated roof; then he pointed the direction.

The problem then was to surround them; but the land afforded a natural trap. A blind gully, its stream long diverted, led down into a shrine to the Goddess of Love. By the time the light gave a rooftop view of the whole park the campaign had begun. With Tark himself, his bed hardly slept in, there on the roof, and Ruslan scowling beside him, each man follows orders to the inch. They're to dot at even spacing the edges of the hundred-acre triangle of grounds to the south of the house, each with his own precise location: along the riverbank, along the boundary wall, on the slope that falls from kitchen garden to harbour.

At the skirl of a shawm from the roof when all are in place each man steps forward ten slow paces; at a second skirl they sidestep to keep an even spacing. The procedure is as punctilious as the previous day's was deranged. Ten more paces at a third blast; re-spacing again at a fourth. Three watchers, still in their trees, by gesture tell the rooftop command of the pair's position and movements.

The wolf bolts to left and to right, in terror at the signals and the soft, sinister footfall, the tidal human odour. He finds the gully and skids down it. Peterkin had been looking for the weakest point in the river-side line, with the aim of bolting through and swimming across to the woods, leaving bow and satchel. Could he swim with the bow? The bow, the knife and the packet of stones. A spare bowstring wrapped – wrapped in what? And how swim with them? These are his thoughts, when the wolf so suddenly corners himself. And Peterkin follows – what else can he do?

The wolf cornered and netted hackles in terror, snarling with teeth bared, thrashing in the cordwork like a landed fish, without the pragmatic nous to so much as chew at its bonds. Its writhing makes tying its legs and muzzle awkward – with cloth strips not to harm it, the boy shown the edge of a sword to persuade him back, then restrained by strong accustomed hands, with neither diffidence nor malice.

The wolf is borne on a hurdle to the harbour. They lay it on the aft-deck and build the cage around it and nail the cage to the deck with broad-headed nails. Asli has come down. She tries to tell the boy all will be well but he turns his face away. His face is wet with tears and his mouth sags slightly open, he wipes his running nose with the back of his hand as he turns away further.

They're trying to untie the cloth bonds through the bars of the cage, then one more foolishly still has drawn his knife. Peterkin, breaking out of a kind of trance, waves them back, gestures to be let into the cage. The men are astonished but Asli and Kuzak nod, and the door is unbolted and slid up and the boy crouches through and it's bolted again.

The crowd is gawping as he starts to untie the cloths; he tries to wave them back and now addresses Asli and she gets the aft-deck cleared, keeping a guard close by as she peeks round the cabin corner to see that the boy doesn't slip the bolt and dive for freedom as soon as the wolf is untied. All the time he speaks to it, in his strange tongue, cajoling, reassuring. A shame, to so lose his trust. But seek not honey in vinegar times they say.

Tark, restless as he watches from the riverbank, steps closer. What's happening in the cage sucks all his attention. Damla, drifting uneasily, joins him; the giant looms a little to the rear, scowling at this crime against nature. All else is forgotten as they watch the boy untie the wolf, murmuring, murmuring, stroking its head. Now the front legs are free and the beast is half upright and the kneeling boy has his arms round it, stroking, murmuring.

Tark's stance becomes a little more haughty, a cryptic smile thins his lips and half closes his eyes. Not at what he's watching, but at the envisaged face of the Emperor's daughter.

Chapter 21: To the Second Cataract

The barque made decent progress for its bulk, with four on the oars and a steady north-west air. They sail all night beneath a filling moon, the broken moon-glade veeing out behind them, the rustle and croak of birds in the reeds. They slip past Mink and Turgutlu on the first night, anchoring shy of Mink till it gets dark, Tark himself in hood and cloak calling a breezy reply to the watchman's question. The faintly moon-gleaming roofs of Turgutlu slide by in the pit of the night with no such challenge. Tark and Damla keep to the cabin by day when other boats are seen, or fishers on the shore.

But the wolf is seen, as they pass the first midland villages, until the spare sail is rigged up as a tented awning. For the Mayor of Lix's menagerie, the steersman cries, but word is out.

And as the barque slides down the wide river, a lazy inconstant sail and Tark's stalwarts rested from the oars in the heat of the day, the word keeps pace, running downstream alongside. Fieldmen drop their hoes and hurry to the riverbank, fishers in rowboats and skin canoes turn their vessels to watch.

There it is! There it is! come their shouts, bold in their anonymity.

Ho there – show us the wolf! Show us the big man! Is he ten foot tall?

But they pass with only the steersman on view, staring ahead impassively. They pass the last habitation and on, into the Mosquito Marshes, the river in the flatlands losing all definition. Straps of sullen channel run black above the peat, meandering through a vast reticulation of reedbeds. Stumpy poles mark the way; even so a boatman perches in the prow, dangling a weighted line.

They anchor when the river begins to come back to itself, banked either side by edgewoods of alder and willow, the ancient willows fissured to the roots, lichen-dangled in senile squalor; but born again in the fresh boles that shoot up where the weary limbs sag into the mud. Hid in vegetation they – all hands but the Baron and Baroness – remove or cover all marks of the Barque's identity, even dropping and dumping the stubby mast (little air movement anyway now), lashing the sail over cabin and all so the boat is sheathed fore to aft as if it bore only goods.

Peterkin and the wolf, in long hours of heat and stench under the spare-sail awning, subsist half-comatose in a kind of dream. As if in the uterine heat and seclusion they anneal still more fully, into a kind of single creature, conjoined by instantaneous understanding, of a kind both less and greater than the affordances of language.

But now and again the trance is broken. The wolf becomes unsettled, or Peterkin does, and the boy calls to the steersman in approximate Megharan – *Are there watchers?* And if the steersman says no then Peterkin opens the cage from inside and ducks out under the sail and peels it back and lets out the wolf, to defecate on the boards and to back-and-forth around the little aft-deck sniffing and leg-cocking and rearing his forepaws onto the rail to watch the water and slowly sliding bank.

The steersman fears the wolf, once snarling and hackling up when the man suddenly shouted to the foredeck. So Peterkin by word and mime gets the man to procure him a length of rope, and he loops one end so the other can feed through but not too easily, and he gives the wolf smell and sight of the rope and gently inures him to its touch on his neck, each stage rewarded with titbits. He progresses the free end of rope through the loop, with the closed circle loose round the wolf's neck. And so in time they come out with the wolf on his new leash, half the width of the boat and barely hindering him, but peace of mind for the steersman. Now and again the wolf twists or baulks and Peterkin makes an affectionate fuss and he tail-wags, acquiesces. In time he shortens the lead and now they are leading each other – the wolf freely, Peterkin warily. Then back under the sail and into the cage, at a call from steersman or foredeck.

Asli comes a few times, also Kuzak. She tries to explain that Tark had to flee, that what seemed a wolf hunt when they first arrived was a mistake, a disaster of bad planning and miscommunication, that they're heading for asylum in the Empire and he and the wolf will be safe there. Peterkin listens sullenly, mistrustfully. His thoughts are all of escape; he even thinks of going overboard in the night, but the lands here are too populous – the wolf would have no chance.

Kuzak when he comes is terse, briskly avuncular.

Why? says Peterkin to him. *This?* Gesturing the boat, the cage.

Kuzak makes a down-palm, okaying sign. Wait and see, he says. Wait and see.

After the marshes a long hot day, that does nothing for Tark's temper, nor that of the oarsmen sweltering on their boards. Ruslan is boiling in his physical immensity, his stroke has become unrhythmed and splashy. He'll never ask for a break.

The big man is overheating Sir, says Kuzak to Tark. Allow me to give him a break.

You, Errant? What are *you,* to serve my servants? Remind me – what are you doing here anyway?

Serving your servant Asli, Baron. Something to do with a wolf.

The wolf is caged, we need no help with the wolf, thank you O versatile and wageless one. So why did you join us?

I was asked to. And we're not in the Emperor's palace just yet. Will the wolf be carried, cage and all, down the Second and First Fall portages, for the world to see? The boy can lead it overland, if we keep him from running off – they could even sidestep Lix, creep down to one of the smugglers' bays between the town and the headland.

And tell me what's in this for *you,* Errant?

I've reasons for seeking the Emperor's goodwill, as have many.

D'you suppose he'll let you pious vagabonds set up stall in the Empire? I think you mistake your man.

The lightest imperial smile would be something. But let me come back to Ruslan – he melts in his sweat. I've seen men die of heatstroke – they start by going clumsy. Watch his oar.

Yah – why ask me, anyway? Take his place if he'll let you. But don't think I trust your little holy beard, enlightened one. You have my forbearance on the word of Asli here (he gestures; she's sitting very still, as if not hearing) – she'll answer if it turns out you're playing the snake.

Kuzak bows an Errant's vestigial bow and turns to Ruslan five yards aft, the boards below him soaked with his sweat. The big man, vague and bleary-eyed as a drunk, gives up his place without argument, then goes down on one knee on the boards as if in thought, staring at nothing. Kuzak, already rowing, checking over his shoulder for the tempo, meets Asli's eye as he turns back and she leaves her discreet corner.

Get him to drink all the water he can. And get Tark's manservant to mop him with a fresh wet cloth – maybe on the fore-deck. Tell him to say it's Tark's word. Get Ruslan's buddy the swordsman to help.

Then the water starts moving faster. They reach the Second Cataract late in the day, hold back until dusk to slide to the pile-borne landing wharf. Some way back from the line of barges, that sit inert and tight-covered. Beyond them the sprawl of porters' hostelry and huts; then the rough-flagged, rough-stepped downward path, on which goods are carried to further rentable barges, to scull with the drift to a second portered drop into Lix, that zigzags by the roar of the final fall.

The Premier Runner, on his way back and exhausted with fifty miles to go, sends sealed word by a subaltern, limping to the palace a day later behind it. After consultation, and with no great sense of hurry, two dozen kingsmen and three Enquirers are sent to Tark's estate; a dozen plus two to the First and Second Cataracts each. Why hurry? The Baron is surely trapped.

The Baron's goods, wolf and all, to be portaged by night down the old stepped path to waiting barges, he and the entourage following. With generous bribes to ensure discretion. From there downriver again; but the party to leave the convoy above the First Cataract, where the river once more and finally hurls its millions of tons through a great gnarly slot in the cliffs, to ease and pool out meekly into the miles-wide estuary that pushes apart the cities of Meghara and Lix. The party to leave the convoy and come into Lix on foot and in darkness, lookouts ahead, by the path that Kuzak had climbed thirty years back to find his second life.

In Lix, with word run ahead, the party to board by night a ship of Tark's fleet, the cargo by then taken down and hauled on rollers by ox-drawn sledge to the nearest free dock, the wolf bound leg and jaw and discreetly sheathed. Then the clandestine ship is rowed in by skiff-tugs for rapid loading; then out and for the Empire on the first tide of morning, and free – Tark's clippers the fastest ships in the Southern Sea.

That was the plan.

But the path, undercut and grown perilous, a rockfall had taken twenty yards of it. Something that happened every few years; a gang would go at it hard to cut back into the cliff and hack out a new stretch, wide enough for a man and his load, a couple of insets for two to pass. A few days of pick and crowbar and hammer and wedge all the hours of daylight and transfer would re-commence. But Tark doesn't have a few days.

Destiny has trapped the Baron, led him here with its promises. He'd felt so sure of it all. And now he is trapped in this vile place, with its noise and squalor of function, the stench from the workers' open latrine in the heat, the stupefying roar of the cataract.

He becomes foul-tempered as the situation sinks in. The terror of helplessness, cornered by the vast logic of nature. He snaps in all directions, but then more and more he blames Asli.

Thus Tark's composure deserts him. His composure: sardonic humour, smooth control, even his quickness of mind.

There is no plan, except wait. Wait. He'd gone down the vertiginous track to the rockfall to see for himself, and the queasiness of the cliff-face situation expanded to raw dread at the prospect. A soft but all-embracing whole-body dread. A half-month's work, were the words that came to him. They'd managed barely five yards of the twenty that had gone, and that looked like the easy bit.

There must be another way. This was your big idea, Madam – find another way.

Track through the mountains? And leave all my wealth to the jackals? How will I get to the Empire?

Cross the river? Hire porters? Through ten miles of thick-peopled country, a village every two? Wake up, wake up, what's happened to you?

Appeal to his mercy? Karaman? Mercy? Too late now, even if he had any. Wake up!

The next suggestion Asli makes he hits her, a great blundering thump on the side of the face, the way an angry tradesman might buffet an apprentice.

That was nothing Madam, don't you dare pull faces. Nothing to what's coming if you don't find us a way.

Chapter 22: Golo, Sujata

he bandit Golo's network of control and information mirrors that of the lawful authorities: in-threads quiver with the news, out-threads with his directives. But its size and geographic range give an agility and speed denied those authorities – he knows what's going on in hours, not days; his decisions are quick, sometimes instant; there's no slack or slant in the force of his will; there's no-one in his world whose face he doesn't know.

He has an informer in the house of Tark, sister of one of his henchmen. The garbled account that comes to him – by way of another sister, just delivered of a child and the visit so approved – is that Tark has gone, seemingly fled; that the senior Baronesses will go too, as soon as their portable wealth is packed. That with one or other there will have decamped most of the guard and half the staff. A single housekeeper struggles to keep order, the Guard Captain dozes while his men play dice.

Golo surmises that Tark has fallen foul, that kingsmen will be on their way. But they'll take a while to arrive, and easy to see coming.

Golo's interrogation of the maid's sister is low-toned but exacting. His eyes never leave her face. Her milk dries up in fear, not flowing again till sunset, drawn by the baby's wailing. By then Golo is slipping through the Baron' unguarded gate with fourteen men, the core of seven – already like him death-sentenced – shamelessly bare-faced, the seven semi-professionals – porters, woodsmen, tavern-bullies – demon-masked for sport and anonymity.

They fan out to survey the house. The Captain of the Guard sits in a cushioned chair he's had moved to the flagstone apron by the great door, to which ascend broad shallow steps. He takes in the evening cool, a fine goblet in his hand. To his left there's an ill-heaped shambles of late-discarded items and content-spilling packages, whose mass exceeded available portage. From somewhere within come cries of reprimand, distant but shrill. The bandits ease forward, spread out wide. The Captain of the Guard is stumbling to his feet; the garnet-studded goblet clanks on the flags, his hand is on his sword-hilt.

You have five arrows aimed at your belly, old man. Drop the sword or they'll fly.

The Captain has spent his life in soldiering. Many times he's been valorous, hauling above the coils of fear. Finding the trick – so hard and cold, but behind it a vivid joy – of handing himself to Fate. The trick that lets you stab at another man's face exactly as he's stabbing at yours. But it's been a long time, and time is what he needs to gather himself, and the strutting cockbird below with his posse of fairground demons gives him no time. He is witless; the sword in his hand feels futile, he can't think how to use it. He can't even think how to drop it, before the cockbird chief, quick as a rat, zips up the stairway and easily sidesteps the angled slash – the Captain's sword arm has suddenly come to life – and zips in and punctures his throat with a blade that barely counts as a sword, as deftly as a heron spearing an eel. The Captain back-steps in physical chaos, blood pumping, his sword arm now awake and trying to fight on its own, and he blunders into his cushioned evening chair and both go down, and the bandit chief is on him and flips him face down with monkeyish strength to not get splashed with the blood.

The last thing the Captain sees with his mortal eyes is face-level flagstones and moon-sheen on pooling blood and the jutting legs of the fallen chair. Then he is above the scene, the monkey-squatting bandit chief above the hefty body that the watcher seems to have left, one hand gripping the hair as he slices off the head.

Golo's big idea is not the mayhem, the leftover port-ables, the maidservants. He wants the whole world to know his name, to think him a demon in shape of a man, a creature free of the bounds of sin because living entirely beyond them, in the way a saint lives within them. He has no fear of his likely terminus: he'll scream curses from the stake, or as they bury him alive – ten thousand will hear his word on the upstart king, the imposter, the fratricide. His laughable inferior in the service of wickedness. His name will live for a thousand years.

His rule of Tark's abandoned domain is brief, and not planned otherwise. The head of the Captain, melancholy, bewildered, is carried on a spear at the front of the pack, the priapic angle drooping with the weight. Golo struts a little to one side. Women lighting lamps run screaming; just three of the remnant Guard escape, the others killed fleeing or hiding with only one bandit loss, and he an unwary part-timer. Male servants prostrate themselves: Destiny decides their disposal, some neck-stabbed as if their posture requests it, others helped to their feet with noisy benignity.

Escapees bawl through the door of the maidservants' hostel: *Bandits! Golo is on us! Run!* But too loudly – incomers follow the sound, round up six from the all-directions flight, drive them to the big house like livestock.

Golo inquires of the post-flight wealth of the house. He knows pretty well already but hopes for gleanings. He sits cross-legged on a table in the Baron's counsel room, as if he'd just dropped from the ceiling.

All that's easily carried is gone, he's told by each quaking interviewee – packed up and gone with the nobles, who each took great care in the matter. He shrugs a shoulder and spits in disdain. We'll search in the morning he tells them. Don't bother to pray for mercy if you're lying.

At least Tark's cellar's is three parts full. There begins a rambunctious celebration. Despoilment is a joy in itself, along with those of alcohol and the flesh: the hall is soon a mess of smashed crocks and slashed tapestries. They urinate in the still-half-full wardrobes of the nobles, in chambers snowy with down from disembowelled mattresses.

But Golo wants more. He wants his antipodes. He wants Sujata to be here. The gaze with which she met his was something new to him. Their early lives were perhaps not so different; but Golo found the sublime in his first murder – the miracle whereby a few seconds' work turns a lively foe into a gawping corpse. So gone, so utterly gone. And the sweet sweet taste of life when it's done, his soul gigantic and taking exquisite ease, soaring above the whole uncoordinate world.

Once he found the trick he gave himself to it. He worships the goddess whose name is The Nameless One, though he never lights a taper nor whispers a prayer. He knows that he *is* her, her avatar.

He wants Sujata to be here, to see him strut through this ruin of smug wealth, this blood-stained testament. He sends four men with Tark's oversized sedan, to bring her in cushioned state.

How came you by the Baron's sedan she asks, when the heftiest bandit has carried her from the cave.

Mother of All, what has he *done*?

Golo has lookouts on the road, and they see the dust of a force three miles away. They come from Turgutlu; a subaltern runner from Maul has brought them the news, they go to secure the estate from robbers and rogues, to keep an eye on the Baron if he's found lurking (there's no order yet for arrest), the same for his wives. For kudos, local pride; and perhaps a little pillaging of their own, small items of a kind easily traded.

A day sooner than Golo had thought, even for a local force. The bandits must leave very quickly. But this is of their nature. The six surviving part-timers slip back to croft and mill with their modest share of portable spoils; those who have let slip their masks, or tossed them aside in various raptures, must tremble when the King's Enquirers come. The other seven go back to the cave to lie low; Golo has picked an interim chief. He has a different plan for himself and Sujata, one that came in the kind of sudden insight he never questions.

You came here to see Tark, he says to her, as his underlings grab up their spoils and scatter. I'll take you to see Tark.

I might have changed my mind. The journey hasn't so far gone to plan.

You come with me, O Crone, or I kill you.

His words are of even tenor, spoken quietly. Sujata smiles into his face and shrugs a shoulder and heaves on her staff to stand.

He doesn't try to hurry her as they piece their way to the little harbour. Behind them come screams as bandit occasionals hunt down housemaids who've seen their faces. The pair of rowboats are skinned against weather with patchwork animal membrane stretched taut; Golo slashes this clear from the nearer boat and slings in his satchel of goods, and helps Sujata in from the steps and unhawsers the boat and heaves off. He rows splashily out, toying with changes of method, showing he's never done it before.

He seems to be trying to cross the river, not head down with the current. They're most of the way when there's shouting from the shore behind, and an archer lets loose a few arrows that plip into the water well short. Golo has seen a long skin canoe tied to the woodsmen's great raft of logs. The rowboat beaches on shingle a hundred yards down and Golo leaves Sujata and runs through shallows and rock to rock and up onto the raft and easily frees the loop-hawsered canoe. He's been spotted both sides now and woodmen are shouting and running but he paddles much better than he rows, and in no time he's back and out of the canoe. He halters to a rowlock and thigh-deep in water he lifts Sujata out in his arms as if she were a child and eases her onto the foreseat of the canoe, and he tosses in his satchel and swarms in himself and unloops and they're off downstream, feeling for the strongest current while woodsmen on their raft shout curses and three intrepid Turgutluans have clambered into the other rowboat and one in a wobbling stance sends a final purely rhetorical arrow.

Golo hides his hat and they slip by Mink unchallenged, small boats are many. He calls a greeting to the watchtower at Turgutlu. A big jovial face shouts a jovial question.

I take my grandmother south, to meet a nobleman. The big face barks a laugh at this nonsense; they pass.

They have no food; evening's come on and they're hungry. This and other things they share, equally or not – the beauty and monotony of the river, its long southward pull, the canoe's discomforts, the nag of bladder, the hot blue sky. A couple of miles past Turgutlu, as if stranded on the eastern bank, is a fisher's cottage with nets drying and patch fields of barley and beans and a milk cow looking over a hurdle fence. Golo ties up and helps Sujata out, then halloos. A man comes from round the back, a woman appears at the door.

Ho brother, sister. We are travellers on the river. May we call on Hospitality?

Yes, and welcome. We only have stockfish, and bread and curd – the rest went at the market today.

More than enough for uninvited guests, we thank you. (The exchange so far follows an ancient formula, backed by unwritten law.)

Three children come to the door and peer round their mother's skirt the way children always peer. The mother motions them back as the guests make to enter. Will you sit outside, she says, in the last of the sun?

The man carries out a bench, the wife two stools. Sujata eases down, Golo takes off his hat, fans himself with it, sets it down beside him. The man offers barley beer, the guests each take a cup. The man's face is closed but his hand is shaking.

Welcome brother. Ours is yours. What do we call you, Sir? What is your trade?

Golo sits square and looks at the man. Sardonic alertness of eye is his only expression. The fisher meets his gaze but keeps himself well back, hiding within the niceties of custom. He has heard of a feathered hat. A spell of time passes, long enough to become a touch uncanny. Then Golo replies.

My name is Golo, Terror of the North. My trade is murder, ransom, thievery. My companion is Sujata, the Holy Crone of the badlands Hermitage. We plucked her from the labours of the road as she travelled to see the Baron Tark, and gave her hospitality, and now that Tark

271

goes south in haste we chase him on the water-road lest he miss his reverend visitor.

The fisher's voice shakes but keeps its depth of tone and his eyes do not plead or look away.

I pray you Sir, in the name of the god, don't ply your trade here.

I never have and never would, bold fisherman, when welcomed in good faith. Drink with me, please. We'll be gone before dawn. The Baron – did you see him pass? Why do you hesitate friend, it's not a trick question. I'm sorry, I didn't ask your name.

I am Kan, my wife is Eser. We live a quiet life and like it so. Out of sight of guardsmen, kingsmen, Enquirers. I pray you don't bring the Enquirers here, and if they're to come don't give me cause to lie.

No-one has seen us pull up here, we've passed no other boat for a mile. I'll go slide the canoe into the reeds. We'll leave in darkness. If you're asked say a fool and a crone came by, the fool said he took the old one to see a nobleman – the words I said to the Watch in Turgutlu. Say you fed them and they left in the night. All that will be true. The Baron – have you seen him? Answer me or not, as you please.

I didn't see him, or his boat. But the talk in the marketplace was, he was seen way south two days ago, with a wolf and a boy in a cage and his Baroness in silk and jewels, and his giant pulling one of the oars and the boat skewing to his might, the steersman a-haul on the rudder. It wallowed, though, for all that, overloaded and ill-made for speed.

Two days? But slow? Aha.

Later the party retreats from the evening plague of gnats. The daughters Yeta and Yilda, twins of six or seven, dance a pretty dance, shy show-offs, and sing a clapping song; the two-year-old son Ferit takes in the guests with his huge infant gaze, then goes back to watching an earwig make its way through the reed-strewn floor. Golo takes out a flask of sixty-year aquavit, taken from the Baron's collection; he and Kan take turns to slug from the neck, Eser tries and squeals and flaps at her mouth, the little one looks up and starts to wail. She takes him reassuring on her lap and the twins hunker in each side and the four make a tableau of motherhood in the dim of the hut. A pottage of stockfish and beans and sorrel, more soup than stew, is a-boil, its pungency thick in the air. Heavy black bread lies under a cloth.

Golo especially is ravenous, but there's more than enough.

It's a time of tableaux, of archetypes. The fisher father Kan grows into himself, with aquavit and a customing to the bandit's presence, as if this is the sort of thing that happens, to be met with a welcome that keeps its self-respect. The hut, in turn, becomes his house again, his presence fills it again like a slow shift of climate. Golo, for all his ego, asks no tribute of humility. He takes his ease, a touch theatrically but with a perpetual bracedness, as if attack could be but an eyeblink away. Even Sujata has something theatric about her, the light dying off into candle and cookfire, the shutters closed against the gnats – a grey severity, precise in its mode and its claims as is the exact-edged fall of her robe.

When Golo steps out to relieve himself the wife leans close to Sujata's ear and whispers, Is there something we should do? Sujata touches her arm and silently mouths No, twice turning her head through a tiny angle. Then she lays a weightless hand on little Ferit, asleep on his mother's lap, and shakes her head again with a quarter-smile.

The door swings open but Golo isn't there. Then half of his face appears and is gone in an instant. Then, content that fisher Kan is not braced a-tremble with bow or axe, he enters with his normal easy swagger.

Were you plotting, when I was gone?

Sujata answers.

I told them that if you fell into a drunken sleep, and someone tiptoed up to chop off your head, The Nameless One would wake you when the axe began its fall, and by the time it landed you'd have rolled aside, and if the axeman drew another breath he'd surely not draw two. Because she looks after her own.

You lie, Holy Crone, I listened and heard no tale of that length. It's a sin to lie, is it not?

I lie in jest, and within the truth. You have the luck of the Devil her servant, and the eyes and ears, and quickness of body and mind. Your end will take a bigger army than that here gathered.

Sweet Crone, you have kept your mouth so piously shut – and now you share with our hosts all you've hid in it?

She's looking down at the sleeping child and she closes her eyes and slightly tilts her head and when she opens her eyes again she is staring into Golo's. And so they remain, eye-locked, as they speak, like arm-wrestlers jammed in a balance of strength. Each searching for fake spirit, a slip of the elbow, determined that the other's no more than human and therefore to be overcome. Each at the same time touched by awe, that such an opponent can be.

We have no secrets from the world, O feather-hat demon. The world will see your deeds at the house of Tark and know all it needs to know. I'm sure you serve darkness better than I serve light, but we each do our best. These people our hosts are the innocent watchers, who've given roof and succour freely and so are untouchable – at least you agree on that. Do you not?

He waves a dismissive gesture.

I am the truth of the world, he says. Darkness and light? What do words mean? You have and I want so I take and now I have instead. You stand in my path and I displace you. You offend my ear and I silence you. Watch the birds and the beasts as they wrangle over their meat – yesterday's friend is today's opponent. The King on his throne is worse than a beast (Eser the fishwife whispers an incantation) – he does as they do, with twice the cruelty, and then concocts some noble cause. All the great fandangle of law and priest and soldiery is but the great beasts taking from the small, and making them fawn while they do. Darkness? Me? I'm just a bold and honest beast, a jackal making his way in a forest of wolves and rabbits.

Honest, says Sujata. She sounds the word expressionlessly, leaves a pause, then she makes it a question.

Honest? Some jackal, running a short track to suicide. You know they'll kill you, and soon (again the wife mouths words) – when the kingsmen come for Tark and find the mess you've made they'll trawl a net that even you won't swim through. Then pray to the Dark One they don't take you alive. Clever beast? What jackal chases its own death? Only one rabid, demon-possessed. Have you seen? – hedgehogged with arrows and still mad for blood.

Possessed – The Nameless One owns you, cossets you, begs you luck from the Fates. You do her will, which is to bring all to nothing. This is *your* will, she tells you, worship your will. And she smiles at your obedience, and she'll smile again at your death.

Golo shrugs a shoulder, insouciantly but not falsely so.

If I'm a rabid jackal then fine. If this is possession let me recommend it. My life is a joy to me. I do as I please – or so I imagine, and what I please is to swirl along under my hat like a twig in a stream, with no past and no future beyond the few yards that lie within my sight. If I'm in the hand of The Nameless One, fine. How would I even know? It's all a joy to me.

Sujata holds her gaze. She smiles a slow puzzled smile, shifting her inquiry from one of his eyes to the other, trying to see in.

Don't you fear Hell?

I fear nothing that's not in front of me, and little that is.

He detaches at last from their locked gaze to look sidewards. Then returns:

Crone, we're imposing on the patience of our hosts. You should be the one to keep note of these things.

Sujata smiles, a warm smile edged with melancholy. She turns to the silent, watching fisher couple, and deepens her smile, not speaking. Then she reaches a stiff age-quivery hand very gently and strokes twice or thrice the head of the sleeping child.

Where the low-laden barque wallowed and toiled downriver the canoe, four-fifths of its weight in the two skinny humans it carries, vees the water sleekly to Golo's tireless paddling. Sometimes he sings, or shouts imprecations, or long boasting litanies of his deeds, as much to the sky and the reeds as to Sujata.

The wife has wrapped bread and cheese for them, and the man a rabbit-skin of mead, and they outpace all news of bandit and crone and sleep next under a tree on a mid-stream isle where the current is quick and the gnats are few. Next morning they reach the marshes, Golo cutting corners and getting jammed, or else bemused in the silent labyrinth, and shouting curses at the gods and working back to the posted channel all the more livened by his fury.

They stop midday at a hamlet on stilts where news is slow to reach the gatherers of reeds and fishers of eel and tench, and they're well fed and questioned about their journey, and Golo gives out lavish fabrications. Sujata keeping silent or answering obliquely, settled in a pragmatic collusion. Again they're given food for the journey; again they sleep discreetly and well fed. Next morning they approach the Second Cataract.

Golo lands by woodland, helps Sujata into cover. Then paddles on warily, close to the bank. Makes a landing.

Chapter 23: Disputations

olo takes off his hat and straps on his half-sword and scabbard and saunters along the wharf to see what's going on. Commotion, a sense of large-scale mess. Heaps of offloaded commodities in burden-sized baskets lie as if discarded. A barge has just cast off and is labouring back upstream, the scullers dour-faced. Another is battening and re-masting in preparation.

Ho brothers, what's up? says Golo to a lounging porter.

Nothing either up or down, says the porter. The gods have broken the path. They like to see our children go hungry.

That great thing there, would that belong to the Baron Tark?

I wouldn't know. A big fat noble, his people won't tell his name. He's very keen to travel on, maybe something bigger and fatter comes after him. Or maybe he's just the impatient kind. He carries wonders – his chief thug's the biggest man you ever saw, also he's got a wolf and a boy who live together like brothers.

I bring a new guest to the fat man, I'm sure he'll be grateful.

Have a care. He already seems vexed by his company.
You'd better watch his temper.

He'd better watch mine.

Golo saunters on, more slowly. He has an easy swagger,
not overdone: the torso slightly swayback and braced,
neck and shoulders loose and cocky, head erect. His
eyes are everywhere, very quick under calculative lids.
He sees a man well known to him ahead, trying to calm
a woman whose voice betrays half-swallowed distress.

Ho Errant! What brings *you* here. Have you traded the
road for a softer bed?

And who are you asks Kuzak with practised coolness,
looking Golo up and down.

Ah! You're ...

His hand takes his sword hilt instinctively.

Move your hand off it, Errant, you know I'd kill you,
says Golo patting his blade. Stay with us Lady! – or bid
the bold Kuzak goodbye.

There's too many for you here, Golo. You've come a
long way for nothing.

I've come with the Crone Sujata. She travelled to see
Tark, I gave her carriage. Now I bring her to him, calling
for a token of his gratitude.

I don't believe you. Brought Sujata here – what, did
you fly? You'll burn, Golo, if you've harmed her.

Harmed her? I've given her hospitality, conveyed her
by sedan and by boat, fed her well on the way, made
many landings at her request. She sits in the shade as
we speak, resting from her journey, ready to meet the
Baron her objective.

If you're telling the truth this is kidnap and ransom.

Words Errant, what are words? You have yours and I have mine.

I want to see her.

I'll take the lady.

You will not.

Do you know Sujata, Lady?

More of this and I shout for the Guard, and do what I can till they come.

Golo takes his lip between his teeth and puts one hand on his head in pantomime contemplation.

Okay, he says, suddenly. You, Errant. But the lady comes to the end of the wharf and stays there while you're gone. What's your name, Lady?

My name is Asli. The Baron will be wanting me.

You'll have a good excuse. Did *he* do that?

Golo gestures at the mouse below her eye, gives a contemptuous smile.

I'll need your headscarf for a blindfold, and your girdle-cord to tie good Kuzak's hands. In exchange you'll keep hold of his sword. I'll take his knife. Don't go for help – if I see Tark's bullies when I come back I cut your man's throat.

And Golo canoes the blindfolded Errant upstream, helps him land, directs him through close vegetation with watchful patience, calls out to Sujata who replies, then pushes up Kuzak's blindfold.

Kuzak, open-mouthed, hands tied behind him, bows deeply.

Oh Sujata are you well? Are you *well*? Have you been ill-used? I didn't believe it – surely not even Golo would try such a trick.

As good or bad as ever. A little stiff and gnat-bitten, nothing worse. Well enough fed and attended. What a strange half-month it's been. And how is the wolf-boy and the wolf?

Oh Sujata ...

He shakes his head. Collects himself.

Wolf and boy well enough though in captivity. *Ach* – you've come into a great mess that's all the greater for your arrival. I don't know how much Golo knows ...

An exchange of information, hurried by Kuzak's concern for Asli. Golo makes his claim: a present of valuables, the best, equal in weight to the present he has brought. Where and when to meet for final arrangements, no Baron's man in sight or arrow-range.

Then he paddles Kuzak back to the end of the wharf and watches as he and Asli return to the barque, Kuzak striding, Asli now and then trotting three or four paces.

For boy and wolf the sun has set three times since the boat became mysteriously still, has set on the semi-translucent awning of cast-over sail, and the skirting of light has thrice eased down through deeper and darker greys till their little world, the foetid cage and its margin of angled space, is blacker than a starless night, and the waves of air that slide in under the skirting have thrice grown cool and then cold so the boy shifts close to the warmth of the wolf and the wolf to the boy.

At first there were shouts from boat to shore and throught he gap he could see the platformed wharf and the legs of unfamiliar men and then familiar ones, and the voices rose in dramatic pitch and then came the voice of the Baron booming exasperation and blame.

Through the first night voices on the boat, a bumpy gravel of voices with sudden upbursts from Tark, curses and imprecations, Asli's persuasive reasoning when an outburst subsided. Under the awning the cold of the night holds through the fore-stretch of dawn. Then the heat comes slowly through the muted light, and the barque rocks with traffic on and off, a deeper duck and lift when the giant disembarks. Voices, in a steady consternation.

The second night, the second day. Deep uneasy lowing of oxen dragging past, breaking to falsetto, stamping, the creaking of harness, a man shouting, the hiss and thump of a heavy whip, the beast heaves forward again. Tappety footsteps, furtive voices: *Wolf!* someone exclaims, *Wolf!* – the word now familiar but the accent new. Tark's voice, swell and fall of rage, Asli's with its strained-jaunty practicality, that the boy can feel is needling the Baron – he barely hears the blow when it comes but Asli's cry of hurt and shock, swallowed incomplete as she grabs back her composure, will stay with Peterkin like an aftertaste – though his concern skins over quickly with a factitious indifference.

When dusk comes on they lift the the riverward side of the awning. The cage door, now kept chained, is opened, and the wolf comes out and defecates and leg-cocks against the balustrade, and Peterkin clears up and swabs; and then Kuzak brings food and a vessel of water and watches them eat together on the starboard aftdeck and says a few clipped words before the bowman guard on the wharf snaps a command and they're gestured back in the cage. Peterkin doesn't try to reply but feels no ill towards Kuzak, his dry efficient composure seems to offer resentment no purchase.

The third day he hears the name Sujata spoken, by Asli coming onto the boat. Tark seemingly furious with her and then his anger flattening out in the face of some new quandary. Also the name Golo, which means nothing to him.

Soon after this he hears the voices of Kuzak and Tark in dissent.

Trap him.

But ...

Trap him I say are you deaf? I say trap him. What is he but a back-country chancer? From the Province with the feeblest, most bribe-happy Guard – anywhere else he'd be dead by now, bones in a gibbet, bones in a gibbet. A chancer, a fool – who but a fool would do as he's done, all those miles of heat and swamp, putting the Crone through it all, nothing but a bone-bag and ninety-nine wrinkles, lucky she didn't die on him. Trap the cocky fool, show unwilling and then give way with reluctance, child's play – how can he pick up his booty without coming near? We've got the best bow in Maul Province, pin that silly hat to his head from a hundred yards. Or *let* him collect, he's toiling upriver the archer hid on the shore, picking his teeth till our laddybuck sweats by, open target, Easy, easy. Trap the fool.

Have you *dealt* with Golo, at all?

Never seen the little chap, hear of his reputation with the peasantry, he's never dared cross *me.*

He's sure dared now. We've chased him around for years, lost three good men and killed but one of his. He can hide in an open field, outrun the best, slip by a guard and cut a sleeper's throat then away and no-one knows till morning. Don't underrate him Sir, please. I've not seen his like in thirty years an Errant.

Know him well d'you.

Never spoken a word until today, but we knew each other well enough by sight. What you see in action stays with you.

How are you going to trap him then, Errant? You sort it out – I'm occupied with thinking up ways to vanish, myself and a boatload of trinkets and a tiresome but essential wolf. Vanish, and reappear on a lean two-master sailing out of Lix, into the gods know what future. You fix it, Errant, you're close to the Crone. Why was she coming to me? D'you believe it?

Yes. Sujata wants you to free the wolf and the boy. It's why she followed you.

Does she, eh. Does she. Maybe we leave her with the bandit, he'll have his ninety pounds of booty to paddle back up with. Free the wolf? Not my plan that. Not.

An upsurge in Tark, a possession. He raises his fists to the sides of his head – they are heavy, be-ringed, clenched very tight. His face between them pulls back in a kind of rictus, both absurd and fearsome. His voice when it comes is strangulated, a wheeze more than a shout.

What *is* this? What *are* you doing here Errant, what's the game? D'you think I don't know there's some game? Guzzled and swilled for free and gawping about as if there's a smell in your nose. What are you *up* to?

Kuzak looks away and then back. Away with the eye of a glazed professional, back with an eye quite different.

No game, Baron. I took the place of the spy you employed, to bring boy and wolf to your property. There'd be no wolf in the question if I hadn't. I'd have moved on if they'd not been met by a pack of imbeciles. I have no love for the wolf; but I stayed for the sake of the boy, though he thinks me now a fraud.

So you are, I can smell it. What's the *game*, Errant, eh? One shyster to another, c'mon. Tell me or I get my men to ask.

They're out of earshot Baron, trying to bully the path-makers into a miracle. You've only got one way out, I've said it – into the hills and south with what your men can carry, slice down to the village of Drof, send your boatmen ahead to hire a barge, they pick up yourself and the rest with discretion a couple of miles downriver. There's the ghost of an ancient track – an Errant secret – that drops into Lix well east of the falls and the portage steps, arrive at night and sail out in one of your clippers at dawn – never seen by curious eye from here to there. A hard journey, but far your safest choice.

And the wolf?

I think forget the wolf.

The wolf is not to be forgot. I land in the Empire with nothing, do I?

A hundredweight or so of stones and trinkets – not nothing.

Tark hisses a sigh.

Where I mean to go it would be. I have a plan for the wolf and the boy.

Does Peterkin know this plan?

Peterkin? That his name? Why would he need to know?

Kuzak exhales and looks down, gives a small shake of his head.

No wolf, no boy. I lead you from here to the pickup down from Drof, we land well back from the First Cataract portage steps and I lead you down and through Lix. With as many of your men as you please, or as few. I suggest your boatmen take the barge back up, as if they've completed their business, which they will have.

That's pretty much the stuff I've heard before. Why no wolf? We could tie the thing up, bind its jaws, take it through Lix in a sack – no?

No wolf. Sujata wants them free, the wolf and the boy. And so do I.

Tark's calculative mind stepped out from his first burst of rage, to run its quick fingers over the modified scheme, even warming to it. But no – unthinkable without the wolf. All his life he's enlarged in wealth and prestige, and now on the lip of ruination this chance to slip through the teeth of Fate into a greater world still. The wolf – he knows how the eyes of the child most spoilt in all the world will stretch and her lip will drop in astoundment to see the boy come into court

287

with the creature on a halter, the boy in smart-turned palace-slave dress to show that they're hers already. To Tark the scene's the golden nub of a secret reality, how can he let it go? He worships two gods only, Destiny and the Sun, and both have shone on him all his days – why not still? His rage returns, a steadier upsurge now, filling his barrel chest, his short wide thrusting neck and heavy face, his half-mad stare.

The wolf comes. By *Hell* the wolf comes. Thanks for the plan, now you go drown yourself and take the Crone with you, I'll get a local to guide us. Get out of my sight, get *out*.

With pleasure, Tark. I'll take my pack from the hold – I won't be coming back. I won't wish you luck.

Tark calls out a servant.

Take this fool to get his belongings. See he steals nothing.

Chapter 24: A Change of Direction

uzak has had a plan all along. He'd take action on leaving the boat, but Tark's three stalwarts are coming back down the wharf. One makes a sarcastic greeting, Ruslan and the other are silent. He nods an inch in passing, toting his satchel, face blank and eyes distant.

He walks to the top of the severed stair-path and speaks with three workers relieved by an incoming shift, sweat-runneled and giving off a dead-eyed taciturnity. They soften when he taps his satchel and says that he too has been relieved of his duties, but permanently, the Baron having no longer the need of an Errant – he shows his ring. The four sit and talk, Kuzak sharing biscuit, pemmican, tributary water, assuming their own flasks are filled from the river.

They tell him that two full days lie between this hot afternoon and a useable stairway, that a seer has foretold that the big man might slip for the unlucky size of his feet and fall into the cataract, whose welcome baulks at no physical limit, and that his two comrades might, in impetuous rescue, follow him soon after. They know there is a wolf on the barque – sneak peerings prompted by the jerking of the oxen, usually of near-comatose biddability. They guess Tark is fleeing but they don't know why or who from. They'll live out this next few days and keep themselves safe in their work, and then move on to less turmoiled times and long after tell the stories.

Kuzak fingers an inner pouch in his satchel and filches out three stones, one at a time. Emeralds, the size of split peas. His words are formulaic: Would that in praise to the God of Gifts your womenfolk might find some use for these. Bows – just head-nods – are exchanged as he hands them the stones. They speak the correlative words of thanks, holding back their astonishment and joy. Once the stones are well knotted into their garments he asks as if in afterthought how passable, do they know, are the back-country tracks hereabouts. Not bad, they say – some fallen trees, the bear-hunters keep them clear enough.

Kuzak bows his farewell. They offer him food and a pallet, being now unroofed, but he demurs the lodging. Though bread and curd to carry would be welcome, or stockfish. When I pass, if I do, with or without companions, few or several.

Soon after Kuzak secretes his satchel and climbs the rising land to an outcrop to look about as he thinks. The numbing complications – ach, the blundering of thought. The seductive pull of some *this is how it will be*, while all the other futures slip by, smirking like thieves in the shadows.

Golo will come. That's been arranged, at their meeting. He might leave Sujata in the hideout – a quarter mile upriver, Kuzak guesses from his blindfold journey; or he might bring her nearer; or – it would be like him –

he might have her in the canoe, shouting his demands, perhaps with a blade at her throat.

And Golo has to die. There's no path ahead with place for a living Golo, not now that Tark has valued the life of the Holy One below any dent in his wealth and his name. Pray that Tark's bowman can pick him off, but Golo has dodged so many arrows that even the wise think him armoured with spells, to demon or the Devil himself or (whisper it) The Nameless One. He has to die, and who knows how it might come, and whether might Kuzak be called on for the doing. He has to die and he will, at last, for he's overreached so wildly that he's surely seeking death. To kidnap a Holy Crone, ransack the house of a King-ennobled Baron, then swagger outrageous demands in his face – he must want to leave this world, now at the crest of his fury, not sink into age as a has-been, holed up in some paranoid cave.

Golo has to die, Sujata must be freed. I need to stay alive myself if she's still in the hideaway, or else she'll surely starve there.

And the boy and the wolf. So much easier, to filch them out of it all, if it weren't for Sujata.

See it. Golo appears, he's told no deal. Me, I tell him. He goes to call on Tark – from the wharf? From out in the river? He waits for the night, sneaks onto the barque? He has Sujata with him: he doesn't? The men are set on him – he runs, and maybe comes back with her head?

No, I must wait to feel the unfolding. Let the future decide itself – it holds so many ifs and if-nots, it's a wonder it can play itself out and never trip over its feet. Watch for your cue, that's all; keep your eyes peeled. Action will call you, and when he does take the moment, and leave all else behind.

So he sat, shielding with his left hand the sun of mid-afternoon, looking down on the scene. The long wharf, four barges only, near the front – word has gone upriver, by punt and leather canoe, to hold back, find a village tavern to sit out the delay. Then at a distance the barque, still awned with the sail to aft, the wolf and the boy in their shaded half-life beneath it. The back third of the wharf is empty – at the far end, on Kuzak's right, will Golo appear (somehow) to hear Tark's decision. Further right still the tree-crowded hills slope down to the water; somewhere their impassable tangle secretes the bandit and Crone. To his left the great river pulls in its sides and hurries to its plunge, a roaring six hundred foot drop in the length of a quarter mile. A boom pier at the cataract end of the wharf hopes to catch any barge that breaks mooring. Across the river tranquil low hills, civilly pieced out and farmed. Behind him begin the foothills to the mountains, trees climbing up to the last inch they can reach, the skyline peaks a god-world of spikes and ice.

Looking south and leftward, the land on this side of the river rises to a shouldery buttress. Somewhere up and beyond it sits the Errant House he will aim for, the very one he first found in the bitter snows of an earlier life.

He soft-chants a prayer, then comes back down to the wharf.

Tark also has a plan, a new one. He and Damla – disappeared, presumed dead. The barque having slipped its moorings in the night – suspicion will fall on the bullied porters. Slipped its moorings and lost to the cataract – to add to its roaring mausoleum, the bones and boat-spars jammed in its crevices, the centuries of unwary enterprise. Gone – he and his pretty young wife and his boatload of wealth – the mortals to carrion-fish it's supposed, the wealth to vulturine looters from far and near (by chance he once watched it happen – the short-strawed of the gang lowered on leather ropes to prise out boulder-jammed knick-knacks in the torrent's slippery deafening slingshot-spumed margin).

Gone, and needing no further explanation. His entourage luckily ashore, billeted to wait out the repairs. Boy and wolf? Who knows? Vanished too, in the cataract or by previous escape, either way unobserved. (In fact gone into the hills, accompanied by Tark's two normal-sized stalwarts, to watch the boy day and night and bring back the pair at a time to be determined, when the dust will have settled and all hue and cry died down.)

But the actual Tark? Damla? His treasure? Lying low in a house – at least two candidates, skeleton-staffed for merchants with itinerant dealings, for many years the Baron was one himself. Arranged by Asli, housing for herself and the staff, the Baron and Baroness to slink in at dead of night, and maybe a couple of hundredweight of the choicest valuables, the rest to go down with the boat, to attract authenticating pillage.

All this to be done tonight. The nobles in due course to make their way discreetly to Lix and the Empire, wolf and boy inveigled as earlier planned.

Yes.

Golo when he feels the time has come helps (in fact lifts) Sujata into the landed canoe, then deadlifts the end her and all and waddles it into the water. They slip warily downstream. Fifty yards short of the upriver end of the wharf the willow and alder thickets give way to open shore. He beaches at the last decent cover and helps out the Crone and leaves her the last of their food, along with a skin of water.

Well then Old One. This might be farewell or it might not. If no-one comes for you by the time the sun has passed yon crest – he point across the river – just shout and they'll hear you, or else pick your way to the wharf and along – you won't miss the Baron's boat. You might not find me in Heaven. Good luck with this wolf-boy.

Sujata says nothing. One last time their gazes meet, each with a question that has no home in words, each with perhaps a quarter-smile. Then he turns and goes.

Kuzak is watching for him, but Golo sees Kuzak first.

Ho Errant. Do you bring my fee?

No Golo, no fee. The Baron was very clear on the point.

Did you say if it doesn't appear by dark I'll come by and take it?

I don't believe I said the words. The conversation was tense, and ended abruptly.

D'you think he cares what happens to the Crone?

294

Not at the moment. He has other worries. Maybe he'll later be twinged with guilt if she fares ill. If he has any later. But for now, no – his only thought is escape, not be dragged before the King. Make it to Lix then flee to the Empire. But *Sujata*, Golo – I take it the hint of threat is in the abstract? She seems well enough for the journey you put her through – do her no harm now.

You threaten me Errant? She came to see Tark, I've brought her to Tark. No, *I* won't harm her. She's one of the few I've ever met who don't deserve the edge of a blade. Not like you, with that little servant's beard, that cabbage-stalk righteousness.

He half-laughs.

Nothing personal, Errant – don't get me wrong. If I kill you it won't be personal. Destiny, just Destiny. So go tell this to Tark ...

We're not speaking.

You'll speak once more, or get someone else to. Tell him – see yon flat-top rock? – tell him to carry the Crone's weight of treasure, in a bag or chest a man can lift, and set it down there. Then his men retreat – I'll be watching – and stay where I can see them. No bow or thegame's off. I'll come and check the stuff, if it's good I'll say where the Crone is, beyond the end of the wharf. Asli can come and check; his bullies stay distant and keep in view. The canoe is right by, I load up, no-one else moves. Then I'm gone.

I'll do it, Golo, but don't be rejoicing just yet. He'll say go to Hell – what then?

Don't say I'll harm the Crone and don't say I won't. If he mentions Hell say he'll be there himself before tomorrow sunrise.

The better of the merchants' houses is a quarter-mile in from the wharf, in line with a nick in the great southern buttress that lets the sun finds it mid-morning. Asli is sent with a purse of persuasive stones, to request etcetera of the housekeeper, a birchslat to the owner in Lix that they'll be on their way as soon as the path is repaired. She's returning with the acceptance when Kuzak meets her on the path. She's hurried, preoccupied; he walks with her and tells her Golo's demands. She passes these on to Tark with diffidence; he says he's heard it already, don't dare waste more time on nonsense, a prize for her if she makes all this work, a sore reward if she doesn't.

Much coming and going from barque to merchant house. Tark's people are briefed to reply to questioners – the Baron requires some privacy, he'll remain on the barque till the stepway is fixed, with a guard and the Third Baroness.

The overheated day slides into evening, the sun enormous in the north-west. The heat of the air takes a skin of delectable coolness. The move has been made, and all are well enough settled.

Sujata sits alone in a steady whine of gnats, whispering prayers.

Asli does what she can with Peterkin's meagre Megharan to tell him what's coming, makes brief introductions of the swordsman and the bowman who will accompany him and the wolf into the hills by a village-avoiding route, the bowman to take Peterkin's bow and knife. The boy and the wolf to take their leisure along with these guardsman companions until their journey can recommence.

Tark goes over his plan with Damla and Ruslan. The nobles to disembark in the pit of the night and wait ashore while Ruslan unhawsers the barque, tugs it by a rowboat attached to its prow, till the midstream current is sure to carry it past the safety boom, there to let it go. Then the three with guidance to softfoot to their new abode.

How well all this might have gone is a question no turn of the world will answer, for Golo had other ideas.

He had indicated to Kuzak the crest in the land, on the far cross-river skyline a good way north of west, that the sun must not pass before his fee is delivered. He knows there's little chance of this sub-clause reaching Tark, and none at all of Tark paying it mind if it does, except perhaps to try and trap him, or fob him off with a satchel of nonsense; but he keeps to the precision of his terms. When the fat sun slides its under-curve a smidgeon past the distant point he ups and slips invisibly into the tangled wood behind him.

He moves uphill quickly, ducking and sidling through

stems, high-stepping the close-woven undergrowth, his body quick-rhythmed behind his razor attention. He comes out more or less where he expected, looking down over croft-fields, habitations, the river and the wharf, the place where the funnelled water bends and disappears as if at the edge of the world. Its roar domineers all other sound, you can barely hear the wind-rustled trees.

Below him he sees Kuzak watching too. They watch together, a distance apart and Kuzak unwitting, each with his steady attention.

Then Sujata appears in the failing light, picking her way to the wharf-end. Precarious among the tussocks, heavy on her staff. Kuzak is instantly up and trotting downhill, jinking with the terrain.

He catches Sujata and links arms with her to the barque, and he stands to one side as she pounds with her staff on the gangplank and sings out the Baron Tark's name and all she can recall of his honorifics. There is a delay. She's about to pound again when Asli appears. Her manner is composed, with its usual well-grooved ease and smile, but even without the bruise to her eye Sujata would read desperation, scuttling within like something cornered.

Asli has been told to fob the Crone off, get her out of sight and earshot. She speaks of the Baron's demanding concerns, of the move to a more comfortable place, she might go there and sleep tonight on a feather bed, the Baron will meet with her in the settled space of the morning. It's but a quarter mile; we'll find a sedan, or else two men will carry her there cross-armed. Sujata would hold her ground, but she hears the note of pleading that Asli tries to keep out of her voice and nods a small bow of concurrence.

I go Asli, the Errant will guide me – he must know the way, he knows everything. But first I speak with your passenger, the wolf boy. I bid you take care, Madam, in uneasy times.

Asli bows with formality. As she turns she glances at Kuzak, their eyes momentarily meet – she sees great anger, quickly flits away.

Sujata has guessed where the wolf is, guesses the boy is there too.

Peterkin? You hear me I think. Sujata. Answer please – are you well?

Peterkin's hardly spoken for days now except to the wolf. His voice is a little off-key when it comes.

Sujata? O Mistress. I okay. I tired this place.

The wolf?

Wolf okay. He tired this place very more.

I'll try to help. Yes? Make things better. I'll try.

You care, care. Is bad people. You care.

Okay, I'll take care. I go now. I'll try to help, okay. I go.

Farewell Mistress, you care please.

Sujata is already on her way when Tark's second and third guards appear with the pieces of a light sedan which they start to construct, bidding her to wait. But she waves them back and carries on, Kuzak taking one arm, heavy on her staff with the other.

Chapter 25: Ask the River

ark curses to hear that Kuzak is still around and involving himself, but shrugs him off and Sujata too as trivial irritations. He gathers Asli and the three guards to repeat the plan. Damla sits at his side.

All except he, Damla and guards to be placed in the merchant house by full dark. Asli included.

The boy and the wolf to leave the barque with the two lesser guards in the early night, as soon as nearby locals are settled in their domiciles – the wolf to run free, the boy attached by a leash to the swordsman, Asli having affirmed that the wolf will stay as near to the boy as if they were brothers. This party to make a wide circuit up and into the wooded hills above. One guard to come to the merchant house next morning when all is settled, the other to live up there with the boy, who remains restrained and weaponless. Food brought up for boy and guard twice each quarter-month, the wolf to fend for itself. The guards to change over at each second food supply. All to continue till further instructions are given, these entailing a guided route through the hills to meet the main party below the cataract. Party by then stripped down to key personnel.

A rowboat has been acquired and discreetly attached to the barque's prow.

Asli now to head to the merchant house, to see that all is well and the nobles' hideaway prepared. When she leaves the gangplank to be raised. Just three now aboard: Tark and Damla to retire, Ruslan to sit by the hatchway, to welcome Golo or any other intruder.

A long wait later, when the moon lifts above the skyline at the midpoint of the night, Asli to return to the barque with a male servant. She to alert Ruslan. The gangplank then replaced, the Baron and Baroness leave the boat, the servant keeps check no locals are astir.

Ruslan then to cut free the now-vacated barque and tow it out and set it adrift, then scull back and re-moor the rowboat. The servant having detected no stumbler to midnight latrine or other insomniac, all soft-foot in darkness to the safe house, Ruslan sword-drawn at the rear.

Early next morning the alarm is to be raised. O, the Baron, his beautiful wife! Who has done this? Golo, Golo was here, the mooring is cut, it was Golo!

And Golo indeed was there, keeping watch. A wolf comes quartering up the hill in the dusk, sniffing and leg-cocking – he draws his blade but it sees him and jerks and detours. Behind a boy and two guards, the boy on a line like a market goat – he shrinks into cover, they pass him unseeing.

When they're by he slips down, taking care as the darkness thickens, bare-footed and feeling out each step. In time he comes to the stony and pot-holed draw-road alongside the wharf. He continues with great care, each foot questions the ground before it settles. Ahead a murmur of voices within the sound-wash of the cataract, a big-sounding man and a woman. Two horn candle-lanterns. One lantern moves away and heads inland, the other jerks and blinks as it rises onto the boat. He sees in silhouette and by momentary lamplit surfaces that it's Tark and the giant who board, Asli who heads inland. He thinks to follow and question her, then not. A single scream will spoil his strategy.

He comes closer, moving more slowly. Asli's lamp is a firefly, jinking uphill; then almost nothing; then nothing. Creaks and a thud as the boarding plank is hauled up and latched. The lantern on the boat blinks in and out of view with the sound of heavy feet on the planks; a momentary woman's voice, the lamp disappears all but a glow, then a hatch slides and clunks and the glow too is gone. Heavier feet: Ruslan feels his way, the thin slick sound as he draws his sword, the whump of his weight as he sits with his back to the hatch.

Golo means to board the boat and cut the big man's throat. And then surprise the Baron. The wife? It offends him a little to kill a woman (he's only done it once, a harridan screaming curses across the body of her man, he told her twice to be quiet). But let them die together, fall into Hell in each other's arms. Yes.

Now his pace is that of a stalking mantis. By inches he reaches the barque, by inches moves alongside it, feeling out its possibilities. It's a starry night, a gleam of the soon-to-rise moon delines the distant skyline. He comes up level with the prow – no boarding point here, he's about to turn back – when he sees the rowboat, a deeper-grey shape that slowly articulates to his gaze. And oars? Oars. A drooping towrope. Some need for tricky re-location perhaps. He looks at the grey rowboat, its pale oars, the businesslike towrope attaching it to the barque. He has an idea. Let them die in each other's arms – let it not be said that Golo lacks human kindness. No.

A mooring cleat either side of the boarding point, by each a thick fender of crocheted rope. First he must kill the giant, if possible use his body to block the hatchway. He crouches by the aft-ward fender and waits a long time, listening. He needs to be sure just where the giant is, absolutely sure. Slowly and by degrees, blending into the cataract, the soft half-snore of the big man's breath. A sudden *huh*, a grunt of small shock, he has caught himself. You can hear the great big hands rubbing the great big face. Then no sound. Then thrice in quick succession the unvoiced letter *p*. Then a husky throat-breath. Then the breath steadies – steadies. The giant is asleep.

Golo moves. His right-foot toes poke into the fender for purchase, he reaches high on the fender's drop-rope, gives it his weight by tiny degrees, lifts himself as smoothly as if he is growing. A silent hand on top of the balustrade, the other beside it. He knows that here a slice of the big man's sword would cut off all eight of his over-curled fingers; he makes himself take his time. An easy mantleshelf move, very slow; a slow astriding leg; he eases down by quarter-inches; his foot is on the deck, it fills with his weight like a slow-filling vessel. Ease, ease, no smurr of sound as he parts from the balustrade, begins his approach. Draws by small and smooth degrees the half-sword that is strapped to the side of his thigh.

The giant is snoring, his head lolled forward. Golo thinks the anatomy – hindrance of the bear-like spine, the musculature. Stab for the carotid, saw through the windpipe. Stab, then saw.

Now.

Asli returns with the rising moon at her back and she can't understand what she sees. The barque has vanished. Did they decide to do the deed early? The manservant, clomping at her side, is too tired to be nonplussed.

Now closer – where *are* they? Ruslan, okay – but is *Tark* out there? She hears excited voices. *Damla?* Why? Only then does she see the boat, faintly in the moonglade, way out in mid- river. Shouts, much louder, the Baron's voice bawling, a frantic edge. Then Damla screaming and screaming.

The rowboat hauling the barque was hidden, but now it swings round and points upriver. Movement on it. Barque and rowboat are being sucked downstream. Then – more lurching movement – it seems they separate. The barque is sliding quickly now on the moongladed sheen of the river. The rowboat is sliding too, with a fierce splashing of oars that looks inefficient even from here.

Asli watches with her mouth wide open as the barque slides faster and faster towards the funnelling mouth of the cataract. Past the boom now, utterly doomed. A small scream escapes her and her hands grip her face.

Sliding out of vision, gone. Suddenly and completely gone, wiped from sight as if it had never been.

The rowboat no longer struggles side-on to the current, aiming for the wharf. It's trying to use the flow to slice a diagonal to the safety boom. It surely can't make it. The oars flap as wildly as a foot-trapped bird. Then – is it there? No. The nose of the rowboat dunts the very tip of the boom and it spins tail-about and is slipping after the barque.

Asli takes her hands away from her face and holds them palms-upward as if in appeal. Then, like a dose of hiccups, snorts of laughter start to rise in her. She tries to stop them, she can't. She has to let go, doubling up in her diaphragm's sudden brute glee.

The dope beside her stands shaking his head, staring out at the emptily sliding river as if he hopes to see it all again.

Golo half-stands in the rowboat and looks for somewhere to jump but there's nowhere to jump. He's hurtling now, the boat on the glassy water a skim-stone on ice. This simply hadn't occurred to him – he'd thought Death would come by sword or by noose or by fire. The water ahead rears up in a barging of great glassy pythons, fighting to leap first over the void.

He screams a long scream from a rictus face, of terror and exultation. Then there is no up or down, in this war of the water-gods; his howl or scream blips out in the immensity of sound.

Part 4: The Errant House

Chapter 26: You Have to Laugh

he river doesn't know what it's done. Its serenity is undinted, just the moonglade's morsel of turbulence out at midstream where transverse ribs take form as the water gains speed. What is more innocent, than a river. Even the cataract's gigantic hiss, is innocent.

Asli's astoundment is not increased when she hears Kuzak's voice at her side. Her mind hasn't found its footing yet, anyone could be anywhere. The thing is she knows where Tark is. Gone. Gone – his goneness fills the universe.

... Golo in the rowboat, Kuzak's saying. The gods are on a rampage. We need to think what next.

She takes his arm, laughing. It's wary and stiff to her boldness even in this extremity.

Mother of All, you're as dry as last year's stockfish. I'm for a drink. Let's see what the fat man put aside for himself.

Shame on you woman, to speak so of the dead, before the gods have even weighed his soul. He can't supress a sniff of laughter.

You're right, old man. We need to make plans.

She tightens her hold on his arm and turns them both away from the river, uphill towards the merchant house. Over a drink.

Kuzak has watched – hidden in brush on the rise of the land, knowing that Golo would come. When the two guardsmen head off with the boy he knows that Tark is underprotected: Ruslan alone is no match for Golo – an entertaining challenge, no more.

Golo as he slips along the wharf is almost invisible, a shadow in shadows, moving so slowly and smoothly you keep losing him. In his slow climb onto the boat he disappears altogether; Kuzak suddenly has the idea he's picked up his presence, is circuiting up and around, to drop on him from behind. The ants of fear are crawling on his back, he has to hold onto himself to keep from bolting.

Then the bandit's head rises up in silhouette, then he's over the balustrade and inching towards the giant.

His rowing was flappily inept, the only thing Kuzak's ever seen him do poorly. But with his absurd strength the barque still moved, creeping very slowly out and out. When it reached midstream it swung downstream in a sudden hurry. Golo unhawsered too slowly, reading the river as if he was in a canoe.

So it all was. Then came Asli, and her slow-witted companion.

A lot to think about. He needs to take some control.

Now he and Asli are climbing the path arm in arm. It feels strangely ordinary, in the dark, on the lumpy path.

I do this, she says, sorry. Disasters, sudden death – I can't help laughing. I *know*, *sorry*. It's that wonderful contrast, between the plan and the outcome. I can read your mind: *jackalbitch*, barking her good luck. True I suppose. That ridiculous boat sliding away, like a fat old duchess on an icy slope. Even the bawling and screaming, you kind of have to laugh. I'm sure he died blaming me. You think I'm a jackalbitch don't you. C'mo*n*, don't give me one of those terse unforthcomings, you *do*.

The truth?

Yeah.

I wasn't thinking about you at all. I was thinking how lucky all this has been.

Kuzak recites an ancient prayer of gratitude to Fate, entirely without embarrassment.

And I'm caught in that strange muddle, of relief and unease, that comes when you've wound yourself up for a fight that doesn't happen. I was going to try and kill Golo. Ambush him, as he strutted back victorious, maybe to go to the house and demand his ransom – Sujata's weight in stones and gold, he'd have bribed the whole of Maul Province with that. Full pardon and all. I didn't give myself better than fifty-fifty, even with a surprise attack from behind. So I'm all a-jangle, Asli Jackalbitch. Your laughter makes as much sense as anything else.

Surprisingly self-knowing, Kuzak of the tight-set teeth. I'm amazed – that you have such feelings at all, let alone that you know about them. I'll have to amend my judgement.

Oh, it's all in basic training – how you're going to feel, if and when.

With this cone of deep-night no-rules candour about to end – they've almost reached the merchant house, the servant a little ahead – she slips her arm and reaches around him, presses her hand confidingly on his side, feeling surprise through the cloth, the tough warm cage of ribs.

Careful with your hands, Madam – I must hold focus, an Errant's course.

A silence. She presses again, with a threat of digging-in fingers.

For now, anyway.

The servant has opened the door. Firelight but no sound of voices. A last squeeze on Kuzak's arm as she whispers.

Mother, what a night of surprises.

They rouse the house. Kinds of the abruptly woken – some instantly alert, some dragging up from depths of gormlessness. Oil lamps are lit, thick shadow boundaries their muted light. Kuzak and Asli wait till all are gathered – Asli peers into the room, poking the air as she mouths a count.

And they tell the story as well as they know it, taking informal turns. Wailing breaks out, of a largely obligatory kind; it soon dips in volume, to not interfere with the telling.

Can we be sure that Golo's dead? asks Sujata.

Just about completely sure, says Kuzak.

Just about?

I know the cataract – it's in our training. Walked and scrambled as near the edge as I dared, both sides. Nothing you could get any kind of grip on, to climb out, once you're past the boom, not even Golo. And not even Golo could live through the drop and the torrent below.

So what do we all do now? says Asli. She's poured herself a large beaker of applejack from which she takes quick sips. Ten of us in this room, plus two guards on the hill with no idea what's happened. Plus the boy and the wolf. The kingsmen could be here tomorrow – Tark was afraid they would be. With the Enquirers in tow.

One plan, says Kuzak – just tell them the truth, they've got no reason to doubt us, given the evidence. Tell them everything. Show them the back-cellar room with the hidden door where they planned to hide up with their riches. Show them just what – don't try and take any.

Not me, says Asli. I'm making a run for it. No idea where, but I've got stones and I can do disguises. I'm too tied in with the Baron – the Enquirers'll turn me inside out. I suggest the rest of you run as well. Karaman can't get Tark now, but he can surely get us. Consolation prize. An Errant too, to tickle his paranoia.

(It's said the Enquirers employ their discourse enhancement techniques with no more than half of their interviewees. But Asli knows which half she'd be in. She wants to be long gone when they arrive. Gone into the wide domain of anywhere but here.

In that domain she – rightly – assumes her talents will get her by. Anywhere – she has no sentimental nest, still warm with the associations of girlhood. A joyless and embittered stepmother, sinking into a dotage of well-deserved isolation; two half-sisters, both married to buffoons, and anyway she was up and gone when they were still children, she hardly knows them.)

So: ten; twelve with the guardsmen, thirteen the boy. Thirteen plus a wolf – good luck or bad? The guards can shift for themselves – eleven. Kuzak has plans for boy and wolf – presumably also his good self – am I right? Nine, the rest of us. What road can the rest of us take? Over to our fine Errant, he knows every rabbit track in the kingdom.

Kuzak takes a more central position, very upright.

We Errants are taught to look for the simplest answer, the one with the fewest sub-clauses, side-tracks. The Baron was fleeing Karaman's wrath. Let's not be the consolation prize (he half-lifts a hand towards Asli), for him or for his soldiers. I recommend we all go as one, at first light, before the kingsmen come. I'll leave you for a while, to find the boy and the wolf. Then we circuit high, above the broken stairway – can't even think about waiting till it's fixed. All (if none disagree) head over the pass on the mountain spur that drops to the cataract. After the pass two choices: take the high track to an Errant House; or angle down to Drof three miles below the falls, where the Baron's ex-boatmen rent a vessel and pick up the others discreetly, and all down to Lix to meld into its streets as have so many, some stipendiary items from the Baron's estate to help things along.

Decide, if you're coming or staying. If you're coming, pray to Fate. If you're staying pray three times over.

Then have a sup of the Baron's liquor to help you get back to sleep.

As the company breaks into fragmented debate, Kuzak suggests to Sujata they speak discreetly. He catches Asli's eye, tilts his head towards a shadowy corner, gives an arm to Sujata to help her up.

Chapter 27: Into the Hills

eterkin had been in the cage for all of the past day, baking under the awning, boredom and a slow sick dread taking turns in him. He's heard the Baron's exasperation through the wall of the cabin, shouts and sputtered threats all the more fearsome for being incomprehensible. Then some sort of conference, the Baron's voice gruff but now controlled; then suddenly they're pulling back the awning, it's early evening, the bowman guard slips the bolt of the cage and gestures him out, re-bolts the cage.

The man slaps his chest stiff-handedly and says the word Sark. He wants Peterkin's bow and quiver, knife too – he's not been told he should leave them here, and they look too good to waste. He shunts Peterkin face-on to the cabin, and winds a long cord around him complicatedly to make a cross-chest shoulder harness. He feeds the long tail of the cord through his own belt. The wolf is hackled and snarling in the cage.

Again the bowman slips the bolt and steps well back. He makes a repeated flapping move, indicating the wolf.

Wolf go, he says, *wolf go*.

The wolf is hackled up, ears back and tail under, every tooth bared in its snarl. The bowman backs round the cabin, keeping a hold on Peterkin's leash, drawing his short-sword with the other hand. Now the wolf can't see him. Peterkin thinks he's surely got it wrong – they want him to free the *wolf*? He tries to check – he repeats *wolf go?* and mimics the flapping gesture, then lifts his questioning arm to the rising terrain.

Yes says the man *yes yes*, wolf go.

It takes a while for the boy to inveigle the wolf from the cage. He finger-lip gestures silence to the bowman, but even so it takes a while.

Then he comes from the cage, ears still down, wary. The bowman guard gives Peterkin leash enough to lead him by the wharf-side of the cabin to the gangplank. A quick skiddy descent and he skitters oddly on the wharf, dancing to one side and then the other. Then suddenly he gets it, and trots onto the wharfside roadway and runs away from the barque on the roadway, and then he swerves off and away uphill in a sudden re-accrual of animal zest.

Follow, says the bowman, now by Peterkin's side, gesturing. The swordsman guard has joined them. We go too – Sark too. Kan (he gestures) – Kan too. Then he says, tugging didactically on the leash, each word paired with an indication or mime: You – run – I – shoot. Boy run – Sark – shoot. *Yes?*

His face has a certain humour to it, brutal but not unkind. The other man is laughing.

The wolf doesn't know what has happened and can't wonder. There was one situation and now there is another. A crease between thickets of spike-bush offers an uphill lead, but suddenly there's a crouching man and he skids and detours, carries on up. The two men with the boy already distant below. The prodigious wealth of running in his legs – but there's a drag on it: the boy, he must wait for the boy. He slips to a viewpoint with cover and sleeks down low and stares between his forelegs at the three slow-footed humans, one of whom is the centre of his world.

He hears the owl-call below, hears the breathlessness in it, he pants as he watches, his tail like some ulterior beast thuds a wizened stem as it wags.

It's dark now, fully dark, the moon not risen. They camp at the side of a trickling stream.

Kan and Sark consider how to keep the boy from escaping. They search his satchel, confiscate flint and steel and his spare bowstrings, the improvised wolf-leash. Throw out some nuggets of old twice-baked bread, some half-festered pemmican. They don't come on his little cloth of stones, tied into his one spare garment, given him by Sujata before the visitors came. They re-work his harness so all the knotting's between his shoulder blades. They wind the long tail of the cord round the arched root of a tree so he's only got a six-foot arc of movement, then tie it off at another root well outside his reach. They use a brand to search the region for sharp stones or anything else with an edge. They don't allow him his own fire; theirs is twenty yards off, enough to let him commune with the wolf without it coming too near.

Their fire is anyway only for cooking and for the pleasure in it. A warm night it is. They take hot salt meat to the boy before eating themselves, with unleavened bread and a skin of water. They move away from the fire and watch him by its light, keeping together. What might it do, a wolf in the dark, a wolf in the night? They watch and the boy low-whistles his dusk-owl call, there's a scrabble by the tree where he's tied and both men reach for their hilts. The boy holds out a hand and the long face with its gleam of teeth darts suddenly into view and the meat is taken, another abrasion of claws on shaley ground and it's gone.

Hey boy, calls Sark. Hey boy, you want more meat?

Yes, is good. I thank. No must cook, wolf happy no cook.

You keep an eye on it, okay? Watch wolf, okay? If it comes at me I'll kill it.

No kill, wolf is good, no kill.

Keep an eye then, yeah?

Sark cuts more meat. He could just throw it out into the dark, but he feels somehow called on to carry it to the boy. He has little fear of the wolf by day, with his half-sword at his hip; but in the darkness a sense of it creeping behind him, sudden scuff of clawed feet on shale and the catapulting attack. It's a long twenty yards to the boy. He lays down the meat on the tree root rather than hand it over, so the boy won't feel any tremor.

From the darkness ahead comes the snarl of the wolf and Sark's hand whips to his sword-hilt – but it's almost a relief, to know where it is. The boy is playfully scolding in his strange tongue – is it the language of wolves, is that his trick? Do they speak too, in a way only he can hear? Sark backs off a little and then continues to watch. The wolf comes half into vision in the light of the distant fire: it takes and gulps the meat from the boy's hand, then licks the hand, then licks the boy's face as the boy yelps a laugh, scolding; then rubs against him, and still pressed against him hunkers down at his side. Is he a sort of wolf himself? Part wolf? Brought up by them? The wolf turns its head and looks at Sark with a steady eye and seems to be thinking of snarling again but then decides not to.

Kan would then have talked about Tark's plans and the whores in Lix and what might the Empire be like, but Sark barely grunted in response and Kan cursed him as a bore, an outsider, and Sark called Kan a dullard and an oaf.

Then they agreed to take turns keeping watch in case the boy tried something on, pointless perhaps with Sark guarding solo tomorrow; and Sark said for Kan to sleep first and wished him foul dreams and a visit from The Nameless One. And they settled down, Sark elbows on knees watching and wondering.

Sujata and Kuzak are here by their different routes for Peterkin's sake, bound in with which is the sake of the wolf.

Kuzak already had a plan, when he was half-inveigled onto the barque: to get the boy and his wolf to the Errant House and there make some arrangement. Maybe a satellite location, one of the retreat huts, and a two-way advantageous system of exchange: wild meat – venison, hare, boar, capercaillie, plus berries, acorns, fungi – for bread and cheese and security, and sundry practicalities. He's three-quarters sure the Counsel will assent, if he puts his repute and service behind the appeal.

But Sujata – back to the Hermitage? How? Is it wise to leave her here with the kingsmen coming? Will they even believe who she is? Or pass her as a suspect to the Enquirers? Is it too late to ferry her over the river? Then the long sedan ride north, six or seven stages at least, some stalwart of the acorn people to head-strap her from the ferry to the sanctuary. With her as she is now, ageing so fast. Spirit yet – but oh, so tired, so frail.

First the greys of dawn, and then the world's colours soak back into its surfaces. The ten making ready – one night at least in the open, says Kuzak, prepare for two. Stumbling and fumbling and cursing, but no resistance – no-one wants to be left behind to be asked where the others have gone. Some of Tark's most portable treasure is portioned out – a pound weight for each employee, a morsel compared with what stayed on the boat and what they'll leave in the house, but a great deal more than enough for sensible needs.

And the little multifarious tribe sets off. Kuzak, Asli, the boatmen bearing Sujata in the skeleton sedan retrieved from the wharf; the butler cum factotum and two maids; the cook – a fat man as befits his calling, by no means youthful; a seamstress who matches his age and physique.

There is a track that serves herd and herdsmen first and wayfarers second, dotted with droppings, weaving through boulders and saplings, on runs of loose shale, over flattened tussocks on peat bog. The pace is set by the boatmen who bear the sedan, not quite slow enough for the gasping and perspiring cook. Kuzak fears for him – goes back and tells him to walk within himself, not try to keep up, let the others wait.

They've climbed no more than a few hundred feet when he orders a break. His authority isn't questioned though it's arisen out of nowhere. He'd expected to meet the spare guardsman, coming back down to the house as prescribed by Tark, but the man hasn't appeared. Kuzak means to look for him.

The remaining nine take their ease, the hillside already warm in the sun. From here they can see the river sunglade, a billion incandescent worms, each one swimming south; they can see the gauze of mist above the fall; they can see the wide farmland of hillocks and dells that gently climbs the river's far side, then tilts away southward. Way across the river but it seems slowly approaching – maybe it's an illusion – a small tuft of dust, kicked up on an unseen road. It might not be a troop of men. Maybe a farmer just, shifting his herd.

Kan the swordsman of Tark's guard, after his night on the hill with Sark and the boy and the wolf, having warmed his cold bones in the sun and taken a healthy breakfast, sets off downhill in the trees and quickly mistakes his way. They camped by a stream and he knows he must follow a stream so he follows the one they camped by. If he'd slanted south and west he'd have come on the right one, running down to the settlement and the merchant house. But the one he follows veers east, reaching the river near the recess where Golo landed Sujata.

He vaguely senses a wrongness but being no scout or tracksman he shrugs and carries on. When he gets to an unbroken view he can't work out what he's seeing, apart from the river sliding below in its flat enormous logic – an awkward rise of the land blocks his view of the wharf, the settlement, the smoky river's roaring disappearance. He traverses to his left for a decent view and he sees way off on the opposite side a thickness of dust with tiny giveaway glints. He knows what it means. They're nearly here; at least the barque is away.

He contours on across rough ground and soon hits settlement and track and then the merchant house. Keeping an eye on the river – nothing yet.

The house is empty. The secret room, empty. No sign of any kind of turmoil. Everyone just gone – *what?* – leaving him and the bowman on the hill? They've been foxed, by this Errant and the rest – shrugged off, left stranded. *Ach*, the *scum*. Each to his own then; his only buddy is Sark up there with the boy.

Then in a hurry he's searching for lootables, filling a skin from the aquavit keg, packing a heavy satchel. Food – most of it gone already, twice-baked bread and pemmican just. Then he's away, checking the river over his shoulder (nothing yet), guessing at the route from here to the camp where Sark'll be scratching and yawning. With the boy – tough little bastard, but let's kill that wolf for a start. A *wolf* – *why?*

He wonders, in a fractured way, where Tark went, the Baroness, big Ruslan.

He's about to leave the thinning path when he comes on the group of nine, slouching in Kuzak's absence, and commences to berate them till Asli tells him what's happened. Then Kuzak is seen well above, gesturing them to follow. Then the bowman Sark; then the boy.

When Kuzak came on Sark and the boy they were getting on well enough, though with Peterkin still on the leash: comparing bows and arrows (Sark careful not to give both at once) – Peterkin tries to draw the war bow unarrowed, and manages for a moment or two, string arm quivering with the effort, to Sark's laugh of surprise.

What brings you here, Errant? he says, standing square-on.

Strange news, Sark of Maul. Plans have changed. Where is the fine Kan? Have we missed paths?

Sark's lips purse as Kuzak explains, and he stares un-blinking at the Errant's face.

How do I know you're not lying?

Come, and see for yourself.

Sark keeps Peterkin on the leash until he sees Tark's household on the track, fat cook and fat seamstress and all. Only then is the boy freed, his bow and other confiscations returned, as baffled by his liberty as he was by his restraint.

The wolf is watching from cover. He'd been quartering the hillside before dawn, enjoying his legs, but wary. In the deep night had come the howl of a pack from maybe five miles. That thin and icy sound, as if drifting above him and watching down.

Kuzak does what he can to explain it all to Peterkin. That Tark is dead in the river, Ruslan and Damla too; that Tark wanted to give him as a present, him and the wolf. He, Kuzak, can take them to a place where they'll with luck be safe and unconstrained; that they can, of course, stay where they are, but this is a world of hunters and goat-herds, not much peopled with lovers of wolves. Peterkin doesn't make sense of the detail, but gets it that Tark is dead and he is free. He too has heard the howl of the pack in the night and thinks to take a chance on the Errant's dim promise of haven, recent events notwithstanding.

When Peterkin sees Sujata in the party he runs down to her on impulse, then stops shyly, the many eyes on him – she heaves up from the deposited sedan (the only decent seat around) and gestures him to her and holds him a long time, stiff with embarrassment though yielding a little before she lets him go.

I've come a long way, he makes out. There is a pause while she looks at him.

I'm sorry, she says. Tark. I thought okay, safe. So stupid. Kuzak (she gestures – he's come part way down the

325

track) – follow Kuzak. He has plan. Trust, he is good, good.

And so the gang of fugitives, comic in its diversity, climbs the crumbly zig-zag track, heading for the pass over the spur that drops from the mountains to end as one wall of the cataract. Where a steep and airy goat-herd path drops away to the right Kuzak leads them on, then goes back and tramples and scuffs a little way down the sidepath, and drops a lapis bracelet where it's bound to be seen.

When they get to the crest of the track he doesn't let them stop till they're over and dropping down, out of possible skyline sight from below.

Chapter 28: Contouring

They have come to a great spaciousness on the southern flank of the shoulder, a huge sky over a fifty-mile view, its clans of stock-still fine-edged clouds. Flatlands below the foothills, flatlands beyond the river that curls and serpentines out from the under-falls pool.

Drof is three miles down, awaiting cargo from the north: a muddle of buildings under the sun, sparse vertical plumage of smoke from cooking fires, a sister village a ferry ride over the river. Tracks to both from their hinterlands. Jumbled hills on the southern skyline, out at the very edge of sight; a cleft where the next and final cataract tilts and goes roaring close by the city of Lix.

Here we must divide, says Kuzak. I'll take the boy and his beast to an Errant House in the hills. Those of you heading for Lix, or your homeland or wherever else, and keen to keep out of sight of the kingsmen – here is your only plan I think. It was Tark's, more or less. You, the boatmen – hire a barge in Drof, there'll be plenty lying idle. Say you left a boat at the cataract wharf and walked round rather than wait for the steps to mend, all true enough. Say you are promised a load in Lix to bring up.

The rest of you – see yonder kink in the river, two miles down from Drof, where a stream comes in? When it gets dark make your way there, the barge will be waiting to pick you up (he looks to the boatmen, checking they're still listening). Till it gets dark, hide out – plenty of thickets (he gestures down the rugged slope that falls away from them) – don't light a fire. Watch the country as evening comes on, see that the locals are settled. When you're sure you won't be seen, carry on down the track to where it bends right towards the village (you see, *there*, a boulder, a sapling growing out of it?). Leave the track at the bend and head across country, keep a line by the stars, when you hit the side-stream follow it down to the river. The barge will be there by then, please Fate and The Lady.

Tie up well to the rear on the wharf above Lix, don't be seen disembarking. Again, wait for the dark. Sneak down into the town. Slip into the inns, in twos and threes – have a good lie ready, for the mead-swillers and the nosy innkeeper's wife. You maids, perhaps, for chaperone, are nieces of the seamstress. Good luck from there.

But who is to descend, and who to go with Kuzak?

Sujata comes first into question. How about this, says Kuzak. You go down with the boatmen – you're a relative: aunt, great-aunt? Ten miles down from Drof there's a west bank town called Mazdaji, where the north-south road comes close by the river. Sedan back north – say you return from a pilgrimage, which is hardly less than the truth.

No, says Sujata. I come with you – with you and the boy, to be sure of the hospitality of the House. I go back later perhaps, if I don't die on you.

With welcome, Mistress, but how will we carry you?

Kuzak shoots meaningful glances around the company. The sweat-soaked boatmen who've borne the Crone so far are to take the other route. Sark and Kan meet Kuzak's eye unobligingly, but then Sark taps his buddy's side and they speak sotto voce. Their faces are well known in Lix, here's a chance to lie low awhile. We'll come, says Sark, but the carrying's shared – with a jerk of the hand at Kuzak, an up-nod at Peterkin owl-calling thirty yards back.

Kuzak scans the company again. A sidelong flick of the eye towards Asli: quick, as if unmeaningly random. On such wisps of demeanour whole lives can turn.

Asli is looking towards him. Her face is almost blank, with the slightest tincture of humour, like someone hearing a very small joke.

Yes, she says, I'll come. If I'm permitted.

So from their halt below the pass the band of refugees splits seven and seven. Seven of Tark's employees to descend: the boatmen to Drof with their plausible tale – they can work up the details in the descent; the five servants to sneak past in the night, directions once more to the cook as senior, the seamstress as back-up, both as logical pace-setters. Kuzak will lead the rest – boy and wolf, Asli, the guards, Sujata – by a deteriorated track, more like the memory of a track, across the hillside and over a second spur and then a dozen more miles of weaving through awkward hills to the House of the Errants, there guaranteed sanctuary. For a month, at least, anyway, by the rules.

Kuzak takes the front of the sedan with Kan the swordsman behind. leading the way. He's thought through the options and wants the boy to carry behind Sark when it's their turn, for best connection with the wolf.

The other group stretches out and dwindles below on their right. The cook is even less happy on the descent than he was in climbing; after a while the seamstress stops and waits for him, and they bring up the rear together. Kuzak's party has contoured a mile curve of hillside before the cook and seamstress join the others, down at a copse where the slope ends and the track levels out onto meadow and heads due south with aplomb till it sees its mistake and sharp-rights for Drof. The boatmen have already gone ahead – from the hill you can see them tiny on the plain; the other five disappear to wait out what's left of the day in cover and cool.

Kuzak's satchel's on a headstrap while he carries the sedan. Not much short of a hundredweight in all; he's fit, but not that fit; Asli nags him to swap his pack for her much lighter one. Peterkin still has just his own satchel and bow; now everyone is struggling but him. He mimes to Sark, who has Kan's satchel as well as his own, offering to ease his load. Sark looks him up and down and smiles lopsidedly and hands the boy his warbow and quiver, so losing little weight but much encumbrance.

On they move, over the second spur with effort, the world of the river now behind them as though it had never been. Kuzak has in mind a campsite a few miles on, leaving a modest approach the following day.

The wolf has followed the little party. Where the terrain permits he skirts high or low, left or right, running in the matrix of hillside odours. Small beasts zip under rocks, into holes; a marmot is too slow and he catches it, kills it in the snap and seizure, trots back to the path with it drooping in his jaw. Peterkin sees and holds back and takes it; the creature is hardly damaged, clean to tie to the top of his bulging satchel.

The wolf picks up old scent marks, then newer ones. They journey towards the hub of the pack's domain. He's closer to the people now, to the boy. No further than fifty yards, watching all the time for an ambush; then no more than thirty.

Crossing the second pass was like leaving the human world. Up here there's no habitation. Ling and spikebush hug the diffident path, that threads between boulders, crosses the deep clefts of diminished streams. Some a trickle, some bone dry. Birch and crabbed pine are the trees, scattered and opportunistic, few of any height.

The scent marks are strong now, only days old. The pack uses the human track. The wolf comes closer still, behind this slow-motion clump of humanity, the old one whom he has never feared sitting in the air between two others. His boy at the back, turning to see him, making the sounds he makes; his tail swipes from side to side.

They come to a better stream and a clearing beside it and all stop at a word from Kuzak and gratefully ease down their burdens. There's a rough arranging of space; latrines are agreed; wood is collected.

The boy has seen goats on a steep rise half a mile off. He points them out to Kuzak.

Goats. People goats?

Kuzak can't see them. Peterkin points and gestures.

Two-top mountain. Under. There, near.

A hint of movement. Kuzak shrugs.

People goats?

Asli is close by, amused. She can't see them either. He's asking if they belong to anyone.

See any people? See any herd-boy? asks Kuzak.

No.

Then no. Wild – they're wild. Not people goats.

We go, says Peterkin, and he's taken his bow and gestures the wolf who watches from across the stream and the two are gone. Kuzak drops his jaw and spreads his arms in appeal, indignant at the defection. Asli laughs at him. She's gotten more publicly blatant, owed indulgence for toting his pack.

In the time it takes for the fire to burn through its early excitements and start to need new sticks, the boy reappears. He has a gralloched and headless goat across his shoulders, bow and quiver tied to it by its own leg-sinews. The sun has fallen below the skyline, all is settling down beneath a cinnamon evening sky.

The party was pooling its dry and functional items for the evening meal. At the sight of the goat there's an outburst of cheering and laughter – the wolf backs off, almost bolts, ears sleeked to the head and tail ducked under. Peterkin makes owl-calls as he butchers the goat, throws a leg from hoof to joint for the wolf to chew on – he's already gulped down the liver and part of a lung, but being a wolf will only demur when his innards are bladder-taut.

Kuzak with a handful of twigs as an improvised scoop takes embers for a cooking fire; chunks of meat are kebabed on peeled and stream-wetted sticks, and the odour of fire-cooked meat swims up and catches in every throat and there's more cheering and praise. Sark waves to the wolf and calls to him and he pulls back in uncertainty and the bowman flips from kebab-stick a chunk of hot meat which the wolf catches and instantly drops and dances about it, snatching it up and dropping it, cringing momentarily at the laughter of the humans, at their cheer when he finally gulps it down.

Chapter 29: A Clear Starry Sky

thin slice of moon is well up in the clear starry sky, a small and varying breeze slips coolness over toil-heated skin, there's a soft reek from the dying fire. Kuzak strolls a little way to a rise, takes a seat on the rough level of a boulder. It might be pre-arranged, though nothing has been said or hinted. But something has shifted, in the intimacy of events. Her squeeze on his arm; his words in reply. The way she nagged like a wife to give her his pack.

Asli lets some time pass and then rises and goes to join him, picking her way without hurry a move at a time.

Well then, he says, Asli of unknown provenance. Here we are.

You have a way with words, O Kuzak. Here we are indeed. What'll happen next, d'you suppose?

Come closer.

What, and sit on these lumps?

Sit on my lap then.

Is that an order, O Kuzak the masterful?

She's rising as she says it, an easy hand on his shoulder sliding to encircle him as she settles herself.

Any other lumps? she says, squirming in exploration.

He nuzzles carefully into the side of her neck, smelling her hair and the woodsmoke in her hair, the smell of their bodies from the long hot day, her odour sharper and lighter and so much more alluring than his own.

Y'r a bold one, Madam Asli. How came you to be so bold?

I'm from Gunyesu in the far south-west, the land of virginweed. Without it by now I'd be mother of four, each with a different father, every one a fool. Not that they're the sum of my adventures. How about you, O Holy One? I have no sense of the lumbering novice. Yet, anyway.

I was married once … no, don't ask, not tonight. Since then – the last thirty years: temple whores, a few merry widows – all within the vows, most folk don't realize. Most of the time just fighting the itch – concentration techniques, all that.

They mouth and face-caress, their hands have easy focus, neither shy nor purposeful. Unhurried, not filching under clothing, happy with this time of first acquaintance. The other's body's mass and personality, its sensate oneness, strangely novel at first touch.

You stink, she says, with a matter-of-factness just slightly short of approval. Her voice is husky.

So do you. Rather pleasantly I think.

When did you fall so hopelessly in love with me? she says, pressing her cheek against his shoulder, feeling the enclosure of his arms.

Hopelessly? Huh. But yes, a gradual business, hard to fix day and time – except your outrageous laughter at the death of the Baron. Such wicked honesty, maybe that was the clincher – maybe. You?

Don't know. Inch by inch likewise. Sleeping with your back to me that time, so firmly composed, you bastard. The way you always handle yourself. At first it's tiresome, boring – then you see the depths and it's so impressive.

Thanks. I doubt I'll live up to all that, but thanks. I must ask, by the way – did you ever go with him?

Who?

The Baron, who else?

Mother, the *Baron? Me?* He doesn't fuck ugly women – *didn't*, didn't. Maybe he'll have to in Hell. They'll give him a couple of thousand to work through, before they let him out.

Don't dare say you're ugly. You're not ugly. You're nothing like ugly.

Well thank you. How effusively you praise.

Stop being difficult.

If you're going to give commands don't give dopey ones. I was born difficult. Who do you think you've got sat on your lap? Mistook me in the dark for one of the maids?

I know you well and wish to know you better, Asli of Ganyesu.

Gunyesu. Carry on, I like the way that was going ...

I'll unvow when we get to the House, we marry ...

Marry? Mother of All here's a turn of speed ...

Marry, what else? Plenty of disused crofts, bothies – make some arrangement, tidy one up, lie low and live a crofter's life awhile, till we find something better. Until or unless. See how we get along.

Marry? Yesyesyes. It's been quite a couple of days. Yes.

They agree, with a humorous reference to detail, not to take the next step in mutual understanding until they're back in a world with warm water, fresh garments and bedding, privacy, no wolf on the loose.

They sleep, nested together, her back against his chest, under Kuzak's cloak, pillowed on their satchels, across the fire from Sujata's prime location. She smiles in the dark at their whispering. In the morning everyone knows, nothing is said.

Chapter 30: A Welcome

The House sits deep in complicated foot-hills, improbable in its size and formal design and yet somehow fitting its locus, where a close and unpromising valley dead-ends and aprons out under steep ascents. It's thirty years and a half since Kuzak came on it by chance; many since have be-wildered themselves in the broken geography (the tale is told of a pilgrim party, saving on guide costs, that wandered for days exposed and hungry  until they followed a stream downhill in a limping line and begged journey home on a comradely barge, their emotions far from spiritual).

Sujata insists on walking the last hundred yards on Kuzak's arm, in her other hand the staff that has come all the way from the Hermitage. Asli, Sark and Kan keep a little way back; Peterkin has been told by word and mime to keep out of view, with the wolf if possible under control. He takes the improvised leash from his satchel, eases the loop over the wolf's head, ties the other end around his wrist. He watches from cover on rising land a little aside from the path.

The only sound is the whisper of falling streams in the steep-sided dish of land. Then Kuzak sings out a formal greeting, through the big open door. Sujata beside him little and buckled, the staff her only sprightliness of line. A youth appears and something is said and the boy goes back in. Before the whispering silence has time to re-settle a man comes, big and physical, immediate in his movements, and he lifts both hands in a florid happy gesture and takes Kuzak's shoulders, they press their faces cheek against cheek and there's a rumbustious bear hug with thumping of shoulders and backs. Peterkin stiffens a little in surprise; the wolf stiffens too, and looks about for a reason. Kuzak introduces Sujata, the big man bows very low. You can hear the boom of his voice, the big heavy vowels.

Then Kuzak extends an arm and Asli and guards come forward. The man bows to Asli and then to the guardsmen. He offers no physical contact but looks inquiringly into each visitor's eyes. Then Kuzak is scanning back for Peterkin and the wolf, speaking as he does, shielding his eyes from the late sun. The others turn to look as well. Sark sees him and points; Kuzak is pulling air towards his chest, making big head-nods. *Come.*

Peterkin shrinks within himself. *Again*, it occurs to him. Here we are again. The big cold stony house, the larger than life, booming-voiced man. In a depth of his mind are the wild goats, the wide empty country.

But Kuzak gestures more compellingly, and Peterkin is up and clucking to the leashed wolf in persuasion, reassurance. As the two make steps back down to the path there comes to his mind the long thin howl of the wolf pack, as if to settle the point.

The wolf drags back on the leash as they get closer, and Peterkin talks to him and then unleashes him, and his ears go up and he skips to the scrub at the side of the track and watches Peterkin's progress very alert. The big welcomer stands arms akimbo, radiating astoundedness.

Peterkin approaches. No sound but the rustling whisper of water. Twice he looks over his shoulder but the wolf has slipped from view. When he reaches the group the big man bows deeply, his beaming joviality a mixture of satire and wonderment. He makes an address which the boy can't understand, though he picks out the words house and welcome, also wolf. Then, and rather unnervingly, the man steps forward and hugs him to his kitchen-odorous smock, with heavily benign flat-hand thumps to the shoulder blade.

When he steps back Peterkin bows and replies.

I come and wolf, look for quiet place. We no harm, we bring meat – wolf good, my friend, wolf good.

Then, to his astonishment and dismay, Peterkin weeps. He clenches his teeth and stares at a place on the stark stone wall of the house, but the salt tears run down his face, sobs arise like hiccups.

Timur the Provisional Master of House – he who has welcomed them, Abbot Gunai being away at Court – discusses practicalities with Kuzak. A wonder has come before his eyes: such is the very nub of Errancy: his welcome is unconditional. But where to put a wolf, while the herd-boys bring in their beasts?

The House has put out shoots since Kuzak's inductee-ship. Outhouses, bothies, huts and hutlets – concoctions of stone and timber and turf, no two of quite the same species, ranging in size from a cottage to a one-man sleep-tube. They chequer the House's surround, the most extreme recessed in gorges, or perched on high and stomach-dropping ledges. Most are empty, provisional – kept for pilgrims and sanctuary-seekers, like the little hamlet below the Hermitage, that Sujata left a bare half-month ago that seems like half a lifetime.

An outlier hut is decided on for the boy and the wolf, until some better arrangement suggests itself. Timur calls out a couple of inductees to make the party welcome in the House, then leads the boy with exuberant gestures across the face of the south wing and around. When all have gone the wolf comes out of cover and stares at the corner of the house where Peterkin disappeared, whimpering to himself.

When Peterkin comes back he is alone – he's managed to convey that he won't be able to manage the wolf with the big man around. The wolf comes up tail low and wagging, drags to a stop thirty yards from the House. The boy has cut morsels from last night's meal and he owl-calls and tosses one, just like the early days. The wolf catches and gulps it, full as he is from his last two copious meals. He crouches and his ears drop at the sounds of window-shutters opening, at voices, but he keeps his ground and snaps a second morsel. Youths' faces are cramming the upper-storey windows; astonished voices, from piping to grunty and all stages between, dart out like missiles; the wolf shrinks back and away. But a man's voice is heard from within and the youths fall silent, and the windows are re-shuttered and all are gone as if they'd never been.

Peterkin tries to lead the wolf a wide-skirting route to a minuscule bridge that leads to the right-hand outbuildings. But the faces and voices have daunted him, and he baulks and whimpers, prawning up, tail under. So Peterkin, telling him all along they've arrived at safety, that an amiable hut sits waiting for them, takes the leash from his satchel again and lets the wolf sniff it and eases on the loop with praise and endearments, and shoulders his satchel and bow and cajoles him along, stopping whenever he baulks to tempt onward movement with morsels from his pocket, and so in time he brings the wolf around and beyond the House and over the bridge and then more easily to their residence.

There are two narrow pallets with straw-filled mattresses and the wolf decides which of them is his. When he's sniffed the hut's small affordance of objects he ups onto the bed and awkwardly turns around twice and settles to rest, chin aligned between forelegs, Peterkin telling him how well he has managed, stopping and heeling back from his cheekbones the tears that are running again, then praising the wolf some more.

Sujata in the receiving room is shown great respect and attentiveness – applejack and honey in a tiny silver goblet, curd and raisins, salted pine nuts. Silk-sleeved cushions anciently insignia'd.

Requirements, tell us your requirements. Rest, O Crone, you have come very far.

Mother of All I have indeed, she says smiling and is suddenly and utterly exhausted.

Big Timur catches the eye of Errant Tanju, discreetly detailed to the care of the Holy One, for want of female help – Asli said some volunteering words which received a smile and a nod but nothing more.

Will I show you to your room, O Crone, when you've taken refreshment?

That would be wonderful. Wonderful. Silk cushions and waited on by men – am I in Paradise then, already? I didn't even know I was dead, though I've once or twice suspected.

Soon Tanju steps smoothly away and mentions certain domestic arrangements to Asli, as the better person to impart them. The only other female in the House, or indeed within three miles. Both go with Sujata to the Strangers' Wing that forms the southern third of the building. She stumbles twice on the way, with weariness and the strong liquor and sudden twinges of joint pain, in collusion with the ridges and dips of a couple of centuries' footfall in the flagstones of the passage. Then an airy chamber, a couch; more cushions, a lambswool coverlet.

Sujata's last question is, how is the boy? She smiles, eyes closed, when she's told, raises one hand a few inches then lets it fall.

Chapter 31: Settling In

Time itself begins to take its ease. The simple mass of stonework, with its climate of perdurant age; the ceremonial rhythms of life: meals, work, training, devotions, gong or shawm to cue the transitions; the timeless call of herd and barley field; high summer itself with its days that might be a single day. Boy and wolf in their edged habitation; the best and least removed north-side cottage made ready for Sujata; Tark's guardsmen Sark and Kan settled in the guest wing. Only Kuzak and Asli remain unsettled.

Kuzak must first unvow – a common ritual, here the requirement for rank and number of witnesses easily met. The wedding itself takes place the next day.

Timur is the celebrant, toning down the boom of his voice and his larger-than-lifeness, though bringing a wry nudge to certain passages. The ritual rotation seals the marriage: in this the couple signify the modes of their new unity, in the tumble and sweep of the ambient world. From their position facing Timur, bride at the groom's right hand, they turn opposite ways a right angle at a time:

Back to back, we face our destiny

Turned away from the world, we face our destiny
In our embrace, we face our destiny
(Here Asli, with a face of bland innocence, digs a knuckle in Kuzak's ribs on the blind side of the celebrant; Kuzak, jaw clenched, whispers a single clipped word; she makes the smallest speculative pout.)
Returning to the world, we face our destiny.

Then Timur, coming closer, puts a hand on the side of each partner's face and speaks into the space between, calling on the gods to show them favour and forbearance. At the moment he breaks touch and steps back they are married. The small congregation cheers and laughs and forms a passage, reaching to touch them as they pass and lead the way to the wedding feast.

Beware false urgency, say the Errants, as much as you beware complacency. Each disturbs the flow of *nishan-kasit*, a term that means roughly 'intent engagement'. So it is that a month passes before a formal meeting is called of the Counsel of the Eastern Errant House. The Abbot Gunai still at King Karaman's palace and no word of a return, it falls again to Timur to officiate. To centre the House's mind in adjusting to recent events, above all to preserve its *nishan*, its *kasit*.

Five chairs in a circle, equidistant. Timur's is nearest the door but has no other mark of prority. Netin the Disciplinarian; Okan and Ozan, respectively in charge of training and housekeeping. Kuzak, technically a guest member.

Netin speaks first:

There are two simple, unbreakable rules here. That only sworn Errants and inductees can have settled residence in the House or its precincts – hence of course no women, no unvowed, no chance strays whether urchin or nobleman's thug. That nothing can be permitted to weaken kasit, disturb nishan, especially with regard to the inductees and their training. The rule-makers somehow neglected to guide us on household wolves, but I draw the meeting's attention to the longstanding Errant tradition of doing our best to wipe the creatures out – indeed a hunt is being planned as we speak, to find the den of the pack we've been hearing of nights, singing of its plans to ease the boredom of winter by carousing with our flocks.

A pause – a chuckle or two and then silence. Then Timur, who's been staring at the floor, raises his head and replies. His tone is forceful but moderate, in keeping with the occasion.

Well put, Netin, as ever, thank you. Issues: seven unexpected guests who might outstay their welcome; the possible unsettling of inductees' morale and focus; wolf. We'll take them in turn. But first I'd like to hear you, Kuzak, as one of the seven who knows the other six, I should think, pretty well. Pray give as full an account as you can of the rather complex events you've been part of, from the Midsummer festival up to your arrival, with particular focus on the character and conduct of our guests. Only give, please, such information about your wife as needed to make the story coherent.

Kuzak begins. The others question him as he tells the story. Why did he volunteer, when the spy absconded, to protect all or any of that dubious threesome? Boy wolf and wife-to-be, of whom he then knew nothing? The Crone Sujata is ancient – why credit her judgement on the vagabond boy? Why benefit the scoundrel Tark? Even stooping to row his boat for him? Why, in your first encounter, did you not face down Golo? With both chief miscreants off the scene, plus Ruslan the giant, why did you bring the remaining strays to us, rather than leave them to the Enquirers of the King? D'you suppose he won't look for them here?

It's more or less what Kuzak expected. He answers evenly, with reference to Errant principles, freely admitting his fond respect for the boy, the same for Asli with obvious extra dimension, the risk of these attachments distorting his judgement. The strays – he repeats the word, with emphasis – have already brought more benefit than he'd expected: high-grade weapons training from the guardsmen, spiritual and doctrinal advice from Sujata, venison from boy and wolf. The Enquirers won't know who they're looking for, or how many, or who went down the cataract in the barque, or who slipped through to Drof and so to Lix.

Which takes us perhaps to the original questions – may I answer before your ask?

Uninvited guests. Myself: I – we – will leave when I'm sure that I've answered my duty to bring the boy to proper settlement. A formulation which must include his wolf, his bond with which is just such a piece of the human spirit as Errancy swears to preserve. We'll settle nearby, for a while at least, if the House is content – this is the only place in the world to which I have an attachment, Asli has none anywhere. The guardsmen will be keen to move on to Lix, for the taverns and the female company – within the month is my guess. Sujata: you must decide. There's an obvious duty to age and reverence. There are precedents for elderly permanent guests, though not I admit for a woman. I suggest, by the way, that the Errants take charge of the Hermitage, whether or not she can and should return there, with her agreement of course – it's presently in the hands of worthy but busy and untutored locals. It would give us – sorry, *you* – a stronger presence in the north-east, and a base for inductees and for Errants of damaged health.

And back to the boy. And the wolf. Consider these suggestions. The boy would, if he chose, make a very fine Errant – brave, resourceful, independent of spirit; physically tough and capable. He and the wolf already bring wild meat. The wolf if it could be managed might keep away lynxes and jackals, especially at lambing and kidding. But a tame wolf is a wonder of far greater potential value – it'd be a wrongdoing to use this one, as Tark planned, to sweeten dealings with King or Empire, but could not the boy tame others? Your plans to wipe out the local pack – couldn't this year's cubs be captured alive?

So guests, uninvited – enough from me for the moment perhaps. Your second question – unsettling the inductees. The boy, his wolf – exoticism, mystery. Where did he come from? – I thought him at first he was a Yoruk, drifted across from the north-west, but he's not. It seems he has the same tongue as some Empire galley slaves, captured who knows where. He has the glamour of a wild, self-pleasing way of life. And another kind of glamour – let us be candid: there'll be a crush or two, which he will be flummoxed by, being I think entirely innocent. I'd guess nothing too tricky. Forbidding contact might be the worst thing to do, boosting up the glamour to a frenzy.

Trickier, glamour-wise, might be Sujata's new handmaid, whose fair-to-middling comeliness is sustenance enough for the daydreams of celibate youths. Sujata, of course, insists that she needs no handmaid; but her adventures have drained her, for now at least. Maybe best wait and see if she gets back the strength she had before all this. If she does, let the maid go; if she doesn't, move both out of the precinct but still as close as may be.

Third, the wolf. I've spoken for the wolf. I have to say I've lost all distaste for the creature, in spending time with the boy. Their mutual understanding is a wonder. The beast has a strange wisdom, it sometimes seems to read his mind. Its greatest fear is of other wolves. As if it's become another creature entirely, halfway between wolf and human. More than halfway perhaps.

There is a silence. Kuzak's opinions, unlike his history, have not been interrupted.

Then Timur speaks.

You're a fountain of decisions, brother Kuzak. No need for the rest of us it seems. We will, of course, make up our own minds. But we thank you for your remarks.

He makes an informal palm-upward move of one hand. All stand, exchange bows, then each embraces Kuzak as he leaves, with greater or lesser warmth.

Well-founded are the concerns of the disciplinarian. As he speaks three of the inductees, in defiance of firm prohibition, are using the brief post-breakfast break to circuit to Peterkin's outlier hut.

He's sitting a few yards below it to catch the sun, the wolf beside him. The wolf hackles at the intrusion, Peterkin signals flat-handed to the youths.

You stop, please. Wait, please.

He strokes the wolf and asks him to lie still, and then raising a hand again he steps into the hut and comes out with the leash, and talking all along he slips it around the wolf's neck and winds it around his wrist, giving no more than a half yard of play. Then he gestures the youths to come nearer.

They come, rather breezy in their boldness, and the wolf hackles again and makes to retreat. Peterkin flat-hands them to stop and speaks with him, gently kneading his neck and shoulder, feeling the gradual easing.

You come slow please, very slow yes. He my wolf afraid. Slow, yes.

The three pigeon-step, keen and breathless, Peterkin speaking to the wolf, feeling his response through the hand that kneads his shoulder.

When the youths are five yards off he gestures them down.

You stop yes, please. Stop on ground.

The youths have been watching the wolf all along, in much the same trance of focus as his in watching them. Two lower on a single knee as if in genuflection, the third squats on his heels. They show both a joy of boldness and a readiness to bolt.

When it comes to it not much is said, before the rancorous sound of the signal shawm begins the inductional day, and the youths are quickly on their feet and bow with hurried formality and are gone. When they'd asked him where he was from he gestured towards the mountains.

Over the mountains?

Yes.

But there is no way ...

Yes, a way. Yes.

So might the smallest of words change the course of the world.

Sujata doesn't know why a maid's been hired for her, but does what she can to keep the girl entertained. She steps out to the dawn service as quietly as she can, leaving

her asleep; she teaches her hymns, prayers, incantations, the girl with her thick accent and incomprehension. The girl breaks a bowl and bursts into tears and Sujata comforts her, stroking her shoulder in a loose embrace.

After a few days they settle into a friendship, preparing meals together, eating them – there isn't much else to do, a single laundry serves the House, their clothes come back impeccable. More and more their time is spent sitting in the sun, in the garden of the cottage, Sujata telling her story. She's rarely spoken of herself before – when she starts it's not so much a dam being burst as one in slow erosion, stone by stone slipping loose, the flow enlarging by degrees. Starting with the boy and the wolf, Midsummer, her error, Golo, the Cataract. But then back to when she was this girl's age, piecing forward from there, sparing only the worst of the horrors. How she met the Hermit; her life with him; her veneration.

Did you marry him?

Sujata laughs. *No*, no. He was given entirely to the gods. And I'd anyway been spoiled for all that, a year out of childhood any appetite befouled. So it was: I have no complaint: I have found great joy in the life I have lived. But the early days were hard – I was troubled with nightmares, the Hermit had spells of madness, ranting at gods and at demons, not yet come to the calm that sweetened his last twenty years. But so it was. I worshipped him, as near as you can a human.

And she told tales of their life together, of his death, of the Hermitage, towards which an Errant and two inductees are now headed, to tend the relics and the beasts, if the good acorn-gatherers have saved them from bandit and wolf.

And so they sit together in the garden, the girl's wonder awoken, the muzz of bees in the honeysuckle, the long arc of the sun.

The Second Cataract might have been made to pulverize boats and bodies – rockface zigzags exploding with spume, the hurtling force a refutation of human size and human works. The underpool is dragged but they only find the bodies of Tark and Ruslan – skull-burst and dislocate-limbed, laid out as things of wonder, the Baron and his giant. Damla, foul in death, is pulled out from reeds eight miles down and a half-month later, and dragged onto a pyre by locals (her rings and remaining necklace discreetly removed) and burned with formal lamentation. Golo's body is never found.

The wharf porter and the local crofters show the house where the party had been. It is left tidy; no-one knows how many went down with the barque, nor where any who didn't have gone. As to the unprovable latter, the kingsmen are too intent on the spoils from the house to fuss with a search. To ease the Enquirers' labours, the simplest version of events is that all went down the cataract – staff, treasure, wolf, Baron, Baroness. All.

The seven who dropped towards Drof have made it to Lix through varied adventures, the first a struggle in darkness through tussock and bog in which the gasping cook felt close to death, and not unrealistically. Their subsequent lives dissolve into the multitude of lesser tales, each of which fills a world.

There comes another meeting of the four senior Errants.

Timur speaks.

Yes, I've reached a conclusion. We take the boy as a non-standard inductee, and as key to the wolf-taming venture, on three conditions. He's willing, he knows exactly what's expected, and he passes the usual tests. All depend on his proper understanding, which depends in turn on his learning our language.

The wolf hunters can't wait for that. This year's cubs will be half-grown already. So we bring him one or two if we can, with as much explanation as possible. Keep him away from the hunt itself, though – he might dislike the murdering.

All agreed? Netin?

The Disciplinarian shrugs his shoulders, his mouth a little sour.

Asli and Kuzak now own a tumbledown cottage, bought with an amethyst ring and three freshwater pearls. Asli is reclaiming the garden and Kuzak's at work on the thatch when an inductee calls to request his presence. The Counsel ...

He calls out and waves as he briskly sets off. Asli returns to her task, reflecting on the role of cottage-wife to a half-Errant. In the time it takes to prise out the complex rhizome of an awkward big burdock her mind has sketched out three alternative futures.

Timur and Netin sit facing the eighteen inductees. They're the kind of large square men whose ease in domineering youths comes partly from being half again their weight, a resource they beam out quite unknowingly.

They're in the main hall. High echoey walls, the inductees three each on six semicircled short benches, the men in high-backed chairs. Netin speaks.

The boy with the wolf, Pita-Kin. Visiting whom. Orders, to which unquestioning etcetera, broken, blatantly almost. Not blatantly enough for names to be named, though a one-eyed tracker could follow the prints. But let it go by – now it's legal. We *want* contact: you fine fellows, the wolf boy. Not any old – our rules, no nonsense. Supervision, while we see how it goes. The good Kuzak, a break from his household duties.

Then Timur. He is in his businesslike mode, with only odd moments of gusty bonhomie.

Here's the idea, or rather two ideas. First, Pitakin is inducted into Errancy. Second his wolf, far from being a problem community member, becomes an asset: for its usefulness in hunting, for keeping off jackals and lynxes, for breeding more like itself – to give or to trade, and so to endow the House. We can't know what sort of Errant the boy might make (though Kuzak has a high regard) till we can have a decent conversation. This is where you come in – to bring on his Megharan and to show him Errancy. And to make him welcome – he's come here by a strange and rocky path. We don't even know where from – some clues here might help. Could hardly not.

Timur looks towards the entrance passage, raises an arm.

So here's the good Kuzak come to address you – is he? – *yes*, aha. Kuzak, welcome. They're all yours.

Chapter 32: Hunt and Capture

Peterkin's first feeling when he gathered that a cub or cubs might be coming was a kind of indignation. Even a sense of having been tricked, again. Kuzak, who has attended to the souls of young men for half his life, senses it and sets out the contingencies, with many simplifications and repetitions.

If you don't want to try and tame any female cubs, say so and the hunters will kill them. A much easier task than bringing them back. I don't know what the leadership will say, but the worst that can happen is you take your wolf back in the hills and live the life you had when you met Sujata. The hills down here are empty enough, since the Empire wiped out the Horuk nomads in the days of the Insurrection, for no better reason than they couldn't be kept an eye on. So no hand on your throat – you do what you choose.

Option one. Try and tame cubs, if any – affection and respect of the House, buddies for your wolf, who must have the usual longings for female company.

Option two, don't agree to try – less of the forementioned affection and respect, hints to find other accommodation perhaps. Your wolf retains its isolation, for better or for worse. We can't ask it what it thinks.

Do you understand me, Peterkin?

Yes I think. Yes.

The hunt goes out tonight. You don't need to make a decision – though if it's a definite no we need to tell the Huntsman to not bother carrying nets. I suggest you wait and see what comes, and then do what you do. Yes?

Now I get back to fixing the roof, or my wife will beat me around the ears with the switch of her tongue. Good day to you. Come visit please, any time, wolf and all. Good day.

The wolf pack has been tracked to its den and is watched with great discretion. It's not yet dawn. Four adults sleep, replete from yesterday's kill, in a clearing in the underslope scrub. Three half-grown cubs and a she-wolf their mother are in the den above, gender of cubs unknown.

This the Huntsman whispers, returning soft-footed to the hunters' position. Downwind, tree-hidden, looking across and down. Sark the bowman has joined the House Huntsman and four chosen inductees. When the skyline is black against saffron and colours are seeping back the party creeps to position, staring at a crack between boulders the Huntsman points out, a slow gesture like a stalking heron. The den's shaley forecourt trodden, a few split bones.

They wait. The day comes into itself, great mountain-gap beams announce the still-hidden sun. Then out come the she-wolf and cubs, skipping and jinking in play. The other four hear and come to join them, tongues lolling from their jaws, ducking and romping, playing at being wolves.

Six arrows are notched. The three big cubs hive off, prance and roll this side of the adults. Loose, says the Huntsman, so quietly the wolves don't hear.

Four of the shafts hit three of the wolves. The elder male, knocked sideways off its feet by Sark's arrow, its ribcage skewered right through, twitches in the shale coughing blood; the two other injured are jerking, ki-yiking. The elder female, not knowing what's happening or from where, yips to the cubs and they scutter back into the den and she follows; an arrow chaps the stones a yard behind her. The other unwounded adult, bolting at random, hurtles unknowing towards the archers, is almost on them in sudden mid-swerve when an arrow whaps in from barely five yards, then two more. The Huntsman points to the injured two now stumbling for cover and shouts and waves on the inductees.

Finish them. Spare them what pain you can, finish them.

The Huntsman then shoulders the trapnet they've carried up, drawing his half-sword in case the female bursts out. He and Sark drape the net so it can't be got round or under, weighting it with rocks, hoping the den has no second entry.

Four wolves dead, mother and cubs holed up – a sudden end to the supercharged moments of action, a vacuum of event, the inductees a-shake with propulsive excitement. The Huntsman sees it and sends them to work it off in skinning the wolves, retrieving the arrows.

Time passes. The Huntsman wants a spyhole into the den through which to locate and kill the mother who cowers with her cubs. They've brought no tools, but by luck a boulder lifts out above the main cranny – the she-wolf rises frantic, gnashing at the gap, then catapults to the entry and into the net, dragging the weight-rocks, hopelessly trammelled. No need to risk the net by stabbing through it – Sark caves her head in with a rock. There's hurried disentanglement to get the net back in place.

The she-wolf is more or less dead but still twitching; the Huntsman calls on the nearest of the wide-eyed inductees to cut its throat to be sure. The youth tries to hide the shaking of his hands, the Huntsman says trouble not just do it, gestures the line to take. The youth sees his hand holding the knife, the knife go in and slice against resistance, as if it's happening in some faraway place, determined by some unseen agent.

The cubs are in chaos. The hurricane of event, angled glimpses of their mother's death, the swamping odour of blood, of the skinless carcases. One suddenly whaps into the net. It's pinned to the ground, extricated with elaborate care. But it's a male. They tie its feet and jaws with sinew and Sark takes it off to one side by scruff and tail, whole-body writhing like a landed fish, to dispose of.

The other two are smoked out, they bolt into the net. Luckily both are female – for themselves, for the enterprise, for the cast upon the future. An inductee is told to cut his shirt into strips: the cubs' legs and jaws are bound, the jaws double-looped to allow them breath but not bite. They're hammocked on head-staps to their new abode, getting on thirty pounds each by weight, along with six wolfskins and all the hunting gear, the lumbered party arriving hot and hungry in mid-afternoon to shouts and cheers which kick the exhausted cubs back into fish-tailing, whimpering, jerking.

When the hunt comes in Peterkin watches them bring in the cubs still with no set idea.

They're brought to a big square goat pen with sides six yards each way and a cubbyhole fold for retreat. He sees the inductees are going to get bitten untying the cubs. He comes forward.

Net, he says. Net. Hold them in net, to do knots. I help? Yes, I help?

Sark exclaims approval, turning to the Huntsman, who nods.

The cubs are in the pen each pinned by two inductees. Still jerking intermittently, scrabbling air. Peterkin stumps in with the heavy net that's been tossed down outside, and he unrolls one side and brings it up dangling to where two inductees are holding a cub, and squeezes between them dangling the edge of the net onto the cub's middle body, and he lowers himself with awkward care to kneel each side so his weight is pinning the cub. All along he speaks to it, cajoling and reassuring. He motions the youth at the head to ease away, and lets down the net right over the head and holds it down and then asks the youth to take over the hold and the youth eventually gets it and holds down the net with his hands where Peterkin's were.

Peterkin frees the cub's front legs with awkward care, then mimes to the youth behind to free the back legs. Then he undoes its jaws more awkwardly still, sawing with his knife between the strings of the net.

It is good he says to the inductees, motioning them to keep the cub where it lies, flat on its side beneath the net. He goes to untie the other, kneeling astride it again but this time trying without the net. When he gets to the head he presses down on the cheek with his forearm to work the knot, murmuring and cajoling all along.

Think it's the language of wolves? says Sark to the Huntsman. If it is the little one ain't listening.

Peterkin, with the jaws untied, holds his press-down forearm while taking with the other hand a firm and careful grip on the scruff of the neck. He tells the cub's now jobless inductees to step right back and when they have he lifts his forearm, the cub squirming and twisting to bite, and he grips the root of the tail with the other hand and rises to his feet. He tries to get the two inductees with the netted cub to do the same, but one gets bitten removing the net and the cub shoots away. It backs and forths at the far side of the pen, then crouches in the furthest corner snarling.

You go, you go, says Peterkin, gesturing the inductees out of the pen with back-shunts of his head. Take net, take net.

When they're out he whispers a prayer to Luck that the beast won't turn on him and shunts and half-tosses the cub he's holding forward and away, and she stumbles and stands astounded for half a moment and then bolts to join her sister and they hackle and crouch snarling side by side while Peterkin's out through the gate and the gate is barred.

The cubs take to the dark little fold and aren't seen again for a while. Peterkin comes and goes; he'll leave his own wolf in the hut and sit against the fence of the pen, talking to the invisible cubs. His wolf will complain more and more at being left alone, an imperative whimpering lifting into occasional howls. A thin sound to the cubs in the pen, muffled by the walls of the hut. The cubs keep silent at first, then the pangs of seclusion override fear and they howl back uncertainly from the hutch and then they are out through the little entry and lifting their heads to the sky, howling and lilting their abandonment.

Peterkin had thought to make his own connection with the cubs before introducing his wolf. But now they've exchanged their first words – before he's even given the little ones meat, planning on using hunger to draw them to him. He watches them at their howling, they twitch back a handsbreadth or so when he moves and then recommence. Zip back into the hutch when he stands, come out and commence to howling again when he's gone.

Back in the hut his wolf is a-quiver with some mix of excitements. Peterkin clicks to him and strokes his neck as he tells him about the cubs, and slips the leash over his neck and takes up the package of skin-wrapped meat he's already cut into morsels and hung outside the hut, and the two head down to the cubs in their fold.

All is heightened, taut with anticipation, strangeness. Since he fled from the river-pack ambush in which his brothers died he's never met another wolf that wasn't trying to kill him.

The fence of the fold is of lashed poles and his wolf immediately sees the cubs and hauls on the leash, supercharged with focus. The cubs are swerving across the little compound, tails between legs and back ends to the ground and making a breathy cascade of fawning whimpers. The big wolf's ears are up and his tail is vertical, his hackles just slightly raised, frozen in his hyper-attention.

When Peterkin unlatches the gate and goes in with the wolf the wolf hauls so hard on the leash he has to sit down and dig in his heels to hold him, the thong tourniquetting his hands. He eases out the leash an inch at a time and the cubs fawn at the wolf's feet and the wolf starts to ease his domineeringness and give the first hints of play. When he's sure enough, Peterkin stands and works his way along the leash and the cubs dart into

their hutch and the boy mutters a prayer and slips off the loop, and his wolf is free and peering into the hutch, and as Peterkin retreats to the side of the pen and sits himself down the cubs keek out and sidle out and there they all are skipping and feinting in play and in sport.

Chapter 33: The Airs of Late Summer

Time has passed. The first touch of autumn sneaks into the airs of late summer, thinning down their plump generosity. Wild goats and deer from the highest slopes are sifting down to easier pastures.

Peterkin is out with his wolves. The cubs are three parts grown, absurdly leggy, entering their wolfishness through a portal of comic exuberance. A while back one caught an unwary marmot and snarled when the boy tried to take it – the male wolf comes in at full height, ears and tail straight up, showing his teeth in a low growl, and the young bitch drops the marmot and flops down fawning and thinly whimpering. Peterkin picks it up.

This time the Huntsman and two inductees are following. The wolves are getting more and more inured to them, the cubs especially. Bold boys took to pocketing morsels of food to flick to them, watch their leaps and darts, their snatch-who-can – it had to be put a stop to, the cubs (now free to wander) were hanging around for more. Peterkin would gather them, in no time they'd be back.

The pattern has come about that the wolves run together in a single intelligence, Peterkin lagging doggedly behind, the party from the House keeping in touch as well as they can. If the wolves have seized prey Peterkin takes over, finishing it off if need be, opening the body and portioning viscera. If the prey dodges and bolts into human sight there's a much-repeated set of injunctions, so they don't shoot each other or the wolves: keep to an approximate line, only loose an arrow well out to right or left, only if there's no wolf in pursuit.

So it goes, and the House has all the meat it needs and more smoked or salted, and the year's kids and lambs kept on to promise a full-bellied winter. So the joining together of men and wolves takes root from its wandering seed, starts to become the way of things, than which there can be no other.

Next year the wolves will breed, the sisters between them bearing seven cubs. After the Three Month War the House will discuss how best to profit the Errancy by way of such marvellous beasts. Hunters, extirpators of jackal and lynx, forewarners of bear and of thief. Prodigies, for court and noble house. The Empire, that mighty bazaar.

So.

Sujata will not know of the new generation, for by the spring she is dead. A fall outside her cottage: she doesn't want to trouble the sleeping maid and so lies a long while before she can climb to her feet. By then the cold is well inside her, working in so deep that her breath is stricken and won't be mended however warm she gets. She watches from within herself as the coughs rack her body, refusing poppy or aquavit, the end to come in its time. She asks for the boy and she holds him, he both embarrassed and blinking back tears, until a burst of coughing makes her let go and she smiles when it's passed and whispers a blessing and closes her eyes and goes back to her watching.

Also to die of pneumonia this winter is Gunai the Abbot in the dungeons of King Karaman, exhausted by ill-usage and the cold, his denial of conspiracy seen by the King as certain proof of it. Karaman's missive announcing his death, taken by runners to each of the five Errant Houses, is flamboyantly insincere, telling with nudging sarcasm of the grief of the royal family, the unstinting care that was given the ageing abbot, the softness of his feather bed, the sweetness of his meat and mead. Timur, now full Abbot, struggles without success to control his rage. A runner goes out in the snow with a sealed message to the Abbot of the Central House, not ten miles from the palace. Burn once read, let no other see.

Sark and Kan, guards to the late Baron, left well before the winter, missing women and taverns and general rambunctiousness. They make their way to Lix with each a decent share of portable treasures, not at all outstaying their welcome, Timur himself with ribald jests as he waves them off. They exchange jovial insults as they walk with their headstrap baggage and weapons the track that curves down and away.

Kuzak and Asli, snugged up in their cottage for the winter, also plan to move on to Lix, though when spring comes the times are unpropitious.

But none of that has happened yet.

Peterkin surges uphill behind the wolves; there's a crashing of sticks, a near-grown kid bolts downhill to his right. He follows the sound with his pointing finger, for the inductees some way behind; rushed fire from both as the kid careers between thickets; both miss and it's gone.

Up ahead the nanny has stood her ground to give her other kid a chance. As she whips round to follow it the wolves are on her and she's almost dead in the moments it takes for Peterkin to appear, torn at throat and underbelly. His first wolf backs off as is now their practice – the she-cubs hold their grips, one almost snarls as the boy comes up but the big wolf is watching and her ears go down and Peterkin cuts the already torn throat and the blood is let loose and the goat's residual weavings and hoofings desist and she lies still.

Up come the inductees, breathless and charged, the Huntsman close behind them. The Huntsman asks Peterkin to let them clean and skin the goat, and the first youth is soon at the task and clumsily a-tremble, not a seasoned butcher and no more adroit for having three wolves at his elbows, keen for the accustomed innards. Peterkin beckons them back; his first wolf complies but the big cubs don't and the wolf growls and snaps and they shrink off. Peterkin guides the inductee – liver to

the big wolf, first; a lung each to the cubs. He names
the parts as he points to them, mimes a two-handed
toss to the cubs so their portions arrive together and no
wrangling, though anyway one is already dominant. The
wolves bolt their gifts with joy, little chewing needed
before each portion yields to the suction of their gullets.

With the goat gralloched the second inductee is given
the task of skinning it. Peterkin looks round for level
ground, clear of the visceral mess and the still-excited
wolves. The Huntsman looks up at him and nods tacit
agreement, the nod of an equal taking advice. All these
long careering days of living by wit and by luck. He
and his brother the wolf – pursued, expelled, impris-
oned, thought nothing of. No-one to trust – not even
Sujata, however well she came through. And now the
Huntsman himself looks to him for direction, now he
is suddenly someone who never much thought himself
anyone, except to himself and his mother long gone.
Now he has a place, where the eyes of others bathe him
in their regard, in their wonderment.

Often these days he finds himself welling with tears,
alone with the wolf in his hut, sometimes when sitting
with him on the hill while the cubs sport and squab-
ble. A swelling of exquisite sadness almost fit to choke
him, deep in his throat and the base of his tongue. The
sudden tears; deep, shameless, unstoppable sobs shake
his ribs. He doesn't know why – there's nothing he's
thinking about.

Now it almost happens again, the sudden lump and
eye-smart. The big leggy she-cubs have guzzled their
pieces and more and are making to hustle the inductee,

who labours with novice hands to peel back the skin from the flesh. Peterkin gestures and calls them to halt, the switch of mode stops his lachrymoseness the way a shock stops hiccups. One half-thinks to defy him, then thinks again and turns around thrice and sulkily settles down.

And the Huntsman is asking a question and then tries another way and Peterkin answers quietly without deference or the reverse, and sits cross-legg'd and composed, around him the strange though somehow homely scene, entirely new to the world, of which he is the genesis, of which he is the centre.

Printed in Great Britain
by Amazon

24774634R00209